MVFOL

Finally, he released her hands. His body was tense in the chair, as if he actually was afraid to look in the mirror. She chuckled at his overly dramatic reaction and gently pulled the towel from his face.

Then she wished she had braced herself for what she saw in the mirror. He was even more handsome than she'd begun to suspect. With all his features revealed and his black hair clipped short, he looked like a freaking movie star.

She furrowed her brow as she studied his face. He actually did look a lot like someone famous, but the name escaped her at the moment.

"Who...?" she murmured.

Who the hell did he look like?

He twirled his chair around, as if not wanting her to see him in the mirror. But that was impossible, since he was right in front of her, his face nearly level with hers.

And she gasped. "You look—"

Dear Reader,

Welcome back to Northern Lakes, Michigan, where the elite firefighting team of Huron Hotshots is still coming under fire. Ethan Sommerly's story starts off with a literal bang. Throughout this series, Ethan has been one of my favorite characters, and I've been looking forward to sharing his story with readers.

I've so enjoyed writing all these books about the Hotshot firefighters. The team is so close that they are like a family. Family is a theme that definitely runs through all my books, probably because I have such a big family of my own. But people don't have to share a name or DNA to be a family. Some of the closest families are people whose common interests and shared experiences draw them together, like the Huron Hotshots, which is why it's so hard for them to consider that someone on the team might be sabotaging it. But is Ethan's "accident" an act of sabotage or a murder attempt?

I hope you enjoy the latest installment in the ongoing Hotshot Heroes series!

Happy reading!

Lisa Childs

HOTSHOT HERO IN DISGUISE

Lisa Childs

HARLEQUIN®
ROMANTIC SUSPENSE™

Recycling programs for this product may not exist in your area.

ISBN-13: 978-1-335-73828-8

Hotshot Hero in Disguise

Copyright © 2023 by Lisa Childs

For questions and comments about the quality of this book, please contact us at CustomerService@Harlequin.com.

Harlequin Enterprises ULC
22 Adelaide St. West, 41st Floor
Toronto, Ontario M5H 4E3, Canada
www.Harlequin.com

Printed in U.S.A.

New York Times and *USA TODAY* bestselling, award-winning author **Lisa Childs** has written more than eighty-five novels. Published in twenty countries, she's also appeared on the *Publishers Weekly*, Barnes & Noble and Nielsen Top 100 bestseller lists. Lisa writes contemporary romance, romantic suspense, paranormal and women's fiction. She's a wife, mom, bonus mom, avid reader and less avid runner. Readers can reach her through Facebook or her website, www.lisachilds.com.

Books by Lisa Childs

Harlequin Romantic Suspense

Hotshot Heroes

Hotshot Hero Under Fire
Hotshot Hero on the Edge
Hotshot Heroes Under Threat
Hotshot Hero in Disguise

Bachelor Bodyguards

Bodyguard's Baby Surprise
Beauty and the Bodyguard
Nanny Bodyguard
Single Mom's Bodyguard
In the Bodyguard's Arms
Close Quarters with the Bodyguard
Bodyguard Under Siege

Visit the Author Profile page at Harlequin.com for more titles.

For my wonderful husband, Andrew Ahearne—
for everything you do every day to love and
support me and for helping me brainstorm the
Hotshot Heroes series!

Chapter 1

With a brilliant flash of light and blast of heat, the stove exploded, propelling Ethan Sommerly into the cabinets behind him. Pain radiated throughout his back, and his face burned. He squinted and blinked, but that blinding light, like a million camera bulbs going off, was all he could see. Ethan could feel, though, the heat of the flames that crackled as they snaked out from the stove. He could also hear the high-pitched beeping of the smoke alarm. And he could smell the acrid scent of singed hair.

His hair.

His beard.

But hell, if he didn't get the damn fire out, he'd have to worry about more than his hair getting torched. He shook his head and blinked again. The light dissipated, leaving only spots that danced before his eyes, but around the spots, he caught glimpses of the flames shooting from the blackened frame of the stove.

What in the world had happened?

He'd just turned on the damn burner. And then gotten burned…

He shook his head again, shaking off the last vestiges of the shock that had momentarily paralyzed him. Finally adrenaline coursed through him, propelling him to grab the fire extinguisher from the wall and direct it at the flames.

The flames dropped lower and lower until only plumes of dark smoke rose from the stove. The alarm continued to peal out, and now the pounding of footsteps coming up the stairwell echoed the loud beeps.

"What the hell…" someone said.

"Do you need the line?" someone else murmured.

"Are you all right?" the superintendent asked. But before Ethan could answer his boss, Braden Zimmer shouted to someone else, "Call for an ambulance!"

Ethan shook his head. "No, don't. I'm fine."

But then a tremor moved through him, making his legs shake. And his face and hands throbbed, pain pulsating through him.

"You look like hell," someone else remarked.

The voices were all familiar, all members of his hotshot team of elite firefighters. But the black spots had spread across his vision, making it harder for him to see anyone. Or maybe he wasn't seeing spots but the smoke that was filling the room.

"You need to get out of here," Braden said. "You've inhaled too much smoke." And he coughed himself.

Until then Ethan hadn't noticed the burning in his chest, in his lungs. But before he could move, his legs folded beneath him, and he began to drop down like the flames had.

Strong hands gripped his arms, holding him up.

"Get Owen!" Braden shouted for the hotshot who was also a paramedic. "And let's get Ethan out of here."

And those hands that held him up, lifted him. Ethan was a big guy—burly, heavy—so there were a few grunts at the effort. He opened his mouth to protest, but no words came out, just coughs as his lungs continued to burn.

How much damage had the blast caused?

He didn't even want to touch his face. The beard he always wore hadn't protected him from the fire. It had probably caused more damage. Ethan wasn't worried about his appearance, though. He was concerned about his disguise.

Was his cover about to be blown?

If that happened, he would lose everything—the whole new life he'd built for himself over the last five years. The life that had probably kept him alive...

"What could that have been?" Tammy Ingles mused aloud as she stepped out of the glass door of her salon. The sound, whatever it was, something between a muffled blast and a whoosh of air had emanated from somewhere close. Tammy's salon was on Main Street in Northern Lakes, Michigan, so there were other businesses close; some even shared walls with hers.

It had been much too close for comfort.

Especially with everything that had happened in Northern Lakes over the past several months. The arson fires, the accidents...

Except those incidents hadn't actually been accidents. Some had been murders and there had been murder attempts too. In fact, somebody she knew had died and other people she cared about had been hurt as well.

She shivered despite the warmth of the summer sun shining down on her. Wrapping her arms around herself, she walked a few yards down the sidewalk toward the firehouse. Everything that had happened in Northern Lakes had had to do with the firehouse and the hotshot team associated with it. Hotshots were elite firefighters who battled wildfires all over the country. This team, the Huron Hotshots, operated out of the Northern Lakes firehouse. A plume of black smoke rose from the three-story building.

She'd suspected that whatever she'd heard meant something bad had happened to the hotshots again. Her pulse quickened with fear. She knew all the firefighters. Most of the town thought that was because she was a firehouse groupie. But, in actuality, she knew the hotshot team because so many of her friends were involved with them. Fiona O'Brien was married to one. Serena Beaumont was engaged to another. And Serena's twin, Courtney, was as good as betrothed to another one of the twenty-member team.

Sirens wailed as a paramedic van sped down Main Street, braking just outside the garage doors of the firehouse. Somebody had been hurt.

Who?

Her heart thudding heavily with dread, Tammy started toward the building. But before she could cross the street, someone ran up beside her. She hadn't opened the salon yet, so it couldn't have been a client…

Fingers clenched her arm, spinning her toward her friend. Courtney Beaumont's dark eyes were wide, and her face had gone ghostly pale with fear. "Do you know what happened?" she anxiously asked. "Who it is?"

Because someone must have been hurt or the ambulance would not have arrived with lights flashing…

"It's not Owen," Tammy assured her as the paramedic who lived with Courtney stepped out of the van. "He's fine."

A ragged breath escaped the other woman's lips, but then she gasped with guilt. "What if it's Cody?"

That hotshot was soon to be her brother-in-law, the love of her twin sister's life. And Serena, Tammy's best friend, had already suffered too much to lose him, too.

Holding hands, they hurried across the street toward those open garage doors. And Tammy gasped now at the sight of the body being carried down the steps into the garage. It was too big, too burly, to be Cody.

A few of the other guys were that big, though. But she knew, with the mad pounding of her heart, who had been hurt.

Ethan Sommerly.

Tears stung her eyes, but she furiously blinked them back to focus on Ethan and the others. The guys who carried him looked as scared as she was. She wanted to rush forward, wanted to rush to his side.

But she didn't know Ethan that well. She doubted that anyone did. Usually he was at his cabin in the middle of a national forest in the upper peninsula of Michigan. He only came down to Northern Lakes for meetings and for when the team was on call—like they were now—to be sent to wildfires in other areas of the country. And when he was here, even when he went out with the rest of the team, he didn't say much. About himself or anything else…

Maybe that was why she was so damn curious about him. He intrigued her in a way that no other man ever had. She was used to guys bragging about themselves, about their accomplishments. And Ethan…

Said nothing.

But he watched her.

She was always aware of when his dark gaze was on her. She could feel it in the tingling of her skin. In the heat that always coursed through her when she was near him. But that was crazy.

With his bushy beard concealing most of his face, he wasn't classically good-looking like the guys she usually went out with, who spent those dates bragging about themselves. Maybe she had been seeing the wrong kind of guys, like her friends had been telling her.

Her friends who'd fallen for firefighters…

Despite the town calling her a firehouse groupie, Tammy wasn't a fangirl of any kind. While she liked flirting and the occasional date, she had no intention of falling for anyone. She'd worked hard for her life, loved how she lived it, and had no intention of changing or compromising to accommodate anyone else ever again.

Courtney tugged on her hand, trying to pull her farther into the garage area of the firehouse. But Tammy held back. "Let's stay out of their way," she said. She didn't want to interfere in any treatment for Ethan, her heart clenching with concern over him being hurt.

"Who is it?" Courtney asked of the firefighters gathered in the garage bay. "Who got hurt?"

Before any of the others could answer her, Tammy did. "Ethan…"

Her friend turned toward her, her brow furrowed again with confusion. "How do you know? I can't see who they're carrying." And she wasn't much shorter than Tammy. She could probably see only what Tammy did—the height and breadth of the man they carried toward those open doors of the paramedic van.

Carried…

He had to be hurt badly—so badly that he couldn't get help for himself—that he had to be assisted.

Was he unconscious?

Panic gripped her heart.

Dead?

She shook her head, unable to consider it. Ethan couldn't be dead. While he didn't live loudly, he lived… *powerfully*. At least that was how he'd always affected her.

And he had always affected her despite her best efforts to pretend otherwise. She didn't like to not be in control of her own reactions, of her *feelings*…of anything, really.

"Who is it?" Courtney called out again to the hotshots, obviously not accepting Tammy's opinion. "What happened?"

Owen had ducked back into his van, but he stepped out now with a gurney that he and the driver slid beneath the body some of his team members carried. He glanced toward his love and shook his head. "I don't know…"

Did he really not know what happened or to whom it had happened? He turned his attention now to the man lying on the stretcher. And released of their heavy burden, the others stepped back—probably feeling like Tammy did, that they didn't want to get in the way.

And now the man on the stretcher was more visible even as Owen fixed the oxygen mask over his heavily bearded face. But the beard didn't look as long and thick and bushy as it usually did. It was bedraggled and burned.

"You're right! It's Ethan." Courtney gasped; then she squeezed Tammy's hand and murmured, "I'm sure he'll be okay…"

Why did she think Tammy needed comfort? Sure, she flirted with Ethan, but then she flirted with everyone. It was just more fun to do it with Ethan since he was so quiet and reclusive. She liked making him flush with embarrassment. She liked teasing him, liked the little rush of adrenaline and power that shot through her when she got a reaction out of him—not that she often got a response out of him. Usually he just stared at her with that dark gaze of his, and she couldn't tell if she amused or appalled him.

Courtney was a friend, so she had to know that Tammy's flirting wasn't serious. She didn't really want Ethan or any other man for keeps. And any woman who actually wanted the happily-ever-after was taking a risk in dating a firefighter because so many of them got hurt.

Or worse.

How badly was Ethan hurt? He wasn't moving. Was he already dead?

She found herself moving closer to that stretcher. Maybe Courtney tugged her that way, or maybe she was just drawn there. But as she neared, the stretcher moved. Owen and the driver lifted it into the back of the van. Then Owen stepped inside with it while the driver stepped back and reached for the doors. Before he closed them, Tammy peered into the back of the van and into Ethan's dark eyes.

He was awake.

He was *alive*.

Relief eased the tension that had gripped her. But that relief was short-lived because she knew that even though he had survived whatever had happened today, he would put himself in danger again.

And again...

She drew in a deep breath and reminded herself that it wasn't her business; *he* wasn't her business. They weren't even friends. And she was the last one who'd tell someone how to live his life because she didn't want anyone telling her how to live hers.

The doors closed, breaking that strange connection between them that she'd felt the first time she'd met him. She'd sensed then that she knew him even though he'd been a stranger to her. But something about him had felt so...familiar...to her.

"He'll be okay," Courtney said as she squeezed her hand again. "Owen will take care of him."

Tammy didn't know if her friend was reassuring her or herself.

But her heart continued to ache with fear and dread, and she kept shivering even when they stepped out of the firehouse and back into the sunshine, walking after the van as it sped away.

To the hospital.

"I'll drive you," Courtney said.

"What?" Tammy asked.

"I'll drive you to the hospital."

Tammy shook her head. "No, no, I need to get back to the salon." She tugged her hand free of Courtney's.

Her friend studied her. "Don't you want to go?"

That was the problem; she did want to go. But she

had no reason to crowd the waiting room for news of the condition of a man she barely knew.

She shook her head. "No. Like you said, he'll be fine." She drew in another deep breath, trying to calm her racing heart, trying to convince herself of that.

"But…" Courtney's voice trailed off.

"But what?" Tammy asked. "He's not my boyfriend."

And even if he had ever flirted back with her when she'd flirted with him, he wouldn't have become her significant other. She didn't want a significant other, just some casual dates. She'd worked too hard to become her own significant other that she wasn't going to risk losing herself in a relationship. And even though she'd gone out with a hotshot in the past, there was no way she'd date one now. But she knew that after her friends had fallen for hotshots, they would expect her to follow suit.

Tammy shuddered at the thought. No. She wasn't going to fall for any hotshot but most especially not Ethan Sommerly, since she'd always felt that unnerving connection with him. After seeing with her own eyes how easily he could be hurt, that bond would break. She would just have to be more guarded with him, more guarded *against* him.

If he survived whatever injuries he'd sustained…

He had to survive.

Even though she wasn't dating him, she couldn't handle his dying. It wouldn't be fair to cut short such a life, such a powerful force…

"He'll be okay," Courtney repeated.

Tammy nodded and turned away from her friend as she blinked furiously at the tears stinging her eyes. "Of course he will," she murmured as emotion choked her.

And she would be, too, because she wouldn't let him get to her any more than he already had.

"He's going to be okay."

Braden Zimmer heard the words Owen spoke, but he wasn't sure if he believed him. If he believed that any of them would be okay until the enemy among them was caught.

"Thanks," was all he replied before clicking off his cell phone.

He hadn't gone to the hospital like the rest of the team had, and guilt weighed heavily on him. But he felt the guiltiest that the *accident* had happened at all—that the *accidents* kept happening and he hadn't been able to stop them. Somebody kept deliberately sabotaging equipment, sabotaging the team.

Who the hell was it?

He'd received a note several months ago that had warned him that somebody on his team wasn't who he or she seemed. But who? It had to be the same person who kept trying to hurt them. He didn't want to believe that because he'd always thought his team was so close that they were more like family than co-workers.

"It was sabotage," Patrick "Trick" McRooney confirmed as he straightened up from behind the stove. He'd pulled the damaged appliance away from the blackened concrete block wall behind it and wedged his big body into the space. "Somebody messed with the gas line."

Like Braden, Trick had stayed behind at the firehouse to investigate instead of going to the hospital. But Braden had had to order him to stay. Trick would have rather gone with his fallen teammate. His face was flushed with anger and frustration, nearly as deep a red as his auburn hair. "Ethan could have been killed."

"You heard Owen," Braden reiterated. He'd had his cell on speaker. "He's going to be fine."

"*Now*," Trick said. "But if these damn incidents keep happening, somebody's going to get seriously hurt or worse."

Trick had had a close call himself recently and not just with their saboteur. A former friend of Braden's wife, Trick's sister, had tried to kill Trick and Henrietta Rowlins. Colleen had tried to kill Trick for never returning her affection and Henrietta because she'd become her romantic rival for the man Colleen had always wanted.

The most dangerous things that had happened to Braden's team had been the actions of people like Colleen and the late Dirk Brown's wife and the deranged state trooper Martin Gingrich and the Northern Lakes arsonist.

Fortunately, those people had all been caught. The saboteur had proven to be much more elusive than them. But he or she was becoming just as dangerous.

They had to find the saboteur and stop this evil before the accidents got even more serious and someone else died.

Chapter 2

The last thing he wanted was to be rolled out of the emergency room like he'd been rolled into it. Of course that had been on a gurney, and this would be in a wheelchair. But when the orderly stopped at the nurses' station to pick up the copy of Ethan's discharge orders, he stood up and, with a bandaged hand, slapped the button on the wall that opened the double doors of the ER onto the waiting room.

His legs shook a little, but he steadied them and walked out to join his friends. Hell, they were more than friends. They were family. The only family he had now.

The only family he wanted.

Ethan wasn't like his other team members who, when they'd been hurt, had had significant others waiting anxiously out here for news of their condition. He didn't have to worry about that; he wouldn't let anyone get close enough to him that they would fret about him. Actually, he *couldn't* let anyone get that close to him or they might do more than worry. They might figure out the truth and expose his big secret.

Which would blow up his life more than that stove had.

"So we just get back from battling one of the biggest blazes to ever hit the West Coast and you nearly get taken out in a kitchen fire," Trent Miles said, shaking his head as if disgusted with him. But there was a curious gleam in his light brown eyes as he approached Ethan. And when he got close, he grabbed him and pulled him into a tight bear hug.

Ethan allowed the embrace for a moment before pulling back. "I already told you that it doesn't make a difference to me that Braden changed the rule so team members are now allowed to date. I'm not going out with you."

Trent laughed just like Ethan had intended. And the tension and anxiety in the room eased.

Carl Kozek, the oldest of the hotshots, stepped forward and touched Ethan's bedraggled beard before sliding a hand over his own smooth, bald head. "You all call me Mr. Clean, but now you know that bald is beautiful and smart. It was your hair that fueled that fire."

Ethan shook his head. "Hell, no, my hair saved me."

Even the doctor had acknowledged that it probably had. Because his hair was still damp from his shower, the fire hadn't been able to devour it all and scorch too much of his skin beneath it.

"You can't leave it looking like that," Henrietta "Hank" Rowlins said from where she stood next to Carl. "You're going to have to shave your beard and cut off your singed hair." She smiled as if happy that he would have to.

She didn't know why his hair was so damn important to him. Nobody did. But without it, he might be recognized.

"I'll just wear it like yours," he quipped.

Her long dark hair was bound in a thick braid that dangled over her shoulder. She chuckled. "You don't have enough left to make it into one. Sorry, Ethan, but you're going to have to bite the bullet and go to Tammy like the rest of us do."

A curious little flutter passed through his heart, and he glanced around for the hairstylist. Not that he would have missed her if she had been there. With her long hair, streaked with blond and red highlights, and her beautiful face and slim body, Tammy Ingles was impossible to miss or ignore. But she wasn't here at the hospital, waiting for news of his condition like his friends' lovers had. And she wasn't his lover…no matter how much he wanted her.

Or how much she flirted with him.

But he knew that didn't mean anything because she wasn't looking for anything serious. With anyone. She was focused on her business and her friends. And he needed to be focused on his "business" as well. On protecting the secret nobody could learn.

Accidents just seemed to keep happening. Maybe all the equipment failures really were accidents, but so many other things had happened as well. They'd lost one of their team. That hadn't been an accident; Dirk's wife had murdered him. Then her lover had tried to take out another member of the team, Luke Garrison. And they'd nearly lost their new member as well when an obsessed woman had come after Trick McRooney and nearly killed Hank, too.

Ethan released a breath of relief. Yeah, he was smart not to get involved with anyone. But those killers and would-be killers had sworn they'd had nothing to do with the other accidents, with the equipment failures and breakdowns. And maybe they hadn't.

Maybe nobody was responsible.

But Fate…

And if Ethan believed his fate, he was cursed just like his ancestors had been cursed. When he was a kid, he'd scoffed about the superstition, but then he'd lost his dad and his brother. And things had begun to happen to him, culminating in him nearly dying almost five years ago, and he'd been forced to take the curse seriously.

So instead of waiting to be killed, he'd killed himself—at least he'd killed off the man he used to be.

But if that incident with the stove hadn't been an accident, maybe somebody else was trying to kill him. But which man was the target? The old him?

Or the guy who'd taken his place?

Tammy swept the broom across the slate floor, wishing she could sweep thoughts of Ethan from her mind as easily as she swept up the hair. But she'd been thinking of him all day, wondering how he was, worrying that he wouldn't recover.

Maybe she should have gone to the hospital and waited to make sure he would be okay. But if he wasn't, somebody would have mentioned it by now. Her business, Northern Lakes Salon and Spa, was the hottest spot for gossip in Northern Lakes. The only place hotter might have been the bar around the corner, the Filling

Station. In fact it had once been so hot that it had burned down and needed to be rebuilt. But that was because of the arsonist. The hotshots frequented the Filling Station when they weren't off fighting fires; they were probably all squeezed into their big corner booth right now.

If Ethan was okay...

If he wasn't, they would all be waiting anxiously at the hospital, which was precisely where she wished she was. Heat rushed to her face with a wave of embarrassment. How would she explain her presence? It wasn't as if she was his girlfriend or anything. She didn't want to be *anyone's* girlfriend; she preferred being her own person and not trying to fit someone else's image or ideal. She'd learned long ago that led only to disappointment for her and for whomever wanted her to change.

"I can get that," Margaret offered. The stylist already had her purse slung over her shoulder, but she reached for the broom. "You're the boss. You shouldn't be doing clean-up duty—though you don't seem to remember that most days." Her brightly painted mouth curved into a smile.

That was why Tammy cleaned up—for the respect of her employees. So they appreciated that she would pitch in whenever or wherever she was needed. But that wasn't why she was cleaning up at the moment.

Her fingers trembled with anxiety, so she gripped the broom handle more tightly. Forcing a smile for Margaret, she reminded her, "I learned from the best."

Tammy had bought the salon from Margaret when Margaret had become a grandmother and had no longer wanted the long hours or responsibilities of owning the place. Not that her former boss looked like a grandmother. Even though she'd let her hair go gray—or actually silver with a streak of purple—she didn't have one wrinkle in her beautiful face.

Ever since Margaret had hired a teenage Tammy to answer the phones after school, she had idolized the glamorous stylist. She had wanted to grow up to be just like her, and she had, with the exception of not having the family Margaret adored. Not that Tammy wanted a family of her own. She enjoyed being single way too much.

And she enjoyed her job. Since buying the salon, she'd renovated the entire building, including her apartment above it. She'd also ramped up advertising with a strong social media presence, and she offered new spa services to draw in clients from many, many miles around Northern Lakes. Some of her summer crowd, the visitors to the many lakes in the area, even came up in the winter to see her.

She was proud of what she'd done here, proud of who she was. And she was happy. Usually...

Today had been tough, though, and since Margaret had known her so long, she could tell when something was off with her. She narrowed her eyes and studied Tammy's face. "Is everything all right with you?"

She nodded. "Of course."

"Are you still shaken up over what happened at the firehouse earlier today?"

Tammy gripped the broom handle even tighter and forced her lips to curve up higher. "No."

But Margaret's eyes narrowed even more, and she cocked her head. "It was that really burly hotshot, right?"

Margaret knew that she had gone over to the firehouse that morning because she'd wondered why she'd found the door unlocked but the salon empty. Fortunately clients had started coming in then and they'd been too busy for Margaret to question her too much about what had happened.

But other people had been talking about it, about *him*, all day.

That was undoubtedly why Tammy hadn't been able to get that image from her mind of Ethan being loaded into the back of the paramedic rig. Even with Owen at his side, he had still looked so alone…like he had nobody.

But that was crazy. He had his team, and they all treated each other like family, which unfortunately meant that they had their fair share of drama, too. Especially lately.

"All of the hotshots are burly," Tammy replied with a nervous chuckle. "Except for Michaela and Henrietta." They were the female hotshots.

"Well, this one's hairy too with that bushy beard that hides his whole face," Margaret continued. "I've seen him when my husband and I have stopped by the Filling Station for dinner. He looks like a mountain man."

A forest ranger. That was his job during the off season and downtime just as Owen James's job was as a paramedic.

Tammy nodded. "Yes, he was the one who was hurt."

How had he been injured? What the hell had happened? Her clients had speculated, but nobody had known for certain. She could have called Courtney and asked. Her friend would have found out after she'd spoken with Owen again.

But Courtney already had the wrong idea about her and Ethan. And if Tammy had called to ask about him,

Courtney would have thought that she was right—that Tammy actually cared about him.

"What's his name?" Margaret asked.

"Ethan Sommerly," Tammy replied because it would be no use denying she knew it. She was familiar with all the hotshots but not in the way that everybody thought she was. Even though she hung out with them, she'd never been with any of them romantically like her friends were. And that was why she wouldn't take that risk, because she didn't want to follow in her friends' footsteps and fall in love with a hotshot. While she was happy for them, she knew that she was happiest on her own.

Margaret suddenly smiled.

"*What*?" she asked uneasily. Did the older woman think that she'd said the name with affection or something? That heat of embarrassment rushed to Tammy's face again.

"He must be all right," Margaret said, and her smile widened even more while Tammy frowned with confusion. She pointed at the glass door behind Tammy. "He's here."

Her heart moved in her chest so suddenly that she gasped. Then she turned toward that door. His big body blocked the evening sun, so he was just a shadow behind the glass. An enormous shadow.

While she froze to the slate tile floor, Margaret moved toward the door. It was glass like the entire front of the building. The other walls were brightly stained pieces of barnwood that complemented the slate floor and gave off the rustic spa-like appearance that Tammy had wanted for the salon. She'd stained all those boards herself to save money when she'd first purchased the place from Margaret.

"What are you doing?" Tammy asked her.

"Letting him in," the older woman replied matter-of-factly.

"But…but we're closed."

Margaret just chuckled, and it had the same tone that had been in Courtney's voice earlier, like she also knew something that Tammy did not.

Okay, that's it! She had to stop flirting with the man. Everybody kept getting the wrong idea about her. But, until the past few years, she hadn't been able to flirt with anyone. She hadn't had the confidence in herself or her appearance back then. But she'd worked hard to change that, to change how she looked and, more importantly, how she felt. So to hell with what everyone else thought…

She lifted her chin just as Margaret opened the door. But when Ethan stepped forward, into the light, she gasped. "Are you all right?"

The black hair of his beard and on his head was scorched. And even his usually long, thick black lashes looked as if the tips had been burnt. She'd seen him on the stretcher, but with the oxygen mask over his face, she hadn't noticed how badly his beard and hair had been singed. But was it just his hair that had been burned or had his skin as well? His hands were bandaged, so those had obviously been injured. What about his face?

"Whether or not I'm okay depends on you," he replied gruffly, which startled her as much as his appearance had.

Even though he'd showed up at her salon, she hadn't

expected him to actually answer her. He so rarely ever replied to anything she said to him, like maybe he was afraid that she was seriously flirting with him. Now he almost seemed to be flirting with *her* since there was a twinkle in his dark eyes.

"Me?" The one word sounded like a squeak as it escaped her lips.

His lips, barely visible through all that singed beard, curved into a slight grin. "Yeah, the doctors couldn't save me, so I'm counting on you."

Margaret chuckled then, and her plump cheeks were flushed with color. "I think that's my cue to leave you two alone."

Tammy gasped again, shocked at her friend's implication. "Hey—don't—" But she was just talking to Margaret's back as the woman headed out the door.

The door swung shut behind Margaret who looked back just as Ethan turned the lock. And her mouth moved as if she was laughing again.

"What are *you* doing?" she asked him now.

"I saw your Closed sign on the door," he pointed out. "You don't want anyone else coming in."

"I didn't want *you* coming in," she admitted, then flinched when a pang of guilt struck her. She'd been so afraid for him all day long. But that was the very reason she didn't want him here; she didn't want to spend any more time worrying about him than she already had. She didn't want to be concerned about anyone but her friends, and with the close scrapes they'd had, thanks to the men they'd fallen for, she was already anxious enough about them.

"Why not?" he asked, and his grin widened. "Are you afraid to be alone with me?"

He was so damn big, and since he'd rarely spoken to her, he was essentially a stranger no matter how long she'd known him or how she'd always felt that even *stranger* connection to him. If he wanted to overpower her, he easily could.

Physically.

But she wasn't just worried about his getting physical with her. She was worried about him overpowering her emotions. No. She wasn't just worried. She was afraid.

Very afraid…

But she was too damn proud to let him see her fear.

Trick was afraid. For Ethan. And for himself. But mostly for Henrietta. She wrapped her arms around him and pressed herself against his back as he stood in the doorway to the damaged kitchen. Her love wrapped around his heart like her arms did his body. Trick couldn't lose her. Not now. Not when he'd finally let himself fall for someone.

But he hadn't had a choice. Henrietta was such a special person that it had been impossible for him to not fall for her. She was so smart and strong and beautiful.

She pressed her silky lips against the nape of his neck. "It's not your fault," she murmured.

But the tight knot of guilt winding his guts didn't ease at all. No. He hadn't sabotaged the firehouse stove, but it was still his fault that Ethan had been hurt.

"Braden hired me onto the team, so I could find the saboteur," he reminded her. "And I haven't done that yet."

"He brought you here to offer him your unbiased opinion of everybody on the team," she corrected him.

"I shouldn't have told you that," he muttered as he

turned in her arms. Everybody else had already left for the bar but them and Braden, so he didn't need to worry about anyone overhearing them.

"You tell me everything," she said.

He did. He'd never had anyone like her in his life— anyone with whom he could be completely honest. He'd never been completely up front even with his own family because he hadn't wanted to add to the burdens they'd already carried.

But Henrietta was the strongest person he knew. She could handle anything. Even him.

He smiled as love stretched his heart even more. "Well, I failed at that, too," he said. "Because I can't be unbiased about you."

She smiled back at him. "I didn't sabotage the stove," she said. "That is what happened, right?"

A curse slipped through his lips. "Yes."

"Do you think it was directed at Ethan or just another random 'accident'?"

He shrugged. "Quite a few of us knew he'd volunteered to make breakfast this morning."

She cursed now. "So you really think it's one of us? That another hotshot is causing these accidents?"

That was why Braden had brought him in for his unbiased opinion—because Braden *was* biased. Despite the note the hotshot superintendent had received, Braden didn't want to believe that a member of his team could be sabotaging them.

Could be hurting them…

And now, after gaining their acceptance and letting down his own guard with them, Trick didn't want to believe it either. That was another reason he felt guilty— for suspecting one of them.

It felt like a betrayal.

But the real traitor was whoever was putting them in danger.

Trick held Henrietta closer. "Promise me you'll be careful," he implored her.

He couldn't lose her.

She nodded. "I always am. What about you?"

"I've learned to keep my eyes open," he said. And, unfortunately, to suspect everyone. He'd even had his doubts about Sommerly until now. Until he'd become the latest victim of the saboteur.

"What about Ethan?" Henrietta asked. "Do you think he realizes it wasn't an accident? Do you think he knows he's in danger?"

If he hadn't figured it out yet, he would soon, especially if he'd been specifically targeted. Because Trick knew from experience if someone wanted to hurt you, he or she wouldn't stop until you were hurt.

And if someone wanted you dead…

Chapter 3

He was in danger—serious danger. He knew it the minute she tilted her chin and gave him the sideways glance out of her smoky green eyes. She was so damn beautiful—with that long, thick hair and those big expressive eyes and that delicately featured face.

He was in trouble.

"You're the one who should be afraid," she said, and a little smirk curved her red lips.

He chuckled, albeit a little uneasily. "And why is that?"

"You know what they say about me…"

He furrowed his brow. "Who's *they*?"

She shrugged. "Everybody that knows me."

"What do 'they' say?" he asked.

"That I'm a man-eater," she said. And she snapped her teeth together in a threatening manner.

He laughed as something lifted in his chest, a burden

he hadn't realized he'd been carrying. She was as funny as she was beautiful. Of course he'd never wanted her to be aware of how funny he'd found her, which was another reason he'd liked his bushy beard. It had made it easier to hide his smile.

Just like the beard was his disguise and his protection, he suspected her flirtatious manner was hers. And since he was about to lose his mask, he decided to rip off hers as well. "The people who *really* know you don't say that," he told her.

Her smile slipped, just a little, before she curved her lips again. "That's because they're too nice to speak the truth," she said. "Or maybe they don't want to scare you away."

"You do," he surmised. "Or at least it seems that's what you're trying to do." He tilted his head now. "So were you the one who rigged the stove to explode when I turned it on this morning?"

She gasped, her green eyes widening with shock. "Is that what happened?"

He nodded. The stove had exploded. He wasn't certain if someone had rigged it or not. But he had a suspicion…

A feeling that it hadn't been an accident, just like some of the other *accidents* that had happened to some of the hotshots hadn't been accidents either. The only thing he didn't know was if someone had specifically targeted him.

Again…

She shivered as if knowing what had happened to him chilled her, while thinking about what had happened to him heated his blood with anger.

"I—I heard something this morning," she told him. "Some weird whooshing noise."

"That's why you came to the firehouse," he said and when she nodded in reply, he felt a pang of disappointment that it hadn't been to see him. She'd just come to find out what the noise had been. That was why she hadn't gone to the hospital. She'd only been curious, not concerned. Why did realizing that have that heavy pressure settling back onto his chest?

"That's what happened to your hair and beard," she murmured, and she stepped closer to him now, so close that her scent reached his nostrils. And he found himself drawing a deep breath—of her, of the fragrance that smelled like rain on roses. So much sweeter and fresher than the acrid odor of singed hair that clung to him.

Her green eyes darkening with concern, she stared intently at his face. "Are you hurt?"

He shook his head. "Just my pride."

"No burns?" She reached out and touched his beard, which crunched beneath her fingertips, and then she flinched as if feeling his pain.

"Just my hair." It had saved him and not just this time. "That's why I need you…"

She sucked in a breath, and her big eyes went even darker—the pupils completely swallowing the green irises.

"You can do what the doctor couldn't." He hoped. "You can save my beard."

She leaned closer and peered intently at his face. And now his breath caught in his lungs, as her scent filled his senses. She smelled so good. *Looked* so good…

How would she feel?

How would she taste?

He found himself leaning forward, lowering his head, as if his mouth was drawn to hers—to her bright lips.

"I don't think so," she murmured.

And he jerked back as if she'd slapped him.

But she was just shaking her head. "I don't think even *I* can save this…"

He shuddered out a breath ragged with relief, that she hadn't realized how close he'd come to crossing the line with her. And with resignation. The doctor had told him the same thing and had wanted to have someone shave off the beard in the ER, so he could check for burns beneath it. But Ethan had refused. He'd wanted to try to save it.

He'd wanted *her* to try to save it. At least that was the excuse he'd given himself for coming here—to her. Not because it had bothered him that, when he'd come out of the ER, she hadn't been in the waiting room with his team. He shouldn't have expected her to be there just because of the idle flirting she did with him. It wasn't as if she was actually interested in him. It wasn't as if anyone had ever actually been interested in *him* even before he'd become who he was now…

She reached up a hand to his hair, which hung to his shoulders and was almost as bushy as his beard had been. And just like his beard, the hair crunched beneath her fingertips. "This is bad too."

Not exactly what he wanted to hear when a beautiful woman ran her fingers through his hair. But he also did nothing to attract women—purposefully. He didn't want anyone getting too close to him, to his secret.

But occasionally he'd let himself imagine being that close to Tammy Ingles, like he was now, with her hand tangled in his hair. No. He'd imagined her much closer than this.

With nothing between them…

Not his jeans.

Not the sexy little dress she wore. The color of the green silk complemented her eyes while the soft fabric clung to and highlighted her every curve. With her figure, she could make even a burlap bag look sexy and stylish, though. He had never expected to find someone like her in Northern Lakes. But it wasn't as if she was lost. This was where she'd always lived, where she'd grown up.

He was the one who'd once been lost. But he had a really horrible feeling that he was about to be found. If he hadn't been already.

He sighed again. "Okay."

"Okay?" she asked, and there was a little catch of excitement in her voice. "You're actually going to let me do it?"

For the past few years that he'd known her, since he'd joined the Huron Hotshots, she'd been offering to cut his hair and shave his beard—in that sexy, flirtatious way she did things, that made him want to do things…with her.

But he'd always refused. Hell, most of the time he hadn't even acknowledged her offers. Even though he knew she was just goofing around, her flirting flustered him—in a way that nobody had ever flustered him before. Unfortunately, his fellow hotshots had noticed how she affected him and teased him about it even more than she teased him.

Maybe, if he was lucky, everybody just thought he was socially awkward from all the time he spent alone in the middle of a national forest. He only ventured out of it when the team was called up to fight fires or when Braden summoned everyone to meetings in Northern Lakes.

They'd been having a lot of those meetings lately and not just about fires but about everything else that had been happening to the team. All the close calls some of them had had.

Was that what had happened to him? Had someone purposely sabotaged the stove like so much of their other equipment appeared to have been sabotaged? Just a few weeks ago Trick had nearly fallen off the boom truck when the bucket he'd been in had come loose from the crane.

"C'mon," Tammy prodded him.

And he realized he had yet to answer her question.

But she must have been done waiting because she grabbed his arm and tugged him past the reception area of her salon into the back. Because of the summer heat, he wore a T-shirt, so his arm was bare, and the contact of her skin with his jolted him to his core, figuratively knocking him on his ass.

Then she *literally* knocked him on his ass when she pressed her hands against his chest and pushed him into a chair. She didn't immediately pull away, not even with as hard as his heart must have been pounding against her palm.

And he found himself drawn to her yet again…

His chest was so big, so hard, so warm…

Tammy's skin tingled from the contact, first with his arm and now his chest, which was like a wall of muscle beneath his bedraggled T-shirt. He must have been wearing it when the stove exploded because it was smeared with soot and torn in a few places, revealing more hair. But the hair on his chest felt soft beneath her hands, unlike his beard. His heart hammered against her palm, and his chest expanded as he drew in a deep breath and leaned toward her—so close that his singed beard brushed her cheek.

And it reminded her of his reason for coming here. She jerked back and with trembling hands reached for a cape. She swept it around him, and the black nylon barely covered his broad shoulders. With a few exceptions, most of her clients were women.

He chuckled, albeit a little gruffly. "I don't need this. I'm not worried about my shirt."

"Did…" She cleared her throat. "Did your chest get burned too?"

He shook his head. "No. I had a flannel shirt on over the T-shirt that took the brunt of it."

She touched his beard. "Actually, it looks like this took the brunt of it."

He grimaced. "You sure you can't save it?"

She didn't want to, but as a stylist, she always tried—despite her personal opinion—to give the client the look they requested. So she reached for the scissors instead of the razor, and she clipped off the singed hair. But even the hair beneath that was singed. "Unfortunately, no," she said. "It's going to have to all come off to make sure your face isn't burned."

He groaned. "That's what the doctor said."

"You really should have let them shave it, so they could see if you have burns that need to be treated. And so I don't hurt you," she said, her voice cracking with concern.

"Just cut off a little more," he said. "Try to save as much as you can."

She narrowed her eyes at what sounded to her like a note of desperation in his voice. He really didn't want to lose his beard. But it was already too late for that; she could see gaps in the hair that went to his skin. But she shrugged and reached for the trimmer. And as she cut off more of the singed hair, she revealed more gaps in his beard and more of his facial structure beneath it. That long, bushy beard had hidden the squareness of his jaw, the sharpness of his cheekbones, and the deep cleft in his chin. He had amazing bone structure.

Why the hell would he have wanted to hide it? When he'd first joined the Huron Hotshots a few years ago, a rumor had circulated that he'd once been in a plane crash, so he might have grown the beard to hide scars. But she didn't feel the ridges of any beneath her fingertips, nor did she glimpse any scars in the gaps where the hair had been singed right down to his skin.

She released a shaky breath. "I don't see any burns. Your skin is just a little red where your beard got totally burned off. And because there are so many spots where it has been, it really needs to all go."

His bandaged hands slid loosely around her waist, and she tensed with alarm that he was about to pull her onto his lap. The alarm wasn't because she was afraid of the thought but incredibly excited about it. He just moved her aside, though, and peered in the mirror on the wall behind her. He shook his head. "This doesn't look that bad…" he protested.

And she laughed. "You look like a teenage boy who can't grow a full beard. Sorry, it's going to all have to come off." Which was what she'd suspected, and had hoped, earlier.

He sighed and nodded.

And she reached for a straight razor.

"*Now* I'm afraid," he mumbled.

She smiled. "I promise it won't hurt a bit." And she brought it toward his throat.

He sucked in a breath.

And she chuckled. "Don't wiggle or it will hurt."

But he lifted a hand, wrapped in bandages, in front of his face. "I haven't done this in a while, but aren't you supposed to put on some shaving cream or something first?"

"Baby…" she murmured, but her smile widened with enjoyment over teasing him. She always enjoyed her flirty exchanges with Ethan, perhaps a little too much. Her hand shook slightly as she put down the razor.

And his breath escaped in a ragged sigh of relief.

"I'm just getting the shaving cream," she warned him. She leaned over and rifled through the cabinet beneath the mirror, looking for one that wouldn't irritate his skin where the beard had been burned completely off. Because, deep down, she didn't believe he was as fine as he insisted he was.

A groan escaped his lips, confirming that he was hurting. When she straightened up and turned around, his face was flushed, and he quickly looked away, and she realized he'd been staring at her ass. Pleasure rushed through her.

After all the years she'd spent being either invisible

or repulsive to the opposite sex, Tammy enjoyed the fact that men noticed and appreciated her now. Thanks to working as a stylist, she'd learned how to tame her frizzy hair and clear up her bad complexion and high-light her best features. She was proud of all her hard work but catching him staring at her brought her more than pride. It brought her a rush of desire.

And that was dangerous—not just to him, since she was going to shave him, but also to *her*. She could not get involved with a hotshot. Any hotshot…or her friends would start planning her wedding like they were plan-ning their own. They would think she would happily settle down like they all were, but Tammy had no in-tention of ever getting married.

Yet she was attracted to Ethan Sommerly. She'd been attracted to him for a long time. And that was why she couldn't give in to temptation—because she might do what her friends had, she might find herself falling for a hotshot. And she didn't want to fall for anyone, let alone someone who was obviously in danger and not just from a fire but from one of these damn accidents that kept happening to them.

Drawing in a shaky breath, she tried to ignore the tension gripping her body and asked, "Do you know why the stove exploded?"

He shook his head just as she lifted her hand toward his face, and the shaving cream on her fingers smeared across his mouth. She could have given him a towel to wipe off his lips. But instinct had the fingers of her free hand lifting to his mouth, wiping the shaving cream from it. Unlike his bristly beard, his lips were surprisingly silky and supple. How would they feel against her lips with his mouth moving over hers?

"Sorry," she murmured as she pulled back her hand.

"You're making me nervous," he said.

"I've shaved men before," she assured him, her gaze meeting his in the mirror on the wall as she continued to lather up his face.

"That's not what I'm nervous about," he muttered.

He must have felt it, too. The tension. The attraction that hung heavily in the air between them. So heavily that she was surprised the mirror didn't steam up like the windows on a parked car.

She didn't have any personal experience with that, though. She'd never been asked out in high school, and the men she'd dated since then, the ones who'd bragged endlessly about themselves, might have been interested in making out in cars, but they hadn't attracted her.

Not like Ethan did.

She drew in another breath and steadied her hand before reaching for the razor. She didn't want to hurt him any more than she wanted to be hurt. So she had to focus on her job, and only her job, which was what she'd been doing since she'd bought the salon. She'd been so busy building the business, remodeling and advertising and training her stylists and spa technicians that she hadn't had time for more than flirting. And even though everything was good now, she had to stay on top of things so she didn't lose anything she'd worked so hard to build. She didn't have time to feel like this.

When she lifted the razor to his face, her gaze locked with his in the mirror. And that tension between them sizzled with heat and awareness.

She closed her eyes for a moment.

And he gasped. "You're not going to shave me with your eyes shut, are you?"

She giggled and opened her eyes. "Don't you trust me?"

"No," he said.

"Ah, then you *do* believe my reputation," she teased him.

He started to shake his head but, seeing the razor so close to his face, he stopped. "No. I don't trust anyone."

She believed him. It was probably why he lived such a solitary life at his ranger station in the national forest. And while she hadn't thought it was possible, she actually had something in common with the hotshot—that unwillingness to trust anyone.

"I promise this won't hurt a bit," she said, smiling despite her twinge of doubt. She didn't want to irritate his skin. So she was very careful and very gentle with the sharp blade, scraping it neatly across his face.

The last of the beard dropped to the floor atop the singed pieces of it she'd cut off earlier. Only thin lines of shaving cream remained on his square jaw and in the deep cleft of his chin. To wipe that off, she pulled a towel from the steamer and wrapped it over his face.

And he groaned again—with pleasure.

Heat streaked through her over that groan. She wanted to feel pleasure too—with him. But she reached for her scissors again. "Your hair is a mess too."

Before he could protest, she sheared off the long, singed locks. He'd worn it past his shoulders, and it was as black and bushy as his beard so that they had blended together. His team had ribbed him about being a mountain man or a Sasquatch. He was going to need a new nickname because the beard was gone, and his thick black hair was clipped short. She reached for an electric trimmer now.

With the towel over his face, he couldn't see what she was doing, but he must have heard the trimmer because he tensed in the chair. "You're not going to shave my head!" he protested.

She chuckled. "Just your nape and sideburns." She cleared away that hair before adjusting the trimmer. Then she did run that over his head to shear off the uneven strands. It wasn't a buzz cut, but it was short.

She sucked in a breath of concern. She hated to disappoint any client with how they looked when she was done. But she especially didn't want to disappoint him, even though he'd never seemed to care about how he looked.

In fact he'd acted just the opposite, like he would rather look his worst than his best. They definitely didn't have that in common. She couldn't understand that, not after all the years she'd spent wishing she was as pretty as her friends, as fit, as confident.

But she'd been the funny one. The chubby sidekick. The tomboy...

She would have given anything as a teenager to look like she did now. But her family was more like Ethan probably was, more focused on what was inside than out. Unfortunately that had usually been junk food rather than values. While she appreciated that they'd accepted her as she was, she wished they hadn't undermined her when she'd tried to be healthier. She wished she hadn't been sabotaged when she'd tried to change, but they'd thought she'd just been reacting to all the bullies who'd picked on her in school. She had started out trying to change for them, but she'd learned quickly that led only to disappointment.

That was why she preferred to be single now. To live alone and worry about making herself happy and no-body else. At the moment though, she wanted Ethan to be happy, too.

"Okay…" she murmured as she reached for the towel. "Moment of truth."

But before she could remove the towel from his face, he lifted his hands to hers. Despite the bandages, his grasp was strong as he held her still.

"Do you need a minute to brace yourself?" she asked curiously. The rumors about him were as wrong as the rumors about her. He didn't have any scars marring his handsome features, no reason for him to be hesitant to see himself in the mirror.

But there was a slight tremor in his hands.

"Maybe you need to brace yourself," he said, the towel muffling his voice. "Maybe I'm hideous with-out my beard."

She knew that wasn't the case. Despite the streaks of shaving cream on his face, she'd been able to tell that his features were as perfectly chiseled as she'd suspected they were when she'd first started shearing away his singed beard.

"Okay, I'll do that," she assured him.

And finally he released her hands. But his body was tense in the chair, as if he actually was afraid to look in the mirror. She chuckled at his overly dramatic reaction and gently pulled the towel from his face.

Then she'd wished she *had* braced herself for what she saw in the mirror. He was even more handsome than she'd begun to suspect. With all his features revealed and his black hair clipped short, he looked like a freaking movie star.

She furrowed her brow as she studied his face. He actually did look a lot like someone famous, but the name escaped her at the moment.

"Who…" she murmured.

Who the hell did he look like?

He twirled his chair around, as if not wanting her to see him in the mirror. But that was impossible, since he was right in front of her, his face nearly level with hers.

And she gasped. "You look—"

"How much do I owe you?" he asked, as if he was in a hurry to leave now.

She shook her head. "Nothing. I've wanted to do this for a long time." She hadn't just been teasing when she'd made all those offers.

Because she'd wondered what he looked like beneath that beard and hair…

She'd had no idea. Or had she?

He had always reminded her of someone. That was why, even the first time they'd met, he hadn't felt like a stranger to her.

"I've wanted to do this for a long time," he admitted. And, suddenly, he reached up and slid his hands into her hair like she'd been running hers through his. With the bandages, he wouldn't be able to feel it, though.

But then he wasn't just touching her hair, he was tipping her face down to his. His touch was light. She could have easily pulled away.

But she'd wanted this for a long time, too, so she leaned forward and closed the distance between them. His lips did feel like silk against hers, and supple and hard too, as he kissed her passionately.

She'd never known him to do much with his mouth since he rarely talked or smiled. Now she knew what he must have been saving it for—kissing—because he was a bona fide expert at it. He nibbled at her lips with his, then swiped the tip of his tongue across her lower lip as if tasting it.

Tasting *her*...

She moaned as passion rushed through her. And he deepened the kiss, sliding his tongue inside her mouth. His hands moved from her hair, down her back to her waist. But when he tried to wrap his hands around her, he flinched, and a gasp of pain escaped his lips—into her mouth.

Remembering that he was hurt, she pulled back, and the heat of embarrassment rushed to her face. She'd forgotten where they were, who they were.

She'd forgotten everything but how much she wanted him. But then she studied his face, which twisted briefly with that grimace of pain, before settling back into those shockingly chiseled contours. Those cheekbones, the deep-set dark eyes, that chin with its deep cleft...

It was all *so familiar* to her.

"Who are you?" she blurted.

He chuckled, but it sounded gruff and forced. "You know who I am."

She shook her head. "No..."

He jumped up from the chair. "You're just not used to seeing me without the beard."

She never had before. Had anyone else since he'd come to Northern Lakes?

"You look so familiar," she murmured.

He chuckled again. "Of course I do. You've known me for years."

But that wasn't true. He was so quiet that she doubted even his teammates truly knew him.

"If you won't let me pay you," he said, "at least let me buy you a drink at the Filling Station. I'm supposed to meet the team there soon."

More heat scorched her face at the thought of walking in with him and what everyone would think…

That they were together.

Courtney already had the wrong idea. And Margaret had seemed to think something was going on between them as well.

Tammy didn't want anyone else thinking that, especially not herself. She shook her head. "I—I have some things I need to finish up here…"

Like figuring out who he reminded her of. When she stared at him, he rubbed his hand across his jaw, and his mouth slid into a frown of disappointment. "Well, thanks again…"

She wasn't sure if he was thanking her for the shave and haircut or the kiss. But he turned and headed out the door, with his bandaged hand still over his face, before she could ask him. Maybe he missed his beard. Or maybe he missed his disguise.

Because that was what it must have been. He hadn't been hiding any scars. In fact he'd been hiding extreme good looks. Like legendary good looks.

She shivered. No. She had to be wrong—because the name that had eluded her when she'd first seen his cleanly shaven face now popped into her head.

Canterbury. One of *those* Canterburys.

Jonathan Canterbury.

But that wasn't possible…because if she was right, she had just kissed a dead man.

* * *

Jonathan Michael Canterbury IV was dead.

He had been gone for nearly five years, but the mansion still looked like a shrine to him with his pictures plastered everywhere. Some portraits hung from the walls of the library and the living room and along the stairwell leading to the second story. And a few pictures sat in pewter or gold frames atop the polished finish of the grand piano in the drawing room.

Leaving his photos on display wasn't going to bring him back. Nothing could, and if for some reason he actually turned up alive after all this time, he wouldn't stay that way for very damn long.

Five years. That was how much time had to pass before he could be declared legally dead. That time was almost up now.

So if he wasn't really dead…

No. Jonathan Canterbury was better off dead. And he was damn well going to stay that way.

Chapter 4

Had she recognized him? It had been so many years since he'd seen himself without the beard, he hadn't been sure he would recognize himself, that he would even look the same after all this time. But the minute Tammy had taken away the towel, he'd stepped back five years into the man he used to be.

No. That man was presumed dead. Even though the wreckage and his body had never been found, he'd died in a plane crash with almost all the other passengers onboard. The only known survivors were a couple of hotshot firefighters. Everybody else, including Jonathan Michael Canterbury IV, had to have died or they would have turned up before now.

But did Tammy Ingles believe that?

Or had she recognized him as the dead man?

She'd looked at him as if she had. Or maybe that had

just been the shock of that kiss. It had shaken him nearly as much as seeing his old face in the mirror. That kiss had been even hotter than he'd been imagining it would be. She'd tasted even sweeter, and her lips...

He groaned. He could have gone on kissing her forever. And that would have been smarter, because if Tammy had kept her eyes closed, he wouldn't have had to worry about her recognizing him.

Would anyone else?

He paused with his bandaged hand wrapped around the door handle of the Filling Station. The bar was dimly lit and usually crowded. It was unlikely that anyone would recognize him in there. Hell, how many people even remembered who Jonathan Canterbury was? He wasn't a movie star or a model or a politician. He was just the son of people who'd done all of those things.

Famous by association but not because of anything he'd personally done. He had to have been forgotten by now.

Ethan certainly didn't remember him.

And he was *Ethan Sommerly* now. He hadn't just assumed the dead firefighter's identity; he had become him and not just to hide but to honor the man who, despite their short acquaintance, had become a good friend to him. The real Ethan Sommerly had had no family, no one to miss him when he was gone. He'd been as good a man as he'd been a friend and hadn't deserved to be forgotten. The real Ethan had saved his life, and he hoped he'd returned the favor by keeping him alive.

He tightened his grip on the door handle and drew in a deep breath. These people—his team—would still see him as Ethan even without the beard. They knew who he really was.

Did Tammy?

No. She'd probably just been staring at him that way because she hadn't been able to believe that he'd actually been bold enough to kiss her. He couldn't believe that he had. But he'd been wanting to for so damn long. And if that stove had taken out more than his beard, he might have missed his opportunity.

And he would have missed a hell of a lot.

She'd tasted so sweet and had kissed him back so passionately. Which intensified his hunger for her. He would have pulled her onto his lap if he hadn't flinched when he'd tried wrapping his hands around her small waist.

He flinched again now as he pulled open the door. The noise of the bar struck him almost like the blast of the stove exploding had. Voices competed with the music blaring from the jukebox. The bar was crowded, people forced to stand on the peanut-strewn wooden floor.

Ethan let the door slam behind him as he walked in, not expecting anyone to hear it. But then the noise suddenly stopped, as if everyone in the bar had frozen. They moved, though, all heads swiveling toward him.

Dread tightened his stomach into knots. This felt like a nightmare—one he'd been having the past five years when he dreamed of being exposed…as a fraud.

An imposter…

Sweat beaded on his forehead as everyone continued to stare. Then a high-pitched whistle shattered the eerie silence. And catcalls followed.

Grinning, Ethan headed toward the corner booth in the back of the bar from where all the noise was coming. Most of the hotshot team, with exceptions of Rory

VanDam, Braden and the boss's brother-in-law Trick McRooney, were squeezed into the booth.

"Hey, I'm not a piece of meat," he said in protest. "Treat me with some respect, would ya?"

"You're not a piece of meat," Trent Miles agreed. "But you can be the beefcake for our next calendar."

Ethan snorted. "*Next* one? When did we do the last one?"

"We didn't invite you to participate in that one," Miles said. "It was featuring firefighters, not Sasquatch."

He snorted but with amusement. Trent Miles had called him a Sasquatch before. Miles wasn't the only one who'd used that nickname for him, just one of the few who'd actually been brave enough to say it to his face.

"Seriously," Michaela Momber said, shaking her head with its short, blond pixie haircut.

Tammy, no doubt, styled it. Her salon took care of most of the town. And after tonight, he understood why. The way her fingers had run across his face and through his hair...

His pulse quickened at just the memory of her touch. And when she'd bent over to rifle through her cabinet, he hadn't been able to stop the groan slipping through his lips. The sexual tension that had gripped him had hurt more than his hands, which throbbed from the burns.

"Seriously," Michaela repeated. "Why would you cover up a face like that with all that gnarly hair?"

Henrietta stared at him, too, almost like Tammy had, with her brow furrowed as if she was trying to place him.

And a chill chased down his spine. Coming here had been a bad idea. He hadn't been eager to return to the firehouse, though, after being hurt there. And he was crashing in the bunkroom while they waited for their next call out to a wildfire. His cabin in the UP was too far away for him to respond quickly enough to a call. But would he even be able to work with his hands bandaged?

Maybe he should ask Braden for time off to heal and to grow back his beard. He reached out and touched his face. Then he deflected Michaela's question the way he'd watched Tammy deflect anything personal—with teasing. "I didn't want you and Hank to lose control around me," he said. "I wanted to make sure you could focus on the job."

Hank snorted. "You should be more worried about Miles here not being able to focus."

Trent Miles was the biggest womanizer of all the hotshots now that Cody Mallehan was about to get married. But unlike Cody, Trent wasn't about to let himself fall for anyone.

And neither could Ethan.

He couldn't risk it—for his sake or for the woman's. But he could still taste Tammy on his lips. He'd never savored anything as sweet or as potentially addictive. He gestured at the empty pitcher of beer. "Anybody save me a glass?"

"You can have mine," Michaela offered. "I haven't touched it." And she pushed it toward the edge of the table.

"On duty tonight?" he asked. She and Henrietta worked out of a firehouse a little north of Northern Lakes when they weren't working as hotshots.

She shook her head. "Nah, I'm just tired." Dark circles rimmed her blue eyes.

Of course they were all tired. They hadn't been back

long from their last call out West. And then this had happened.

Another accident.

He wasn't the only one on edge over it. But now he had to be on edge about his identity, about anyone discovering the truth. Then the life he'd built for himself would blow up like that stove had, and the repercussions would be far worse than some singed hair.

"You screwed up," Trent said, "so it's your turn to buy."

That was their rule. If anybody messed up on the job, they had to buy drinks for the rest of the team.

But he chortled in protest. "I just turned on the damn stove."

"That was your first mistake," Carl remarked. "Trying to cook…"

"Not everybody's got a wife like yours," Ethan reminded him. Carl had been married a long time to a woman who loved to cook and bake. Fortunately she often shared those goodies with the team.

"If you would have shaved off all that hair years ago, you'd be married, too," Michaela said.

"Good to know you're so shallow," he teased her. Michaela and Henrietta were like his sisters. Well, not like his sister since Melanie was rude and superficial and patronizing, but he wished she'd been like Hank and Michaela. They were fun and smart and strong.

This team was his family now—his *real* family. "I'll get the pitcher," he said, and he turned to head toward the bar. As he walked away, he thought about just continuing right out the door.

But he'd already disappeared on one family. He

couldn't leave this one as easily as he had that one, especially now when they were in danger.

And he had no doubt that they were. All the accidents that had been happening lately couldn't have really been accidents. Somebody was trying to hurt them.

Or just *him*?

Tammy *had* to have him. She had to…

Kneeling on the floor, she flipped through the stack of magazines in the reception area of the salon. Because her clients were all so different, with so many varied interests, she subscribed to nearly every magazine still available in print copy. From *Country Living* to *People* magazine.

And of course all the celebrity gossip rags. She was the one who actually liked those, though. She liked reading about the rich and fabulous, and it was on one of those that she thought she'd seen the face she'd seen in the mirror tonight when she'd shaved off Ethan's bushy beard.

The stack of magazines she'd picked up slid from her lap onto the floor, so she just fanned them all out across the slate tiles. And that was when she saw it again— Ethan Sommerly staring up at her. But he wasn't Ethan.

He was Jonathan Michael Canterbury IV, and nearly five years ago, he had fallen victim to the family curse of dying young when he'd been presumed killed in a plane crash.

"What the hell…" she murmured as she reached down for the magazine. She skimmed her fingers along the square jaw she'd shaved, over the deep cleft in his chin. It had to be him. They looked too much alike for it to be a coincidence.

Pounding at the door startled her, and the magazine slid from her grasp. She glanced up and saw Courtney standing on the other side of the glass, waving at her. Then she saw double as Serena appeared beside her twin. Only their faces were the same though. They wore their black hair differently, Courtney's in a short bob and Serena's in a long braid like Henrietta Rowlins wore hers.

Could Jonathan Canterbury have been a twin? No. Then there would have been two faces on the cover. And it wouldn't have had the headline *NEARING ANNIVERSARY OF DEATH OF LAST MALE HEIR TO CANTERBURY DYNASTY AND CURSE.*

The twins at her door knocked again and called out, "Let us in!"

She straightened up and put the stack of magazines back on the table. But before she headed toward the door, she slid the magazine with his picture beneath the pile, so nobody else would see it.

She paused with her fingers on the magazine. Why had she done that? Why shouldn't she talk to her friends about it? She talked to them about everything. About their lives…

Occasionally about hers. She had less to talk about than they did with their recent romances and Serena's upcoming wedding and Courtney's new shop in town. Tammy preferred it that way, though; she'd rather hear about other people's lives than share about her own.

She especially didn't want to talk about Ethan or Jonathan or whoever he was. Especially not after the morning and the kiss…

She jerked her hand away from the magazine and headed over to the door. Her fingers shook slightly as she turned the dead bolt, unlocking it. "What's up?" she asked. "Hair emergency?"

They both looked perfect, though, just as they had back in high school when Tammy had looked anything but perfect. She stepped back to let them inside, but the twins remained on the sidewalk.

"Another kind of emergency," Serena said.

And dread stole Tammy's breath. When she could draw air back into her lungs, she anxiously asked, "What? Did something else happen?"

One accident after another kept befalling the hotshot team. Or were they the curse?

Jonathan Canterbury's curse? Had he brought it to Northern Lakes with him?

"We have to go to the Filling Station," Serena said, and she reached out and clasped Tammy's hand, tugging her through the open door.

"Henrietta called and said there's something we need to see," Courtney added.

Something. Or *someone*?

Ethan had said he was heading there when he'd left her. He'd invited her along for a drink, but she hadn't wanted to walk in with him and get the gossip going.

But if she walked in with her friends...

And if one of them recognized who he was...

Then she wasn't the one who'd given up his secret. That was why she'd hidden the magazine; she didn't want to expose him since he obviously didn't want to be found. But with his disguise gone now, it was only going to be a matter of time before the truth came out. Whatever that was...

"Let me get my purse," she said.

"You don't need it," Courtney told her. "I'm buying."

"Why?"

"Because I pissed you off this morning."

She furrowed her brow. "What are you talking about?"

"You got mad at me for thinking that there was something between you and Ethan," Courtney said.

"I—I didn't get mad," Tammy stammered. But she had been embarrassed and unsettled and...

Worried—so damn worried because he'd been hurt. She'd spent the entire day fretting about him.

And she hadn't even known who he was.

Now anger coursed through her. How dare he lie to her? To them...

Tammy tugged free of Serena and stepped back into the salon. She thought about snatching that magazine. Instead she grabbed her purse from the back and her keys. Jangling them in her hand, she explained, "I have to lock up."

Northern Lakes wasn't the safe town it had been when they were all growing up. Over the past year, they'd had arsonists, killers, and now a Canterbury...

Every time he thought he was living his worst nightmare something else happened. Losing Dirk was still the worst. One of his team dying had nearly destroyed Braden. But Dirk hadn't died because of the saboteur.

Ethan could have, though.

That was why they had to stop him or her—whoever the hell it was.

And that was why Braden didn't have time to deal with this reporter. "I'm sorry, Ms. Townsend," he told the woman standing outside the door of the firehouse. "There is no story for you here."

The curly-haired brunette narrowed her eyes and studied his face as if she could somehow tell that he was lying. Too bad the streetlights were so bright around the firehouse, and fluorescent lighting spilled out the open door in which he stood.

"There was an explosion here today," she said.

How did she know that?

Of course the entire town had probably been talking about it, so she'd undoubtedly overheard something at the coffee shop or the bar.

He shrugged. "It was just a mishap with a stove."

"In a *firehouse*?" she asked doubtfully. "And what about the other incidents that have occurred? I heard that you lost one of your team members earlier this year."

As if he needed to be reminded of that, as if he would ever forget...

"That was the result of a domestic situation, Ms. Townsend," he said. "Rehashing that will only add to the pain Dirk Brown's loved ones have already suffered."

Since Dirk and his wife had had no children and little other family, the loved ones that would be hurt the most would be Dirk's team members. They all missed him so damn much.

"But that's not the only bad luck that's struck your team lately," she remarked.

How the hell did she know so much?

Did Braden have a rat on his team? Was it the person he'd already been warned wasn't who he thought he was?

Maybe this person wanted attention for all the damage he'd caused. Maybe that was why he'd contacted this ambitious, young reporter. And if he'd reached out to her, she could have a connection to him.

Braden studied her now. She worked for a television station in Detroit, which was where the firehouse was that Trent Miles worked when he wasn't out with the hotshot team.

Was Trent a traitor?

But just because they were from the same city didn't mean they knew each other. Anybody could have tipped her off to what was going on. And maybe they'd reached out to a Detroit reporter to make Trent look complicit.

Braden hated this. He hated suspecting everyone he knew of being the enemy. That was why he'd brought his brother-in-law Trick McRooney onto the team. He'd wanted Trick to suspect everyone, so he wouldn't have to.

But he was the superintendent. It was his job to protect his team—from the saboteur and maybe now from this reporter.

Chapter 5

Ethan should have kept walking earlier when he'd gone to the bar to buy the next pitcher. He should have just kept on going out the door and out of the city limits of Northern Lakes.

He knew, the minute she walked into the bar with her friends, that staying had been a mistake. The Beaumont twins looked like black-haired bookends to the bright-haired beauty that she was. And he wasn't sure if he should have run because of how damn much she affected him or because she knew the truth.

He saw it on her face the minute he met her gaze. She looked at him, and the recognition was there. It had been there earlier, but then she'd also had some doubt, some confusion, as if she recognized him but didn't know why he looked so familiar. But now...

There was certainty.

She *knew.*

But before she could say anything, the bar erupted with applause. Her brow furrowed beneath a fall of her tawny hair, and color flushed her face. "What…?"

All of the hotshots, except for him, stood as they applauded her. "You've done what we all thought was impossible," Trent Miles told her. "You made this ugly ogre good-looking."

Ethan laughed, like he was meant to, but dread settled heavily into his gut. What would she say? Would she give him up to his team?

Would she tell them the truth he'd kept from them all these years?

Her lips curved into a smile and she bent over in a dramatic bow. "Thank you. Thank you," she said. "It's nice to be appreciated for my talent."

She did have talent—immense talent—for making people look their best and feel more confident and happier. He'd seen her work, had seen the joy she gave people.

But for him…

Looking like this—looking like he used to—didn't make him happy. It made him miserable as hell just like he'd been as Jonathan Michael Canterbury IV. That empty, pointless life had been the lie—not this one.

"You are a freaking magician," Trent continued, heaping on the praise. "Who the hell knew he could look like this?"

"Who *does* he look like?" Henrietta asked, and she turned toward her friend. "You are the queen of pop culture, Tam. Who is it? It's been bothering me since he walked in…"

He'd seen her get on her cell phone earlier; she must

have called the others to come to the bar. Tammy had agreed to come with her friends, but she'd refused his invitation.

Was it because he'd crossed the line with her? Because he'd kissed her...

Or because she'd recognized who he really was?

"Who does he look like?" Hank prodded her.

A tightness gripped Ethan's chest, as panic squeezed his heart.

But Tammy said nothing. She just smiled and shook her head.

Hank sighed with disappointment. "I thought for sure you would know. Anybody else?"

"It's driving me crazy too," Michaela said as she studied his face.

They all stared at him. Hell, they'd been staring at him since he'd walked into the bar.

But for Tammy...

She didn't look at him now—almost as if she couldn't look at him—because she knew. She didn't have to try to figure out who he was anymore.

Why didn't she share his secret with the others? Did she want something from him?

Money, like everybody else in his old life had. That was all they'd wanted, wealth and influence, that had been his only purpose. For them...

He'd had no purpose of his own.

Not like Tammy did. She was successful, so her salon had to be profitable. If she wasn't interested in his money, could she be interested in...

No. She'd pulled away from him earlier, and she hadn't seemed nearly as affected by their kiss as he had been, as he *still* was. His body was tense and not just because of everyone staring at him.

His body was tense because it ached with want. He wanted her.

What did Tammy want?

With her apartment just above the salon, Tammy didn't have far to walk from the Filling Station back to her house. Both were on the main street of Northern Lakes. So she'd insisted on seeing herself home—before anyone could offer, anyone like Ethan.

But this man wasn't Ethan.

She shivered as a cool wind swept down the street, between the buildings and through the thin material of her dress. Even summer nights tended to cool off this far north in Michigan and this close to one of the big lakes as well. Lake Huron was less than ten minutes from the town that had a number of smaller inland lakes as well.

As she hastened her step, her heels clicked against the concrete of the sidewalk. She wasn't hurrying because of the sudden chill in the air but because of the unsettling sensation that she was being followed. And then she heard it—the footsteps echoing hers.

She already had her keys out, in her hand, to use as a weapon if need be. She could gouge out the eyes of whoever was stalking her…if she hadn't had some idea who it might be. No. She didn't want to use the keys as a weapon. She wanted to use them to get inside her apartment before he caught up with her.

Her hand trembled as she extended the keys to the door. This one wasn't glass like the one for the salon. It was a steel door to the stairwell that led directly up to her apartment. Before she could jab the key in the lock, a shadow fell across the door.

He was so tall, so broad, that he blocked out the glow of the streetlamp, leaving her in the dark. But she wasn't...

She was the only one who knew. The only one who'd figured it out. Was that why he'd followed her?

To compel her to keep his secret?

But he was the one who asked, "What do you want?"

Him. After that kiss, she wanted him—but she wasn't about to admit that, especially now when she knew how impossible it would be to date him. Even more than if he was really just a hotshot firefighter. But he wasn't. He was so much more. And she didn't need that kind of complication in her life.

So she would resist this attraction she felt for him, the attraction she shouldn't feel knowing what she knew now, how he'd deceived them all for years...

After all the lies she'd heard growing up from her family, from her friends, that she was beautiful, that she was perfect as she was...and then the others who'd told her she would be perfect if only she'd lost some weight, if only she'd dressed better, or did more with her face and makeup...

So many people had been dishonest with her for so many reasons that she struggled now to believe anyone. And knowing now that he'd lied to everyone, he was the last person she would ever trust.

"I want to go inside," she said. "I want to go up to my apartment and—"

His bandaged hand covered hers, guiding the key into the lock. Then he used his other hand to turn the knob and open the door.

Tammy sucked in a breath. She'd wanted to go upstairs alone, so she could think or maybe not think. It
wasn't really any of her business anyway that he'd been
lying to everybody. It wasn't as if they'd been dating.
All they'd ever done was flirt and kiss…

And that kiss hadn't happened until tonight.

Had he done that then to distract her, so she wouldn't
notice who he was? What the hell kind of game was
he playing?

His kissing her had damn well made it her business
now. She wanted to know what was going on, but she
didn't want to have that conversation where someone
might overhear them. While she hated lies and secrets,
it wasn't her place to reveal them.

So she walked through the door he held open for her
and, after flipping on the lights, started up the stairs.
When no heavy footfalls followed her, she turned back
to where he stood blocking the doorway with his enormous body. "Aren't you coming?"

"Am I invited?"

"I'm not going to send you a written invitation to
come up to my apartment," she said. "But I want to
talk to you."

He stepped inside then and closed the door behind
him. And it was clear that he didn't want anyone else to
overhear this conversation either. He didn't want anyone else to know his secret.

Was she the only one who'd figured it out?

Maybe she shouldn't have invited him into her apartment after all. But it was too late. He was already inside, and he turned the dead bolt, with the door locked
behind him.

She turned away from him and hurried up the last

of the stairs, rushed so much that a heel slipped from a step, and she would have fallen if not for his grabbing her waist and steadying her. Even through her dress and his bandages, she felt the heat of his touch.

The strength in his hands…

He could overpower and hurt her so easily. She'd thought that before, the first time they were alone in the salon, but back then he hadn't had a reason to hurt her. Now, if she was the only one who knew the truth about him, he had a reason…if he was determined to keep his secret.

"Careful," he murmured, his deep voice a low rumble in her ear.

She shivered again, at the sensation of his breath stirring her hair, and at the warning. It was too late to be careful. Or she wouldn't have let him into the salon earlier, she wouldn't have kissed him…

And she certainly wouldn't have let him inside again now—so late at night. She pulled away from him and walked up the last couple of steps to the kitchen which was aglow with light from the pendants hanging over the granite island that separated it from the living area.

The apartment looked a lot like the salon—rustic chic—with slate floors and warm wood finishes. She loved her place, loved living in the heart of the city—such as Northern Lakes was. It was busier now with summer bringing many tourists to the area. While some of those visitors were wealthy and a few of them had even been famous, nobody as infamous as him had ever come to town before.

"What are you doing here?" she asked, walking around the island to put space between him and her.

She didn't want him to touch her again, didn't want to feel the heat of his body or the thrill that ran through her…

"I want to talk to you," he said.

She shook her head. "No, what are *you* doing here—in Northern Lakes?"

His already dark eyes darkened more. "I work here, remember?"

"Why?" she asked. With all his money, he never had to work—anywhere—let alone in as dangerous a profession as a hotshot.

"Because we're on standby for the next wildfire," he replied.

"Stop being so literal," she said. "You know what I'm asking you. You know that I know who you are."

"Ethan Sommerly," he said, and his deep voice went even deeper with vehemence.

She shook her head. "No, you're not."

"Yes," he insisted. "I am." He moved around the island of blue-stained cabinets that had been topped with a slab of granite with veins of blue and copper running through white.

Fear quickened her pulse and she backed up, away from him. But the wall behind her stopped her as her butt bumped into the apron of the copper, farmhouse sink. He followed her, looming over her.

"It's only a matter of time before everybody else figures it out, too," she said.

So he would have no reason to silence her…if that was his intention, his reason for stalking her around her own kitchen.

"Henrietta and Michaela are already wondering…" And now Serena and Courtney were, too. "It won't be long before someone finds a picture of you online." Or on the magazine in the lobby of the salon…

He expelled a curse. But he stopped his denials. Without the beard, he couldn't hide his face and his expression anymore. Nor could he hide his identity.

"People are going to find out the truth," she insisted. But she wondered what that actually was. What the hell had happened that he'd wound up here—as Ethan Sommerly—when everybody else thought he'd died in a plane crash?

"What do you want?" he asked again.

"The truth," she said. So many questions flitted through her mind. But he was so close, so hot, so distracting…that she struggled to think at all.

"I mean money," he said. "Do you want money?"

She wrinkled her nose at the thought. "I don't want a damn thing from you." But she knew that was a lie. She wanted him, even more so after that kiss…

"Then why didn't you say anything when everybody was asking you who I look like?" he asked, his dark eyes narrowing with suspicion.

Like she harbored some ulterior motive for keeping silent.

But when someone was as rich as a Canterbury, a lot of people probably wanted something from him. The only thing she really wanted was the truth. But that might not be worth the risk. If she knew more about him, she'd get closer to him, and she couldn't afford to get any closer without the risk of feeling something for him.

"It's not my secret to tell," she explained matter-of-factly. "It's yours. But, like I warned you, it's not going to stay secret for long—not in this town." And since

Henrietta and Michaela were wondering who he looked like, they must not know his real identity. His team would be devastated when they learned the truth, that he'd been lying about who he was all this time.

For some reason she felt as betrayed as they would all probably feel. And she wasn't sure why because she hadn't ever really known him. Apparently nobody had.

"I will pay you," he offered, "to keep quiet."

She snorted over his attempt at a bribe, but just like every other time someone had hurt her feelings, she was too proud to show her pain. So she reacted with her usual humor. "I know I talk a lot, but nobody's offered me money to shut up before."

"I guess there is an easier way to keep you from talking," he murmured as he lowered his mouth to hers.

His kiss jolted her—just as it had earlier. Passion heated her blood and hammered in her heart. She'd never felt such a surge of desire before—had never wanted anyone as much. She lifted her hands to his head and ran her fingers over the softness of the newly shorn hair. In contrast his body was so hard, so muscular, as he pulled her up against him.

His erection strained against the fly of his jeans, making it obvious that he wanted her.

Or did he just want to keep her quiet?

He had never kissed her before today, despite all of her flirting with him. Except for his intense stares, he'd never really expressed any interest in her until now. She'd always thought it was because he was reclusive and shy. Now she knew that it was just because he was too good for her, too rich and famous to dally with a small-town hairdresser. At least he hadn't said so, like some of the other guys who'd visited the area and wanted to sleep with her but nothing more…because she wouldn't fit into their big, high-society lives. She didn't want to fit into anyone else's life, though, not after she'd worked so hard to build her own here.

But of all those guys who'd said that to her, nobody had been as blue-blooded as Jonathan Canterbury IV, so what was behind his sudden interest in her? Was he just trying to seduce her into keeping his secret?

She pressed her palms against the solid muscles of his chest and pushed him back as she pulled away from his kiss, from the potent force that drew her to him. She shook her head in denial of that attraction and his ploy to silence her. "It's not going to work…"

"Oh, it will work," he assured her, and his lips curved into a cocky grin.

She gasped at his blatant innuendo. If he was still just Ethan Sommerly, she might have laughed at the bawdy humor. But now she knew who he really was and how little he probably thought of her.

She shook her head again. "Not with me."

His dark eyes glittered, almost as if she'd challenged him. And he intended to accept that challenge. "I could change your mind," he threatened.

He could—with another kiss, with a touch, maybe with just another intense stare.

She braced herself to fight the temptation that was Ethan Sommerly. No. He wasn't Ethan Sommerly, and that was the problem.

"There is a story here," she murmured as she stared out of the window of her hotel room at the small town of Northern Lakes.

Even if her source hadn't let things slip to her, Brittney

Townsend would have known just from the hotshot superintendent's reaction when she'd questioned him.

He was worried.

Not about her…

Well, maybe about her.

But he was most worried about his team. She had seen the concern on his face and in the tension gripping him. The thing was—she was worried, too.

She didn't want any one of them getting hurt—but most especially not her source. Maybe the best way to protect that person was to get everything out in the open…to expose all of the secrets of the Huron Hotshots.

Chapter 6

He awoke with the taste of her on his lips. Or was he only dreaming? Maybe he'd dreamed it all—everything that had happened. He lifted his hand to his face though, and even through the bandage, he could tell that his beard was gone and most of his hair as well.

The blast had happened. But kissing Tammy Ingles had shaken him up more than the exploding stove had. He didn't know if she scared him so much because she was the only one who knew who he really was or because of how much she'd made him crave her.

His body ached, and it wasn't because of the uncomfortably thin mattress of the bed in the bunkroom. It was because of her.

He shouldn't have left her. What he should have done was kiss her over and over again until she wanted him as much as he wanted her. But she had kissed him back;

she'd touched his hair. She'd seemed as passionate as he'd been…until she'd remembered who he was.

Or at least who she *thought* he was. That had always gotten in his way before. The women he'd dated in the past had always been more interested in his money and his family name than in who he was as a man. Even his fiancée…maybe most especially his fiancée.

He sighed and pushed thoughts of Helena from his mind, which was easy since he hadn't thought of her in years. But Tammy…

Ever since the first time he'd met her, he thought of the gorgeous hairstylist. And now he couldn't get her off his mind. Keeping his eyes closed, he savored the flavor of her, and despite the obnoxious snoring of some of the guys bunking near him, he tried to imagine he was with her—in her room…

And he nearly fell back to sleep.

Until loud barking jerked him fully awake.

He opened his eyes, but darkness still enveloped him. Curses rang out along with the barking.

"Shut up, Annie," somebody grumbled.

But the barking got louder like someone had turned up her volume. Or the big sheepdog-mastiff mutt had gotten closer. Was she chasing someone?

Or had someone started another fire?

Ethan jumped up from his bunk and rushed toward the door, nearly tripping over the dog in the process. She growled low in her throat. And she *never* growled.

"What is it, girl?" he asked. "Is somebody in here?"

"There's a lot of somebodies in here," Trent Miles muttered. "And we're all trying to sleep, so tell her to shut the hell up."

But Ethan flipped on the lights instead. And more curses rang out.

Annie barked even louder than she had been as she lunged toward him.

He pushed her down and asked, "What is it? Do you smell smoke?"

She wasn't the typical firehouse mascot Dalmatian, but she could sure as hell sniff out a fire. She'd saved the life of Cody Mallehan's fiancée, Serena Beaumont, as well as Stanley. Stanley was the nineteen-year-old who did odd jobs around the firehouse.

Annie was usually with the boy, so he must have come in early today to clean up the mess the kitchen fire had caused the day before. Maybe the lingering smell of that fire was why the overgrown puppy was barking now.

But the guys started laughing, and Trent pointed out, "She doesn't recognize you without your beard. She thinks you're an intruder."

Ethan bent over and ran his hand over her bristling fur. "It's me, girl. It's Ethan."

For now…

Until someone else discovered his true identity. Then his whole world would explode, not just the stove…and he'd lose everything he'd come to love. His job. His friends. Maybe even his life…

If he was right, if that plane crash hadn't been an accident five years ago…

And if someone had figured out who he really was, maybe that stove blowing up hadn't been an accident either…

The loud barking hadn't awakened Trick. He'd already been awake and down the hall in the firehouse kitchen, trying to find what he'd missed. *Hoping* to find some damn clue that might finally reveal the identity of the person behind all the mayhem.

But Annie's unusually urgent barking compelled him to run back to the bunkroom. With so many of the hotshots sleeping there while awaiting the next wildfire call, it would be the perfect place for the saboteur to strike next. The intruder had not counted on Annie being at the firehouse, though, and she had cornered him near the doorway. Lunging at him, she pushed her paws against his chest and trapped him between her and the wall.

Who was the guy? And when had Annie become such a guard dog? She opened her huge mouth and…

Swiped her tongue across the guy's face.

"See," Trent Miles said. "Even Annie thinks you're better looking now."

"Now that she recognizes me," the man replied as he pushed the dog back down onto all four of her legs.

"*Ethan*…?" Trick said in surprise. He hadn't recognized the hotshot without his bushy beard. But for some reason the guy almost seemed more familiar without all the facial hair.

Trent chuckled. "McRooney didn't recognize you either."

Ethan lifted one of his bandaged hands to his face, almost as if he was trying to hide behind it. Was that what the beard had been—a way for him to hide?

Because it wasn't as if he'd needed it for any other reason. The guy didn't have scars like someone had told Trick he did from a plane crash that had happened nearly five years ago.

He narrowed his eyes and studied Ethan's face or

at least what he could see of it. He really did look so damn familiar…

"You see it too," Miles remarked. "It's been driving Hank crazy trying to figure out who he looks like."

Henrietta…

Trick automatically wanted to correct him because there was nothing masculine about Henrietta. She was beautiful and sexy and drove him absolutely crazy, so crazy that he didn't ever want to leave Northern Lakes. And he sure as hell would never leave her.

Except for that morning when he'd had to slip out of her bed early to come to the firehouse and investigate. He didn't want her being the next one to get hurt.

He had to stop this saboteur, and trying to find out who the hell was responsible for all the *accidents* was also driving him crazy.

"Didn't Hank mention it to you?" Trent asked him.

Trick shook his head. "No. We have better things to talk about than ol' Ethan here." Actually they hadn't done much talking at all last night. They'd been so happy neither of them had been hurt that they'd celebrated. But they *had* spoken about what had happened with the stove and who might have done it.

"Good to know," Ethan remarked. But his dark eyes narrowed with suspicion and he asked, "But what are you doing here if you have so much to talk about with Hank?"

Trick shrugged. "Just getting an early start."

"Damn early," Ethan said. "We'd all be sleeping if Annie hadn't woke us up."

"Now that she knows who you are, she's settled down," Trick pointed out. "So I'll let you all go back to sleep." He turned away from the door, but he didn't make it far down the hall before Ethan joined him.

"What the hell's really going on?" the injured hotshot asked.

Trick shrugged. "Like Miles said, Annie must not have recognized you."

"I'm not talking about Annie and you know it." Ethan gestured toward where Trick had strung a caution tape across the doorway to the kitchen. "That stove blowing up like that wasn't really an accident, was it?"

He shrugged again. "How would I know? My sister's the arson investigator—not me." Sam had come to Northern Lakes to find the arsonist and had found her soul mate as well. She was the one who'd convinced Trick to help out his brother-in-law with this investigation of his own. But he hadn't been too damn successful yet.

"So you're admitting it was arson," Ethan pressed.

Trick sighed. "I just told you I don't know."

"But you *suspect*."

"Talk to the boss," Trick said, deferring to Braden's wish to keep the whole thing quiet. Though he agreed less and less with that decision, his brother-in-law was in charge of the hotshot team and the investigation, not him.

"I was lucky yesterday," Ethan said, "that I just lost my beard. I could have lost my whole damn head. And I might if I'm not prepared for the next attack. And it was an attack, wasn't it? Just like all those other things that have been happening to us?"

"Some of those things were caused by bad people," Trick reminded him. That was how the spot had opened up on the team for him to join because a hotshot's wife had killed him. That hadn't been an accident nor had all the things she'd done to try to take out Owen James too. And then her lover had first tried to frame then kill Luke Garrison.

Frustration coursed through Trick over what everyone had endured since he'd joined the team. "It's like we're cursed or something," he remarked.

And all the color drained from Ethan's face.

Alarmed, he reached out and grabbed the guy's arm to steady him. "What's wrong?" he asked. "Are you okay?"

Or had the hospital released him too early?

Ethan drew in a deep breath before nodding. "Yeah, I'm fine…"

But clearly he wasn't. He looked as though he'd seen a ghost. After the close call he'd had the day before, maybe he'd seen his own.

Footsteps on the stairs echoed through the apartment, making her pulse race. Was it Ethan?

No. She'd locked the door to the street after he'd left the night before. But these footsteps weren't coming from the stairwell that led down to the exterior door. These were from the stairs that led directly to the salon. The salon receptionist, Amber, appeared in the doorway between the mudroom and the kitchen. "Tammy, you have to come down here." The young woman's face was flushed with excitement.

"Why? What is it?" Tammy asked.

"*Who*," Amber corrected her. Her blue eyes twinkled now. "It's someone famous…"

Had Ethan come back to the salon—not as Ethan—but as his true self, Jonathan Michael Canterbury IV?

But Amber was so young she probably didn't even know who he was—unless she'd found the magazine. Her heart beating fast, Tammy cautiously asked, "Who is it?"

"That reporter from Channel 9 out of Detroit."

"Avery Kincaid?" She was the wife of one of Braden Zimmer's assistant superintendents, Dawson Hess. But she'd recently moved to New York for a job opportunity with a national news broadcast.

"No, she's not there anymore. It's the younger one— the one who started out as an intern with the station. Usually she covers parties and concerts and stuff like that…"

Which was how Amber knew who she was since that was the only *news* that interested her.

Tammy smiled. "That's great. But what in the world is she doing here?"

"She wants to do a story about the Huron Hotshots," Amber said. "She's asking everybody about all the stuff that's been happening to them lately."

Tammy cursed and jumped up from the stool. She knew the hotshots well enough to know that none of them would welcome the media coverage, but most especially not Ethan.

Or Jonathan…

She cursed again.

Amber's eyes widened with shock, probably over Tammy swearing instead of being excited, and the young woman seemed frozen at the top of the stairs. So Tammy had to ease her aside to run down the steps. Fortunately, she worked out, or she might have been panting for breath when she rushed into the salon. As it was, she was able to speak succinctly when she found the reporter standing in the back near the chair of one of the gossipiest young stylists on Tammy's staff.

"You can't be back here without an appointment," Tammy told the reporter, before turning to give Caitlin a meaningful look.

The reporter, Brittney Townsend, had curly brown hair and unusually pale brown eyes. Tammy had caught a few of her broadcasts as well—about parties and concerts.

What the hell was she doing in Northern Lakes?

"This is the boss," the stylist told the reporter. "She knows the hotshots better than just about anyone else in here." And then Caitlin's purple-painted lips curved into a smirk. Her lips matched the color of her hair.

"You should be focusing on your client," Tammy admonished her, pointing to the woman in her chair. "Not gossiping."

The smirk slid away from Caitlin's mouth. She wasn't used to Tammy reprimanding her. Maybe she needed to do it more often because the young stylist stopped talking and turned her attention back to her client.

"You can't be back here," Tammy told the reporter again, and she gestured toward the lobby. But then she felt a flash panic that the woman might see the magazine and then see Ethan...

She followed Brittney into the waiting area and glanced at the stack. A few had been lifted off the top, but the one with Jonathan Canterbury IV on it remained hidden.

"Sounds like you're the person I should be talking to anyway," Brittney chirped with a friendly smile. "You know all about the hotshots." She said it with none of the innuendo Caitlin had, but Tammy still bristled with indignation.

"You're wasting your time in here," Tammy reiterated. "If you want to know anything about the hotshots, you need to speak with them."

Brittney sighed. "I tried, but the superintendent isn't being forthcoming with me. And I know there's a story here…"

The reporter was young, but her instincts were good. There was *definitely* a story here—a big one.

But Tammy just shrugged as if bored with the conversation. "I don't think so. I'm sure you'd find that every other hotshot team has the same experiences." She was surprised the lie slipped so easily through her lips.

The brunette's brow furrowed. "What kind of experiences?"

Brittney was good. Too good…

Tammy shrugged again. "You know. Whatever they experience fighting fires and all."

"There was some kind of explosion at their firehouse yesterday," the reporter persisted. "Do you know what happened?"

Tammy shook her head. "Just something with the stove…"

It wasn't as if a burner had caught a potholder on fire, though. The stove had exploded. And like before, Tammy had the gut feeling that it might not have been an accident.

Especially now that she knew who'd been hurt in the explosion. Of course there had been other accidents—so many other accidents—that had affected other hotshots besides Ethan.

"Like I said, you'll have to talk to them for details,"

Tammy said as she walked through the lobby and pushed open the door. "But since you don't have an appointment, you will need to leave."

The woman's eyes narrowed. "You seem in a hurry to get rid of me."

"Just having a busy day," Tammy fibbed.

"Too busy to take a walk-in client?" the reporter asked. "I could use a trim." Her chocolate-brown locks were wound into perfect spiral curls that looked as though they'd recently been styled.

Tammy smiled. "Not in my professional opinion."

And color deepened the woman's naturally tanned complexion. She'd been caught in a lie, and she knew it.

But she was unrepentant. As she passed Tammy in the doorway, she pressed a card into her hand. "My cell is on there. Please call me when you decide you want to talk. A report from me about your salon could do wonders for your business."

"My business is doing just fine," Tammy assured her as she pulled the door closed behind the woman, leaving her on the sidewalk looking in at her.

Actually, her business was doing better than fine. Every service the salon offered was booked out for months in advance. She literally had no openings for the reporter as a walk-in client unless she'd wanted to personally take care of her. But clearly the woman hadn't wanted a haircut. She'd wanted a scoop. And if she inadvertently ran into Ethan, she would get one.

Just as Tammy had warned him, his secret was going to come out.

Chapter 7

Doubt bombarded Braden as he stood at the podium in the conference room on the third floor of the firehouse. Even with the windows open, the smell of smoke hung heavily in the air like the humidity hung outside the windows. Sweat beaded on his brow and trickled down his back between his shoulder blades. But he wasn't sure if he was sweating because of the heat or because of what he was about to do.

Was it the right thing?

Not long after Trick had joined the team, he'd tried to talk him into being open and honest with all of them. That was something Braden had always been until he'd received that ominous note.

That damn note…

Ever since he'd received it, he hadn't been able to look at any of the hotshots the same way he once had.

Now he regarded them all with suspicion. Maybe it was time to get it all out in the open.

But first...

"We have a problem," he said, and began the meeting.

Several of the team nodded in agreement while some murmured, "We sure as hell do..."

"A reporter from Channel 9 is in town trying to do a story on us," he said.

"My wife already did a story," Dawson Hess interjected.

"About you," Cody Mallehan remarked with a teasing smile.

That story about Dawson and the arsonist terrorizing them had brought about her job offer for the anchor position in New York. Maybe that was why the young reporter from her previous television station wanted to do a story on them—because she thought her career might follow Avery's trajectory.

"Her name is Brittney Townsend," Braden continued, as if nobody had interrupted him.

But he was disrupted again when Trent Miles audibly gasped. And his light brown eyes widened in surprise.

"Do you know her?" he asked. Trent and Brittney both worked out of Detroit—albeit the city had millions of other people in it as well whose paths had probably never crossed. But he'd already wondered...

Trent just shook his head.

"Why is she here?" Ethan asked.

At least the voice sounded like Ethan even though the face didn't look at all like him anymore. Without his bushy beard and long hair, he was a whole different man. Braden furrowed his brow as he stared at him.

Ethan sat in the back, in his usual place, and he kept

lifting his bandaged hands to his face. While it was a little pink in a few spots, it didn't look seriously burned—not like his hands must have been.

"She's here," Braden replied, "because somehow she got wind of everything that's been happening around here lately." Did she have a source within the firehouse?

Or was her source with the state police post that had arrested the perpetrators of some of the things that had happened to the hotshots?

Since one of those perpetrators was one of their own, Braden doubted any of them would have been talking to the media. But…

It could have been anyone in town. Everybody knew that a lot of *accidents* had recently been happening to the hotshots. But they didn't know everything, and he wanted to keep it that way…with everyone else but his team.

Only the hotshots deserved to know the truth.

Just like Trick and now even his wife had urged him to reveal. He'd been reluctant to share all the facts with them because he hadn't wanted to tip off the saboteur. But keeping the note secret hadn't kept any of them safe or led him any faster to finding out who was responsible for all these incidents.

As Trick had pointed out the past several weeks, not disclosing the truth might have actually put them in more danger. Trick most of all since the saboteur had probably realized Braden's real reason for hiring his brother-in-law. To find him…

Or her…

"Too damn many things," Carl Kozek grumbled from his seat in the front row. "My wife's getting on me to retire from the hotshot team too." He'd already retired from the firehouse where he'd worked in the off season.

"She's not the only one," Donovan Cunningham remarked. "Holly's trying to get me to quit, too."

Braden glanced over that man's head to Trick who sat behind him. Their gazes met, and Braden nodded. "I should have addressed this sooner," he admitted. The weight of the guilt on his shoulders made them slump.

"You're always telling us to stay safe," Michaela said in his defense. "Accidents just happen…" When everyone turned toward her, her face flushed with color, and she defensively stammered, "Well, they do…"

It was clear she was probably the only one who still believed that the things that had happened were not intentional.

"I wish that was the case," he said. "But there is enough evidence to indicate otherwise."

"What?" Ethan asked. "What are you saying—that someone actually tried to kill me yesterday?"

"I don't know if the intention of the accidents is to kill anyone," Braden said. At least he hoped like hell that wasn't the case. "Or just to wreak havoc…"

"Havoc wreaked…" Ethan muttered.

"The only *casualty* of these accidents has been your beard," Braden pointed out. So far…

And that was why he had decided to come clean with the team. But he had to wait until the others stopped chuckling over his remark.

"But I do want everyone to be extra cautious," he commanded. "And I also want to find the person that isn't who I think they are…"

Braden drew the note he'd received so long ago from a folder on the podium. He raised it up high enough, so they could all read the words spelled out in crude block letters.

"Who is it?" he asked. "Who was I warned about?"

It was his nightmare all over again. Like in the bar, everybody stopped talking, but they didn't freeze. They all turned to stare at him where he sat in the back of the conference room.

A curse slipped through his lips.

Had they figured it out just like Tammy had warned...did they know who he really was?

"Why are you all looking at me?" he asked defensively. "I didn't send that note." The last thing he'd wanted was for anyone to suspect that he wasn't really Ethan Sommerly, but someone must have figured it out a while ago and sent Braden that note. Or they'd been there when the plane had crashed and knew the truth. He glanced over at the only person, besides him, who knew...

That person was the only one in the room not staring at him. His blond head was bent, his shoulders slumped, as if he was trying to disappear like they had all those years ago when they'd been lost for months in the mountains.

Ethan continued, "And I sure as hell haven't been tampering with our equipment because I wouldn't have sabotaged myself."

"The stove was rigged to explode." Trick finally confirmed what Ethan had suspected.

But everybody kept glaring at him as if he was guilty of something.

"The two things could be unrelated," Michaela said. "Maybe the note is just about someone pretending to be someone they're not and it has nothing at all to do with the sabotage."

If the note was regarding him, that sure as hell was the case. But there was someone else it could be about. Before he did anything too drastic, though, he needed to talk to that person. So all he did was insist, "The note isn't about me."

He was Ethan Sommerly now—the man he'd been for the past five years, the one they had all come to know and trust. And while he hadn't been completely honest with his teammates, he hadn't hurt any of them. He hadn't betrayed that trust. Instead he'd tried to protect them.

But maybe he'd failed.

Maybe, even though he'd changed his name, his family curse had still found him. And his team...

She'd made a mistake. A horrible mistake. She knew it the moment she opened the door to him. Just seeing him, filling the doorway with his big body, had the heat of desire rushing through Tammy.

But she hadn't called him here to finish what he'd started the night before with his kisses. She'd called him here for something else entirely.

"Are you going to let me in?" he asked as she continued to stand in front of him. "You invited me, remember?" A glint passed through his dark eyes.

Or maybe it was just the light as she stepped back and waved him inside. She closed the door quickly behind him, hoping nobody had seen him enter the stairwell leading up to her apartment.

"I called you here to warn you," she said, making

it clear that was the only reason. To herself as well as to him.

"About the reporter?" he asked.

"You've seen her?"

"No. Braden warned us all this morning," he said with a heavy sigh.

"What are you going to do?"

He shrugged. "Stay away from her."

"It's not going to be that easy," she said. "Brittney pushed her way into the salon this morning, asking questions about all of you. She seemed pretty convinced that there's something going on with the hotshots."

His big body tensed. "She was here? She came to see *you*?"

Heat rushed to her face. The reporter must have heard that Tammy was a firehouse groupie and had thought she would reveal all the hotshots' intimate secrets.

Tammy only knew one secret, though, and as she'd already told him, it wasn't her place to reveal it. She headed up the stairs, knowing he'd follow her. And as he did, a groan slipped through his lips. Startled, she turned toward him. "Are you okay?" she asked. "Or are you more sore today?"

She'd had that happen after a car accident. The first day she'd felt fine. The next she'd felt like a bus had run over her. Maybe it was the same with the blast he'd survived.

A muscle twitched in his cheek. Some stubble had grown back, shadowing his jaw, but the squareness of it and the deep cleft in his chin were still clearly visible and sexy as hell. Since he was standing a couple of steps below her on the stairwell, they were eye to eye.

And that glint sparkled in the dark depths of his gaze again. "I'm sore that you made me leave last night," he rasped. "I wanted to stay. I wanted to be with you."

Her pulse quickened, and even more heat rushed through her, pooling in her core. She could not deny the attraction between them. But she didn't want him to use that to distract her from the truth he kept denying. "That's not why I called you," she repeated.

"I know. The reporter…"

"I didn't tell her anything," she assured him.

That muscle twitched along his jaw again. "What's to tell?"

"Who you really are," she reminded him with a pointed look. "I know."

His lips curved into a tight smile. "You think you know…"

"I *know*," she reiterated. And she forced herself to turn and continue the rest of the way up the stairs. But knowing he was watching and that her tight skirt clung to her every curve, she swayed her hips as she moved. She wore a tight tank top with the skirt, in deference to the heat outside, but also because she knew he was coming.

She was just flirting, though, like she always flirted. She couldn't actually go beyond that, not with a man who hadn't even been honest about his identity. Even now he kept trying to deny it. So she put the island between them again and picked up the magazine from the granite countertop.

After seeing the reporter out of the salon, she'd smuggled the magazine up to her apartment, so nobody would stumble across it. This issue was an old one, so it wasn't as if it was still out on newsstands or in the stores. She held the magazine up next to his face. Despite the passing of five years and the stubble on his jaw now, he looked exactly the same.

"I have clients who'd kill to age as well as you have," she murmured. Then she flipped the magazine around and showed him the cover.

He grimaced as if he couldn't bear to look at himself. Then he shook his head again. "That's not me. I don't know—"

"Stop lying!" she interjected, her patience with him wearing thin. She hated being lied to. Her parents had lied to her for so many years.

You're not overweight.

Your face will clear up.

Your hair looks pretty...

So many lies. The lying had only added to her already low self-esteem. Sure, your parents were supposed to love and support you, but not delude you. Then there'd been the other side of that: the mean kids in high school who'd told her she was ugly and gross. And they'd been lying just like her parents. Because even as she'd struggled through her awkward phase, she'd never been ugly...not like they had been. But because of all those people and all those untruths, she struggled even now to trust what someone said to her...

Were they telling the truth or only what they thought she wanted to hear? She didn't want anyone trying to fool her for any reason. And Jonathan Canterbury IV had already fooled her for years.

"I'm not that man anymore," he said.

"Yes, you are," she insisted.

He shook his head then clenched one of his bandaged hands against his chest. "Not in here..."

Fine. Tammy could believe that he'd changed. She had changed, too, from the person she'd once been. But she'd had every reason to want to change, to improve herself while he had already been somebody people had respected and envied.

"I don't understand what happened," she said, as she tried to make sense of why he would have assumed another identity. "Or how it…how you—"

"Became Ethan Sommerly?" he finished the question for her.

She nodded.

He uttered a ragged sigh before pulling out a stool and settling heavily onto it. Dark circles of exhaustion rimmed his dark eyes.

Feeling sorry for him, despite herself, and wanting the whole story, Tammy turned and pulled a beer from her refrigerator. "Want one?"

"Is that a Pinot Grigio in there?" he asked.

He was a *wine drinker*? Putting back the beer, she pulled out the chilled wine instead. She opened and poured them both a glass.

He took a long sip before wearily admitting, "I'm not even sure where to start…"

"How about with why," she said. "Why would you want to let people think you were dead?"

She'd read the article a few times since bringing the magazine upstairs. The article had reminded her about his devastated mother who'd already lost her husband and his brothers and her other in-laws along with her younger son before the plane carrying Jonathan had crashed. She'd also read about Jonathan Canterbury's heartbroken fiancée. And she remembered all the news coverage from when his plane had gone down.

"How could you do that to your family?" she whispered, her voice raspy with sympathy for them. "To your friends? How could you let them think you're dead and put through them so much pain?" She'd been with her friends when their significant others were off fighting wildfires and knew how much they worried about them, how afraid they were that they might not come back. Fortunately, they always had, unlike Jonathan Canterbury IV.

He snorted. "You don't know my family…"

She nearly snorted, too, thinking of herself mixing with people like his rich and privileged family. "No, I don't. But I read the articles, saw the interviews…" While his beautiful fiancée had given many tearful interviews, the Canterburys actually hadn't spoken directly to any reporters. They'd just released statements through a representative, pleading for privacy and for prayers for his safe return. "They were desperate to find you. But when you and Rory VanDam were finally found, you claimed to be Ethan Sommerly."

"I was lost for months in those mountains, so my family and friends already thought I was dead by the time Rory and I were finally rescued," he explained. "They had already mourned me as much as a family like mine mourns, and trust me, it wasn't for long or very damn hard."

She sucked in a breath at the bitterness in his voice. His family life obviously hadn't been ideal, but with all the tragedies the Canterburys had had, that was probably understandable. "Why do you think that?" she asked. "Is your relationship with them that bad?"

He sighed. "What relationship? Even before that plane crash, I was already dead to them."

"I'm sure that's not the case…"

"You don't know my family," he reiterated. "When my dad died, my mom shipped me right off to boarding school."

"Isn't that what rich people do?" she asked. "Send their kids to boarding school?"

"I was ten, and we'd just buried my father," he said, his voice gruff with emotion, and tears sparkled in his dark eyes.

The pain inside him resonated with Tammy, and she reached out, sliding her hand over the one he'd fisted on the countertop next to his wineglass. "I'm sorry. How did he…"

"Heart attack," he finished for her again. "Then there was David's death…"

"Your younger brother."

He nodded. Then he cleared his throat and said, "He was in boarding school when he died. He was just fourteen…"

"That article didn't really say how he died…" And she hated to pry, hated to put him through any more pain than he was obviously already feeling.

A muscle twitched along his jaw, and he pulled his hand from beneath hers, as if rejecting her comfort. Or did he think it was pity? "Drug overdose," he replied hoarsely. "But my mother and sister and brother-in-law worked really hard to keep that from getting out. They care more about appearances, about family tradition than each other." He blew out a rough breath. "I got disowned because I dropped out of law school. I didn't want to follow in the footsteps of anyone else in my family. I wanted to be someone else. *Something* else.

That's why I signed up for hotshot training. That's why I was on that plane with the other hotshots."

"A hotshot?" She couldn't process that someone like him, someone from such a privileged life would choose a profession that was so hard physically and so dangerous emotionally…for the hotshot and for his family and loved ones. She shook her head at the thought of that and asked the other question that had been niggling at her since she'd first figured out who he really was. "So why Ethan Sommerly? Was that a name you made up or a real person?"

Sadness darkened his brown eyes again. "Ethan was real, and he was on the plane, too. I went through hotshot training with him. He was a good guy. A loner with no family, but he was a good friend to me through training. When the plane started having mechanical issues, we all put on our parachutes and got off. Or at least I thought he and a couple other guys escaped with me and Rory. But maybe the others didn't have time, or they weren't found. I don't know… I never saw him again. I didn't even find Rory right away. We got separated…" He shuddered.

And she nearly did as well, thinking how awful that must have been, being lost as long as he'd been. Being alone…

But then even after he'd been found, he seemed to prefer to be alone, off in the woods working most of the time as a forest ranger.

"You really went through hotshot training?" she asked, circling back to the reason he'd been on that plane in the first place—a reason she couldn't understand. "As Jonathan Canterbury? Why would a billionaire heir want to fight fires? Were you doing it just to piss off your family?"

He chuckled and admitted, "That might have been part of it. I also thought it sounded cool." He chuckled again. "It's not nearly as glamorous as it sounds."

"Your life as a Canterbury was glamorous," she said. "You were always in the news, attending movie premieres and gallery openings—"

"My life was pathetic," he interjected. "With no purpose, no passion…" And as his gaze met hers, that glint in his dark eyes flickered into a blaze.

The heat in his gaze raised her temperature, had that passion he'd mentioned rushing over her now, overwhelming in its intensity. She couldn't remember the last time she'd felt like this, if ever. And while she knew it was dangerous, she also knew he wasn't going to stick around…not now, not when his secret was certain to come out.

So she would be safe to take what she wanted, and she'd wanted him for a long time…just not for keeps. She smiled and leaned across the counter towards him, fluttered her lashes at him like she always had, and licked her lips. And his gaze got even hotter as he stared at her. "So you joined the hotshots looking for passion, Ethan…" she murmured, as her pulse quickened. "Or should I call you Jon—"

Before she could finish her question, his mouth claimed hers. He nibbled at her lips with his before pulling back to murmur, "Ethan. Call me Ethan."

"Ethan—"

She barely got the word out before he was kissing her again. The taste of the wine on his lips made her feel as light-headed as if she'd drank the whole bottle herself. But she'd barely had a sip.

She wanted more though—of Ethan, not the wine. She wrapped her arms around his neck, clinging to him as he leaned across that island. Then he stood up and lifted her right over it and into his arms.

She tore her mouth from his and protested. "Don't hurt your hands."

His voice gruff with desire, he replied, "They're not hurting." But it was clear that he was; his body was rigid with tension.

She could relieve that tension for him—*with* him—as well as the tension that wound tightly inside her. Last night she'd stopped him because he'd refused to be honest with her. So far tonight, with just the limited amount of information he'd shared, he'd laid his soul bare to her.

Tammy felt like she knew him better than anyone else did, and that gave her a sense of intimacy that made her entirely comfortable enough to tell him, "Take me to bed." She pointed through the living room to the open door off it.

"Are you sure?" he asked.

She nodded. "Very sure…"

He lifted her into his arms, and as he passed through the bedroom doorway, she flipped on the switch that turned on the chandelier dangling over her bed. The space was very feminine. And he looked huge and out of place among the pale pink walls and sheets.

But he didn't seem to notice the room at all. He just stared at her, his eyes dark with desire and that glint of passion had turned into a hint of trepidation. She could tell he was worried about something, too.

"I'm not going to change my mind," she assured him.

"Or are you afraid of what I might do to you in here?" She chuckled at the ridiculous thought of her intimidating such a muscular giant of a man.

But he nodded in agreement. "I am very afraid of you."

Probably because she was the only one who knew his secret. Or *was* she?

Before she could ask, his mouth brushed across hers again. He kissed her as he carried her the last few feet into the room. After laying her on the bed, he stepped back—leaving her fully in the light of the chandelier.

And old insecurities rushed over her. Would he see the stretchmarks from when she was bigger? The scars from the acne? Maybe she shouldn't have turned on the light. Other men had seen them, had made remarks, had made her feel not good enough. She knew they were wrong; she was better than good enough. She was happy as she was. And she wasn't about to change for anyone. Not even Jonathan Canterbury IV.

"It's fine if you've changed your mind," he told her. His voice though gruff with desire also held tenderness for her. "I'll leave."

Tammy shook her head. She wasn't changing her mind. Her heart quickening, she pulled her tank top over her head and tossed it onto the floor. The top had had a built-in bra in it, so now her breasts were bare.

Ethan groaned as if he was in pain, and he stared down at her with awe on his handsome face. "You are so damn beautiful."

Usually she felt that she was, but occasionally those old insecurities crept back in. But they were gone now, as she stared into his eyes and saw the admiration, the raw desire in them. Emboldened, she pushed her skirt and panties down her hips.

And Ethan's big body shook slightly. "You're going to bring me to my knees," he ground out.

"You don't have to beg," she assured him.

"I would," he said. "I want you that badly…" Then he stripped off his jeans and his shirt, and she could see how badly he wanted her.

His erection pulsated with need. And when she reached out to touch it, he jerked back. "It's been a long time for me…"

"Then get over here," she told him.

But he shook his head. "I need a minute." He stood beside the bed, drawing in deep breaths that made his huge chest swell even more.

She couldn't wait, though. She needed to feel him next to her, needed to touch him, so she grasped his forearm, above the bandages on his hands, and pulled him onto the bed with her.

"Take these off," he said as he held out the bandages to her.

They were the only thing either of them wore. "But… you need them."

"What I need is to touch you," he said.

"You don't need your hands for that."

His lips curved into a faint grin as understanding dawned. And he used his mouth, first on hers with more of those passionate kisses. Then he moved down her throat to her breasts. And he kissed them before closing his lips around a nipple and gently tugging.

Tammy arched up from the bed as pleasure streaked through her. And a moan slipped through her lips. She wanted him so badly…

But when she reached for him, he slipped from her grasp as he moved farther down her body. He kissed her everywhere before finding the spot that throbbed with desire, with *need*, for him. And he made love to her with his mouth.

She arched up again, crying out at the intensity of the pleasure, before her body went limp. And he disappeared from the bed.

"Where did you go?" she wondered aloud.

He held up his jeans in his bandaged hand. "I can't get the condom out of the pocket."

She grinned as she helped him, first with the pocket and then the packet. When she rolled the latex over him, he groaned.

Touching him had her throbbing again with desire. She leaned forward and kissed his sexy square jaw and the cleft in his chin, then she slid her lips down his throat to his massive shoulders. He was so damn handsome, so perfect.

She pushed him onto his back, so she could straddle him. And despite the bandages, he gripped her hips and helped guide her onto his shaft. He was so big.

So hot, so hard…

She groaned at the sensation of this man filling her so completely. Then they both began to move, frantically seeking a release to the tension that had built inside them. The smoldering sexual attraction that had simmered between them for so long…

And she regretted now that they'd not done this sooner. Sure, she'd been worried about getting in too deep, about falling for him. But now, knowing who he was, she knew that wasn't possible. He wasn't going to stay in Northern Lakes; he wasn't going to stay a firefighter, not when Braden and the others learned the truth. Unless they already knew…

But she doubted that. Before any other doubts could creep in, the passion overwhelmed her again.

He arched up from the bed and sank deeper into her. Then he kissed her again before sliding his mouth down her throat to her breast. His lips closed around a nipple before his tongue swiped across it.

Pleasure streaked through her. She came again, and his name slipped through her lips.

"Ethan…"

But that wasn't his name. That wasn't who he was.

But that was the man with whom she'd made love. He was the one she knew. Jonathan Canterbury IV was a stranger to her, and she suspected he would stay that way.

A guttural groan tore from his throat as his body tensed and then shuddered with his release. Then, instead of pulling away, he clutched her against his chest and rolled to his side to hold her like he intended to never let her go.

But she knew that wasn't possible. Once someone else discovered who he was, and they *would*, everything would change. He would have to return to his old life and leave Northern Lakes.

And her.

And a night like this would never happen again.

Chapter 8

Maybe he hadn't changed that much, at least not as much as he'd thought he had. Maybe he was still the spoiled rich kid he'd been five years ago: the one who hadn't appreciated what he'd had.

Because what he'd just experienced with Tammy...

He'd never felt that much before, that intensely, but instead of staying to tell her how much he'd enjoyed being with her, he snuck down the stairwell in the dark, carrying his shoes in his hands so the sound of his footsteps wouldn't wake her. She'd fallen asleep in his arms, and they ached now. Not from holding her, she was so slight, but from wanting to hold her all night.

But he shouldn't have held her at all. Even though she'd called him over, he should have stayed away from her. He was in danger and not just of his identity being revealed but in *real* danger.

Somebody had sabotaged that stove and the other equipment. Was it one of the team like the note Braden had received seemed to imply?

Or had that note been about him?

He knew of only one person who could have sent it then. But he hadn't had a chance to talk to him. That hotshot had slipped out of the conference room right after the meeting. Maybe he would be in the bunkroom tonight.

Which was where Ethan needed to head before anyone figured out where he'd been. Tammy had a reputation as a firehouse groupie because of gossip, not fact. She hadn't earned her reputation, and Ethan didn't want anyone believing that she had because of him.

He wasn't sure why she hadn't changed her mind, why she hadn't sent him away. Had the kisses they'd shared the day before made her as needy as he'd been?

But even though he'd just experienced the most intense pleasure of his life, he wanted her still. In fact, he paused with his hand on her door as that desire built inside him again. But desire wasn't the only thing he felt; he felt dread, too.

She was right.

His secret was going to come out.

So, after stepping back into his shoes, he forced himself to push open the door and walk away from her. It was for the best—for her.

But not for him…

His body ached again as tension filled him. He stepped onto the sidewalk which, despite the lateness of the hour, was awash in light from the streetlamp. And now another kind of tension flooded through him as a chill raised the short hairs on the nape of his neck.

The night was still warm and humid, so he wasn't cold. But he was chilled for another reason because he suddenly felt as if he was being watched. But when he glanced around, he saw nobody else on the street. Of course he was in the light, casting everything else in shadows.

Somebody could have been standing out there, stalking him. Was that why the stove had been sabotaged?

Had someone discovered who he was even before the beard had been burned? Had they been trying to get rid of him before his true identity could be discovered?

Something scraped across the asphalt, sending a pebble rolling over the street.

"Hello?" he called out, his voice echoing eerily in the night. "Who's there?"

He peered around again, looking for any sign of the person who was out there, watching him. He saw only a quick flash of light in the shadows.

"What the hell..."

It could have been from someone's phone. Or perhaps from a gun: the flash of the bullet as it left the barrel.

He ducked low and hurried off down the sidewalk, hoping he could make it back to the firehouse alive.

What the hell was that?

Tammy jerked awake, tangled naked in the sheets of her bed. Alone.

He was gone.

She shouldn't have been surprised but she was. He'd been holding her so tightly, as if he never intended to let her go. But he had.

Once she'd fallen asleep, he must have snuck off. Was he ashamed of what they'd done? Of her?

A small-town hairdresser might have been good enough for a hotshot firefighter. But she wouldn't be good enough for a Canterbury. His ancestors had been presidents and movie stars, billionaires and American royalty.

So what was he doing hiding out in a national forest, coming out only to battle wildfires with his team? What was he running from?

Himself or from whomever had tried to kill him?

Maybe the plane crash hadn't been an accident. And maybe the stove explosion hadn't been either. Maybe Tammy wasn't the only one who knew who he really was.

So what was that noise she'd heard, that had jerked her awake?

Had it just been the sound of his footsteps on the stairs? Or the door opening and closing as he crept out in the night? But what if it had been something else? Someone trying once again to take him out?

Awake and worried, she threw on her robe and headed toward the stairs. Her bare feet nearly slipped on the steps, but she had nobody to catch her this time, nobody to steady her.

She'd had no intention of sleeping with Ethan tonight. But then he'd kissed her, and she'd known that the desire was there—that it had always been there—for him. While she flirted with just about everyone, she'd only wanted him. And that was crazy...

He wasn't the sweet, quiet man she'd thought he was. He wasn't Ethan Sommerly. That man was dead.

What about this one?

Her hand trembled as she opened the door. Then she peered out into the darkness. Nothing stirred, not even a breeze. He was gone.

Like the ghost that he was.

* * *

His ghost was everywhere—on every wall and in every picture frame in the house. Maybe the only way to truly get rid of every trace of him was to burn down the place. To torch the estate that would have been his inheritance...

Had he lived.

But he was dead.

Even though the wreckage of the plane had never been found, his body never recovered, he was dead. Only a couple of survivors had made it out of the plane before it had crashed: a couple of elite firefighters. That was how they'd survived months lost in the mountains.

Old Jonny boy wouldn't have survived. He'd had no skills. Hell, no common sense...since he'd figured he could actually fight fires.

There was no way he had made it out of that wreckage alive. But the law required five years before he could be declared dead. And that five-year anniversary was only a few weeks away now.

Then, whatever hope there had been for his return, would die, leaving only his ghost behind. A lighter flipped on in the darkness, illuminating the picture frames atop that grand piano.

Soon enough it would be able to go up in flames, leaving the past, and every last trace of Jonathan Michael Canterbury IV, in ashes.

Chapter 9

He was a dead man, and guilt weighed heavily on Ethan for lying about it. Knowing that Tammy was right and eventually somebody else would figure it out, he trudged down the steps from the bunkroom on the second floor to Braden's office on the first floor. He drew in a deep breath, bracing himself, before he raised his bandaged fist and knocked on the door.

He didn't even flinch at the contact. The burns were healing fast. Pretty soon he'd be able to remove the bandages on his hands and resume his hotshot duties...

If he still had a job after he told Braden the truth.

Nobody answered his knock, so maybe he'd been given a reprieve. But just to make sure Braden wasn't distracted, he knocked again.

And somebody grunted, "Come in. You have to see this..."

Just as he pushed open the door, Braden spun his laptop around on his desk, and Ethan's face stared back at him from the computer screen.

It wasn't the picture from the magazine that Tammy had shown him. This picture was from last night, of him standing outside her closed salon. The flash he'd seen must have been from a camera.

But just like the magazine, the picture was captioned with the name Jonathan Michael Canterbury IV. Whereas the magazine had been announcing the upcoming anniversary of his death, this article announced his resurrection from the dead.

Braden glanced up at the doorway, and his face reddened when he saw him standing there. "I thought you were Trick." He swore. "But it's you. For the past three years that you've been part of my team, I thought you were Ethan Sommerly. You lied to me."

"I didn't lie," Ethan insisted, his heart hammering with fear and panic and regret. His life, the last five years of life that had mattered to him, that had mattered, was about to end. "I just let you believe what everyone else believed. And everyone believed that's who I was when I was found."

When the engine on the plane had started sputtering out, the real Ethan Sommerly had strapped a parachute on him and pushed him out with a backpack of supplies. He'd thought the man was going to follow him out after strapping on his own parachute. But maybe there hadn't been time or maybe there hadn't been enough parachutes. The real Ethan's wallet had been in that backpack. And after being lost for months, he had looked eerily similar, with the bushy beard and long hair, to the photo on Ethan Sommerly's driver's license.

Braden glared at him. "Same thing as lying. You didn't tell anyone who you really are." He shook his head. "I can't believe I've had someone like you out fighting fires with my team."

"Like me?" Ethan repeated, as his pride began to sting. Being a hotshot meant everything to him; he had never felt as sure of anything as he was of his profession. *Of his purpose.* He'd never had that before, and before joining Braden's team, he'd never had a real family before. He didn't want to lose his job, but most of all, he didn't want to lose his family. "I went through an intensive program to become a smoke jumper—the program your father-in-law taught—before I even became a hotshot. I worked for almost two years as a smoke jumper and a forest ranger before I came here. And that was after I survived all those months lost in the mountains. Since I've been here, I've held my own on every call we've ever had. You know that. You know me."

Braden clenched his jaw. "I thought I did."

"You know me," Ethan insisted. "I am not that person…" He pointed a bandaged hand toward that computer screen. "That's not me." Not anymore.

Maybe not ever…

"I never fit into that life," he said. "I never fit in anywhere like I have on this team." And just like last night with Tammy, he was tempted to beg again. Beg for his job, beg for Braden's forgiveness…

Maybe most especially for Braden's forgiveness. He had always respected the superintendent, had always known how much the team meant to him. But it meant a lot to Ethan as well. After giving up his old life, family and friends, the team was everything to him now.

But then a memory of the night before flashed through his mind, of Tammy in his arms and then straddling him.

He groaned and pushed a hand over his short hair. "I'm sorry, Braden," he said. "Really sorry." He knew an apology wasn't enough, though—not for years of what the superintendent probably considered deceit.

Braden shook his head, refusing to accept his apology.

"I am truly sorry," he insisted. "I didn't think I was hurting anyone."

"Does your family know that you didn't really die?" Braden demanded.

And Ethan flinched. "No. But months had already passed by the time I was rescued. They had already mourned me."

"So you don't think they would have been happy to find out you had actually survived?"

He shrugged. "I don't know if they would have been happy or disappointed," he admitted. "I don't know why that plane crashed. But just like the stove thing, I'm not convinced that it was an accident."

And Braden was the one to flinch now. "You think somebody was trying to kill you?"

"The plane crash wasn't the first close call I'd had," he admitted. "There were other stupid things. A car nearly ran me down outside a club. The brakes failed on my car. Hell, maybe all those things that have been happening to the hotshots has been because of me…"

"Because of the Canterbury curse?" Braden asked.

Ethan snorted, albeit uneasily. He didn't used to be superstitious, but so many people in his family had been lost that he'd begun to at least respect the curse if not entirely accept it. But maybe someone else had decided to take advantage of it. "Is it a curse or just an excuse for someone to try to get rid of me?"

"Why would they want to?"

He shrugged. "Money, love, jealousy... I don't know. But I only wanted to die once—that's why I didn't want anyone from my old life to find out that I'm alive."

Braden pointed again at that picture on his computer screen. But he said nothing. He didn't need to; the picture said it all.

If they hadn't already known, they would now—that he was alive. So how long before the *curse* struck again?

Tammy had opened up the salon but had hurried upstairs again before any of the stylists or clients had arrived. She'd needed to repair the damage her sleepless night had done to her face. So she'd concealed her dark circles and painted on a smile before she'd headed back down to the salon.

It hadn't been open very long, but it was already abuzz with chatter, which was so loud it even rose over the drone of the dryers. But the moment she stepped out of the office and into the styling area all conversation ceased.

Her smile slipped, and she lifted her hand to her face. Had she not done a good job? Were her dark circles still noticeable? "What?" she asked. "What's going on?"

"You tell us," Margaret said as she raised her eyebrows. "How long have you known what he was hiding underneath that beard?"

Ethan...

Of course. That was all everybody had been talking about since she'd cut his hair and shaved his beard—how damn good-looking he was.

And trying to place who he looked like…

"Not what—who," Caitlin corrected the older stylist. "He was hiding some famous dead guy."

Tammy froze now. "What are you talking about?"

Caitlin held up her phone, which had a large screen on it, and Ethan's handsome face filled that screen. "This…"

With a smile at the client sitting in Caitlin's chair, Tammy walked up to the young stylist and took her phone from her hand. "What is this?"

Along with a picture of Ethan, there was a new article—a clip of a scoop from the reporter who had stopped into the salon the day before. Tammy touched the Play button, and Brittney Townsend's voice emanated from the speakers on Caitlin's phone.

"For five years the world has believed that the Canterbury curse claimed the life of Canterbury heir Jonathan Michael Canterbury IV when his plane crashed in the Rocky Mountains. Miraculously he survived the crash and has been living as an elite firefighter in northern Michigan. But apparent from the bandages wrapped around his hands, it seems as though the curse has struck again—"

Her finger trembling, Tammy stabbed the Pause button. But she didn't want to just pause it; she wanted to delete it. Delete the story, delete the picture, delete what had happened last night.

No. She didn't want to erase that. She wanted to repeat it but not with Jonathan Canterbury IV. She wanted Ethan Sommerly. But he was dead.

Unless he'd survived the crash and started a new life like Jonathan had, he had probably been dead for nearly five years now.

"Why didn't you tell us?" Margaret asked, and a trace of hurt replaced her earlier amusement.

Tammy shook her head. "I didn't know."

"He lied to you too?" Caitlin asked, her voice softening with sympathy. The young woman hadn't had much luck with the men she'd dated either.

But for some reason Tammy felt compelled to try to keep his secret. "Who says he's lying?" she asked.

"I think we can all say that now," another voice chimed in.

Tammy hadn't hit the Play button on Caitlin's phone again. That voice didn't come from the speakers this time. It came from the doorway between the lobby and the back of the salon where the reporter stood.

"You could be mistaken," Tammy snapped. "Just as it was a mistake for you to come here again. I already told you that there are no open appointments."

Caitlin opened up her mouth, probably to offer to fit her in, but before she could say anything, Tammy glared at her. The last thing she wanted was for this pesky reporter to hang around any more than she had already been. Ms. Townsend must have planted herself on the sidewalk last night to get that photo because the windows of the salon were visible behind Ethan's head.

"I didn't come here to get my hair done," the reporter admitted. "I came back to get your side of the story."

Tammy shook her head. "There *is* no story."

The reporter smiled, her pale brown eyes bright with excitement over her discovery. "Jonathan Canterbury is alive. Surely, even in this town, people must realize that's news."

Offended on behalf of her hometown, Tammy sucked in a breath.

And the young reporter's face flushed. "I didn't mean that to sound…"

"As patronizing as it did," Tammy finished for her.

Was that why Ethan had hidden out here? Where he thought everyone was too backward to be aware of who he was?

Her pulse quickened with anger. But she wasn't sure who she was angrier with—Ethan or this reporter. She'd known him longer, though. With the other hotshots, he'd protected Northern Lakes from the arsonist that could have destroyed the whole town.

So she felt compelled to protect him for some reason. "And it's only news if it's true," she said. "Sure, they look alike, but plenty of other ordinary people look like famous people, too. Caitlin here looks like Selena Gomez." She lowered her voice as if whispering but spoke loud enough for everyone else to hear. "But I don't think she gave up her fame and fortune to work for me, do you?"

Caitlin giggled. "I wish!"

The reporter's face turned pinker, but she insisted, "This is different."

"How?" Tammy asked. "Do you have DNA evidence proving that Ethan Sommerly is Jonathan Canterbury?" She shook her head. "I doubt that. You have speculation only."

"I have the picture I took outside your salon last night," Brittney Townsend persisted.

Now heat rushed to Tammy's face. But hell, everybody already thought the worst of her. And she and Ethan were consenting adults, so what did it matter if anyone knew what they'd done last night?

It wasn't as if either of them was married. Actually, Jonathan Canterbury would have been—had he not died. He had been engaged. What had happened to his fiancée? Was she still mourning the man she'd loved?

A twinge of guilt struck Tammy's heart. She hated to think of the pain that Canterbury's family and friends must have felt and hated even more to think that he'd needlessly put them through that pain.

Of course months had passed before his rescue— months in which they'd already suffered, and he wouldn't have been able to spare them that.

But it wasn't as if someone got over the loss of a loved one in just a few months. Tammy's friends, Courtney and Serena still mourned the death of their mother and it had been over a year now.

Tammy shrugged. "Your picture proves nothing, Ms. Townsend."

"My picture proves that you know Jonathan Canterbury very well."

Tammy shook her head. "I don't know Jonathan Canterbury at all."

He was not the man she'd slept with the night before. She'd slept with the hotshot she'd known and flirted with for the past few years. But that man was dead now—thanks to the photograph the reporter had taken. Everybody would know now that Ethan Sommerly had died. While he'd left behind no family or friends to mourn him, she acknowledged, as a twinge passed through her heart again, that she was going to mourn him. That he'd meant far more to her than she'd realized…

Maybe it was best that the truth had come out—because she couldn't fall for a man who was already gone.

Braden's office door opened again, but this time there was no knock. That was how he should have re-

alized his earlier visitor hadn't been his brother-in-law.
Trick rarely ever knocked.

Trick released a ragged sigh. "So now we know who
your little note was about."

Braden nodded. "I guess we do."

"You *guess*?"

He shrugged. "Until the note writer comes forward
and tells me that's who it was about, I'm not sure. Who
else would have known that Ethan wasn't Ethan?"

Then he remembered who else had survived that
plane crash. Neither of the men had been working for
him when it happened. Ethan and Rory VanDam had
bounced around other teams, as smoke jumpers and
hotshots, before joining his team three years ago.

"But this only complicates things more," Trick said.

Braden nodded in agreement. He'd been worried
about one reporter but that damn picture was going to
attract a hell of a lot more than one.

"Ethan—Canterbury—whoever the hell he is—he's
not the saboteur," Trick insisted. "He sure as hell didn't
rig that stove to blow up and blow up his disguise along
with it."

"I know," Braden said. "So if he's not the saboteur,
is he the target?"

The other man shrugged. "This is the first *accident*
that almost took him out."

The last one had nearly taken out Trick. That was the
problem—the next one could target anyone.

"What did you do?" Trick asked. "Did you fire him?"

"How can I fire a man who really never worked for
me?" Braden asked.

"He worked for you," Trick said. "He worked at least

as hard if not harder than every one of us has worked for you."

Braden smiled over Trick's defensiveness and over how his brother-in-law had finally become part of a team. For years the hotshot had gone from team to team—only filling in as a substitute, never joining. Until now...

Now this team was as much his as it was Braden's. "So you don't think I should fire him?"

"What if he is the target?" Trick asked. "Then he's going to be in even more danger if he's out on his own. As a team, we can try to keep each other safe."

"Except for whoever is causing these accidents..."

And even though the note was probably about Ethan, it didn't mean that the saboteur wasn't still a member of the team. With everything that had happened, it was becoming clearer and clearer that it had to be one of them.

But which one?

Chapter 10

He'd expected Braden to call a meeting. Or to fire him...

Or to fire him and then call a meeting...

All day, while he'd hidden out in the national forest that encircled the town of Northern Lakes, Ethan had waited for that call to come.

You're fired.

And maybe he was. Maybe Braden had thought it went without saying that he'd lost a job he never should have had in the first place. That he wouldn't have had had Braden known the truth about him.

But he had to know, no matter how it turned out, if he had a job or not. If he was no longer part of the team...

So when the sun began to sink into the forest, Ethan came out of the woods and headed back to town. Since he was a ranger, he'd been assigned a US Forest Service pickup. Something else he would have to give up if he'd lost his job.

He drove to the firehouse and parked in the lot. But dread held him back from heading toward the three-story concrete block building.

What if Braden was inside? Would he use the opportunity to fire him now?

No. It would be better to head to the Filling Station. Leaving the pickup in the firehouse lot, he started off down the sidewalk toward the bar. It was late enough that the team would have all gone there—at least the ones who'd been staying at the firehouse. With the kitchen damaged, they had no way to make food for themselves, so they would have gone to the bar to eat, if not to drink.

As he walked toward the bar, Ethan glanced around him—looking for that damn reporter who must have taken his photo the night before. Was she skulking around in the dark again?

And where were the others?

He was sure many more reporters would descend on the town once they saw the picture. And then he wouldn't be able to hide anywhere—not even in the woods.

Except for calls to wildfires with his team, he'd spent much of the past five years hiding there. But now he had another place he wanted to go...

And it wasn't the bar. It was Tammy's place.

His body ached as he thought of her, of last night...

And despite the picture and the early meeting with Braden, she had been on his mind the most today. Hell, she'd never been off his mind. Even now he had to stop himself from turning and walking the other way—toward her salon.

But he couldn't put her in danger again. And just being around him had probably done that.

What if all those accidents that had happened to the team had really been targeting him? Maybe he shouldn't wait for Braden to fire him; maybe he should just quit.

He would be smart to take off before more media descended on Northern Lakes. Or worse yet, the authorities arrested him for identity theft. What laws had he broken when he'd let everyone assume he was another man? He was less concerned about legal ramifications than what he was about to do right now.

He hesitated just outside the door to the Filling Station. Then he drew in a breath and reached for the handle. He couldn't leave without saying goodbye to his team.

To his friends...

Just like the first time since Tammy had shaved his beard, the bar fell silent the minute he stepped inside—before the door even slammed closed behind him. It was as if they'd all been watching it, waiting for him to show up.

But unlike last time, there was no whistle, no one calling out to him. No one said a word even as he walked up to that booth in the back corner.

Once again not everybody was in it. Tammy wasn't there. And even though she wasn't a hotshot, she often joined them in the booth along with her friends.

Trick and Braden weren't present either. They were probably in a meeting about him, trying to decide if he was the saboteur. Hopefully they knew that he had never—knowingly—put his team in danger. He might have unwittingly done so, though.

"I'm sorry," he said.

"You should be," Carl Kozek bit out, his face flushed with anger. "You've been lying to all of us for years."

Trent Miles snorted. "Lying and laughing at us."

He shook his head. "I am a hotshot. I went through the training. I have the experience. I have had all your backs on every call I've been on."

He waited for more snarky remarks. But nobody said anything for a long moment.

So he sought to fill the awkward silence the way he and Trent Miles always did. "And you were the only one I was laughing at," he teased his friend.

But Trent didn't even crack a smile.

"What about Tammy?" Hank asked. She'd obviously seen the salon in the background of that picture of him. "She deserved to know the truth."

"She does," Ethan said. He wouldn't have slept with her if she hadn't known. But he wasn't about to share that with Hank despite what close friends the women were.

"She did recognize you," Hank murmured. "I knew she would."

He'd probably just gotten Tammy in trouble, too.

"This doesn't change anything," he insisted.

"You didn't write that note? You're not the one who's been sabotaging us?" Carl asked skeptically, his eyes colder than Ethan had ever seen them.

He shook his head. "You know I'm not. It's my world that's gotten blown apart."

"Not just yours," Hank said.

"Have reporters been harassing you guys?" he asked,

and dread coiled in his stomach as he remembered how miserable the paparazzi had made his life. His *old* life. He hadn't been able to go anywhere or do anything without his picture getting taken, without questions being fired at him.

"That one from Detroit keeps coming by Tammy's salon trying to interview her," Michaela said. "I was there when she showed up today."

Tammy was the last person he wanted harassed like he'd once been. She was the one who'd warned him.

Michaela chuckled. "But Tammy keeps tossing her out."

"We're not worried about the press," Owen James said. "This is a hell of lot more serious than that."

"The accidents…" That dread coiled more tightly in his stomach.

"Braden finally admitted that's not what they are," Carl reminded him. "We're in danger."

Ethan wanted to deny that it was because of him, but he didn't know for certain. It could have been that damn curse.

"We trusted you," Luke Garrison added softly. Not too long ago the team had mistrusted him because a former state trooper had tried to frame him for attempted murder. But Luke had done nothing to earn their mistrust.

However, Ethan had when he'd kept his true identity from them. Regret churned with the dread in his stomach. "That stove thing wasn't the worst thing that had happened to me," he said. "The plane crash was, but that wasn't the first. I really believed someone was trying to kill me, and that the only way to get them to stop was for them to think they'd succeeded."

"The Canterbury curse," Hank murmured.

He shook his head. "It wasn't a curse that tried to run me down in the street or take out the brakes on my car..."

Owen gasped. It wasn't too long ago that someone had tried to run him and Courtney Beaumont down as well. He nodded. "Okay, I'm starting to understand."

"You still can trust me," Ethan reiterated. "This doesn't change anything." Unless Braden fired him, which he probably would. But that really wouldn't change anything either. "I'm a hotshot. That's all I want to be. A member of this team."

"It does change something," Trent Miles said slowly and seriously.

His heart beating fast, Ethan asked, "What?"

"From now on, you're buying," Trent replied, and his mouth curved into one of his wicked grins.

Ethan was gone.

He had to be. If he wanted to keep his anonymity that he'd gone to such great lengths to protect the past five years, he would have had to leave town the minute that picture had hit the news. Maybe he'd gone back to the national forest in the upper peninsula. Or maybe he'd gone back to the mountains where Jonathan Canterbury IV had disappeared all those years ago.

Tammy didn't know where he'd gone, but she didn't expect him to stick around Northern Lakes. If she had, she wouldn't have agreed to meet up with her friends at the Filling Station. So the minute she stepped into the bar and saw him standing by the booth in the back, she froze. Even though the place was crowded, he was easy to see since he stood so much taller and broader than anyone else in the room.

Memories of the night before flashed through her mind, of that big body lying naked beneath hers. Of all his muscles rippling as he moved…

Tension spiraled inside her, and her pulse quickened with excitement.

No. With dread…

She didn't want to see him. Not now.

Not ever…

"Tammy!" Michaela's voice was loud despite her surprisingly small stature for a hotshot. But she was deceptively strong, and that strength was in her voice. "Join us."

Joining them meant joining him because he'd just slid into the booth next to a grinning Trent Miles. They were friends. Or they *had* been.

But from the looks of it, they obviously still were. Had Trent known all along, or had he just found out and forgiven him for the subterfuge?

No, it was more than that. Didn't they all realize how serious this was and that nothing would ever be the same? But she wasn't sure if that was because of Ethan's true identity being exposed or because of what they'd done last night. She felt exposed, vulnerable, in a way she hadn't felt since she was a teenager.

Tammy had vowed to never be that vulnerable again. She had once wanted so bad for her peers to accept her, to respect her, but she'd learned the only one whose respect she really needed was herself. The only person she really needed was herself; she needed to stay single, unattached…invulnerable.

He should have left already because there was no

way he would be able to stay. Especially if he was in danger…

Tammy couldn't stay here. She shook her head and whirled around on her heel. Since she wore them all the time, she was used to them. She could run in heels if need be. Not that she expected him to chase her down.

If he'd wanted to see her after…what they'd done, he wouldn't have slipped out of her bed and crept out into the night while she was sleeping. But he hadn't snuck away stealthily enough. He'd been caught on camera leaving her place. Heat rushing over her face and body, as images of that night kept flashing through her mind, she hastened her step and headed toward the door. But when she pulled it open, she couldn't go through it. Someone blocked her escape.

The woman wasn't much bigger than Tammy was, but she was relentless. "There you are," Brittney Townsend began. "I was hoping to run into you again to ask you more about your relationship with Jonathan Canterbury IV."

Her heart beating fast over seeing him again, grinning and laughing with his team members, Tammy lost the grip on her usually mild temper. "Leave me alone!" she shouted at the woman. "I have nothing to say to you. Stop stalking me for your damn story!"

The reporter must have realized she'd pushed too hard because she stepped aside to let Tammy past. But a few people crowded the doorway behind Brittney. People that Tammy had never seen in Northern Lakes before. But she knew who they were. She'd seen them on the news and in that magazine article she'd found about the upcoming anniversary of Jonathan Canterbury's presumed demise. His mom, Edith Ludington-Canterbury. And his sister, Melanie Canterbury-Bergman. And the man with the thinning blond hair who stood behind them must have been his brother-in-law, Wesley Bergman.

"Who is she?" Mrs. Ludington-Canterbury asked the reporter. The woman had to be sixty but looked no older than forty with her black hair and flawless complexion. She was beautiful, so beautiful in fact that some of her family had been movie stars, another had married a prince. And in her own way, so had Edith Ludington when she'd married Jonathan Canterbury III. He had been American royalty: the nephew of a president, the son of an ambassador, the grandson of a business tycoon.

"This is the woman whose apartment your son was leaving when I took that picture," Brittney Townsend replied.

The reporter had already infuriated Tammy but now she'd humiliated her. Tears stung her eyes, but she was too proud to shed them. Instead, she glared at Brittney and warned the new arrivals, "I wouldn't believe everything this woman says." Then she tried to squeeze through the doorway.

But Mrs. Ludington-Canterbury grabbed her arm. Her grasp was surprisingly strong despite the small size of her delicate looking, perfectly manicured hand. "What—isn't that man my son?"

"He can't be," Wesley Bergman answered before Tammy could. "Jonny is dead. He died five years ago."

Now the woman blinked back a sudden rush of tears. And moved by the pain on her beautiful face, Tammy covered the hand on her arm with hers.

"No," she said. "He's not dead." She turned and pointed

toward that booth in the corner. "Your son is sitting over there."

Drawn into the bar—toward him—the group moved away from the doorway. And Tammy was able to make her escape. Yet she hesitated a moment as she watched Ethan's family and that reporter walk across the peanut-strewn floor to approach him.

He stood up, and over their heads, he met Tammy's gaze, staring at her like he always had. No. It wasn't like he always had. There was more intensity in his dark eyes than she'd ever seen before.

Was he angry with her?

He had no right to be.

She wasn't the one who'd been living the lie all these years. At least not the kind of lie he'd been living. She might have let people believe, with all her flirting, that she was desperate to date. But she wasn't. She preferred to live alone rather than to let anyone close to her, like she'd let him close. She'd worked too hard to build a life for herself; she couldn't risk letting anyone else in. But a strange pain clenched her heart now, squeezing it tightly.

But it wasn't broken. And she would make sure that she never risked it again—especially not on a man who wasn't even able to be honest with himself.

Trick had had too many close calls since joining his brother-in-law's team. And when he entered the Filling Station, he had yet another one as someone slammed up against him.

Although she was slight, she was moving so quickly that Tammy Ingles nearly bowled him over. He caught her shoulders to steady her, and when she glanced up at him, tears sparkled in her green eyes.

She was a close friend of Henrietta's as well as most everybody else on the hotshot team. He'd never seen her without a smile on her face that was reflected in her eyes.

"Are you okay?" he asked her with concern.

Her throat moved as if she was trying to choke down sobs, and she only managed a faint nod.

"What is it?" he asked. "What's wrong?"

She glanced back toward the booth in the corner of the bar. But Trick couldn't see it for the group of people gathered around it. Hell, the only one he could see in the corner was Ethan—or *Jonathan*—since he stood head and shoulders above everybody else.

Anger passed through Tammy's eyes when she caught sight of the man, too. And Trick realized that Braden was right. No matter what he called himself, his teammate was in a hell of a lot of danger.

Even the always happy-go-lucky hair salon owner looked like she wanted to hurt him. And who were the other people, the ones gathered around him, looking up at him with a mixture of shock and horror?

Before Trick could ask, Tammy slipped away from him and through the door to escape from the bar, from Trick's questions but most especially, Trick suspected, from the man none of them had ever really known.

Who was he?

And how much danger was he in now?

Chapter 11

Had those been tears he'd glimpsed in Tammy's beautiful eyes? She'd stayed so far away that Ethan couldn't be certain, but concern twisted inside him, compelling him to run out the door after her.

But a hand on his arm drew his attention back to the woman standing before him. And when he glanced down at her, he had no doubt that there were tears in *her* eyes.

Shock gripped him. He'd never seen his mother betray any sign of emotion before. Not when she'd shipped him off to boarding school or even when she'd buried his father or his younger brother.

But then she blinked, and the trace of moisture disappeared. Maybe he'd only imagined it.

"It *is* Jonathan," she murmured as if she was speaking to someone else, not him. But then she'd rarely spoken to him. Their relationship had not been close.

Ever.

He'd been close to his dad, or at least that was how he remembered it. His dad had died when he was ten. And then he'd been sent away, shortly after the loss, so maybe he'd only romanticized those memories of his father.

He glanced again to the door through which Tammy had disappeared just moments ago. Had he romanticized last night too?

"Jonny?" His sister patronizingly called him the name that had always made him flinch. And when he reacted as he always had, she gasped. "It is you!"

"You don't have proof of that," Wesley said. The esteemed lawyer was always so careful and cautious.

Ethan smiled at how conservative his brother-in-law still was. He fit more perfectly into the Canterbury family than *he* ever had. Wesley was also fiercely protective of his wife and his mother-in-law, which had always impressed Ethan. He appealed to his brother-in-law's protectiveness now. "Wes, we can't have this conversation here. I assume you've checked into the Lakeside Inn." It was the nicest place to stay in Northern Lakes.

Predictably his brother-in-law nodded.

"I will meet you all back there, and we will privately discuss this situation," he said with a glance at the stranger who stood among them.

She had to be the reporter. "I'm Brittney Townsend from Channel 9," she introduced herself. "Your family contacted me after they saw the photograph I took of you last night."

"When you were sneaking around in the dark," Ethan gritted out with a nod. "Yeah, I have nothing to say to you."

He actually had plenty, but he knew she wouldn't care about the disruption she'd caused him. This woman clearly cared only about her career and furthering it no matter the expense to anyone else.

She narrowed her eyes, which were a pale brown that looked oddly familiar. Maybe he'd met her before.

"I'm the reason you're reuniting with your family," she said. "I should be allowed to report on the reunion."

He cursed. She'd blown his world apart, and she wanted to squeeze every last bit of blood from him. He shook his head. "No way."

Undeterred, she turned away from him to focus on his family. "We had a deal," she reminded them.

His mother sniffed and coldly informed her, "I don't make deals with reporters."

"You are not welcome," Wesley repeated for Ethan before glancing at him as well. From the cold look in his pale blue eyes, it was clear that Ethan wasn't welcome either. They'd always gotten along before the plane crash, so Wesley must not have been as convinced as his mother and sister seemed of his identity. In addition to being protective, the lawyer was just naturally suspicious.

Maybe if Ethan had been more like him, the plane crash wouldn't have happened and lives wouldn't have been lost. But he hadn't wanted to believe that the incidents before the crash hadn't been just accidents. Or that someone else might have been making sure that the legend of the curse lived on and that Jonathan Canterbury IV did not.

Wesley looked away from him to focus on his wife and mother-in-law instead. "Let's return to the hotel," he told them. "We don't need an audience for this discussion." He glanced dismissively at the booth full of hotshots before guiding Melanie and Mother toward the door with the reporter trailing behind them like a dog yapping at their heels.

"Wow," Michaela said, as her blue eyes widened with awe. "It all kind of makes sense now…"

The reason he'd taken another man's identity, his life…and not just to save his own. He nodded, glad that they understood. His family would not. But Mother, Melanie and Wesley weren't his family—not really. And because he'd been so young when he'd been sent off to boarding school, he really didn't even know his older sister. And his mother…

He doubted anyone knew her. Maybe even herself.

"I'm sorry," he told them again. "I didn't mean to deceive anyone. I just wanted to stay safe—"

Luke Garrison snorted. "As a hotshot?"

"I really wanted to be one," he said, and he glanced at Trick who had joined them. He would know if Braden intended to fire him.

"You *are* a hotshot," Trick told him. "My father trained you."

"Don't you mean he trained Ethan Sommerly?" Carl asked. The older hotshot hadn't been nearly as accepting as Trent had.

Trick shook his head. "No. I called Mack, and the old man confirmed that he trained Jonathan Canterbury in the same class with Sommerly. He said Canterbury was the one who worked harder than anyone else in the program."

"Still does," Miles murmured with a nod at Ethan.

He had to talk to Braden as well as his supervisor with the US Forest Service. It wouldn't be easy, but he had to make sure that he didn't lose the job that meant so much to him. But first he had to talk to his family.

His *biological* one. He had to get them to understand that this was his life now, that Northern Lakes was his home. And that he was not going back out East with them, to the estate that had never been his home.

"I'll talk to you all later," he promised.

But Hank asked, "You won't leave without saying goodbye?"

"I won't leave," Ethan promised. Not if he could help it.

Even if Braden fired him, he couldn't banish him from town. Now if he or anyone else pressed charges against him for fraud…

Hell, maybe it was a good thing his brother-in-law had come to Northern Lakes. Since the man was a lawyer, he could represent Ethan. But he probably wouldn't defend what he'd done.

Ethan sighed. It probably was indefensible that even though he hadn't thought his family cared about him, he'd let them think he'd died. His shoulders slumped as he turned and headed out of the bar. His feet dragged on the sidewalk as he walked back to where he'd parked his truck at the firehouse.

The Lakeside Inn was on the other side of town, on the shore of the biggest of the chain of several lakes that had earned the place its name. So he would need his vehicle to drive there. Not that he was in any hurry to meet with his biological family.

They were unlikely to understand and forgive him like his hotshot family had. Well, most of his hotshot family had. Not everybody had understood how badly he'd wanted to be a hotshot, how badly he'd wanted to have a normal, productive life out of the spotlight of the media. How he'd wanted to do something purposeful, something meaningful.

He glanced around for her—for that damn reporter who'd turned his world upside down. But like before, he didn't see anything, not even a flash in the darkness now; she wasn't following him. But then she knew where he was going, and she'd probably already beat him to the hotel.

He hastened his step as he neared the firehouse. Light spilled through one of the open overhead doors of a garage bay. The bright neon yellow engine gleamed in the fluorescent lights. But Stanley, the kid who kept them gleaming, stood back and studied it, as if looking for a spot he'd missed.

"Looks good," he called out to Stanley.

The kid turned and grinned at him.

Ethan glanced around for the kid's furry shadow. "Where's Annie?"

Stanley shrugged his thin shoulders. "She ran off barking at something a while ago." He shrugged again. "Probably a cat or a raccoon." Stanley used to run off after her, but he trusted now that she always came back to him.

Ethan lingered a moment outside the garage, not for the dog to reappear but for Stanley to ask him about the picture on the news. But the teenager looked at him as he always had—even when Ethan had had his beard. And he seemed to have no questions about his identity. But then he might not have even seen the news.

It was only a matter of time before he did, though. Ethan considered giving him a heads-up but then he realized he was probably only looking for an excuse to stall that talk with his family.

"See you later," he told Stanley.

The teenager grinned again before turning back toward the engine. And Ethan headed around the corner of the firehouse to the parking lot in the back where he'd parked his truck. Before he could near it, though, something bounded out of the darkness. He braced himself as the dog leaped at him, barking as ferociously as she had that morning.

"Shhh, Annie," he told the mutt. "It's me. You need to get used to me." Or maybe she didn't. Maybe he wouldn't be around much longer.

Thinking about that, about how he may be fired soon, had him running his bandaged hand over the dog's thick fur. "I'll miss you, girl," he murmured gruffly.

She licked his face as if agreeing with him. "What were you chasing?" he asked. She must not have caught it because she had nothing in her jaws but drool. He wiped a dribble of it from his chin as she licked his face once again.

Sighing, he reached into his pocket for the key fob for his truck. He needed to get this damn meeting over with. But when he tried to push Annie away, she leaped right back up. "Come on, girl, I have to go…"

He didn't want to. But he had to.

However, Annie persisted in her affection. Maybe if he hit the remote starter button on the key fob, he could distract the dog long enough to get away from her. But when he clicked the button, the truck exploded with a blast so powerful it was the last thing he remembered before his world went black.

The windows rattled within their frames, the glass trembling as if on the verge of shattering. Even the floor shuddered beneath Tammy's feet. This wasn't like the disturbance the other day. This was louder. More intense…

And it left Tammy with no doubt that this was another explosion, one even bigger than the incident with the stove the other day.

Ethan had been hurt that day. Had he been hurt again? Because she had no doubt this blast had been meant for him…

While she stood in shock, a wine bottle clasped in her hand, her friends looked around her living room as if they expected to find cracks in the wall and debris strewn on the ground. But the explosion hadn't happened here.

"What was that?" Serena asked. She lived farther from the firehouse and hadn't been close enough to town to hear when the stove had exploded.

But Courtney had. Her face had gone as pale as Tammy's probably was. She'd recognized the sound as well, but she seemed to doubt herself because she asked, "Do you think that was…?"

"It was an explosion," Tammy confirmed.

"At the firehouse again?" Courtney asked, her voice cracking with fear.

"They were all at the Filling Station," Tammy reminded her. As she'd walked out of the building, her friends had been walking up to the bar. They had known her too long to miss how upset she'd been, so they'd insisted on coming back to her apartment with her instead of going inside to meet their significant others. "Nobody is hurt."

She had doubts about that, though. Serious doubts…

So many in fact that her body trembled as fear overwhelmed her. Before it could slip from her shaky grasp, Tammy placed the wine bottle on the coffee table. Then she headed toward the stairs. Her friends rushed after her.

"We're going with you," Courtney said.

Tammy nodded. She didn't have to say where she was heading. They all knew now where the explosion had happened. They just didn't know what had blown up. This time.

Or whom…

But Tammy had her suspicions. No. She *knew*. It was Ethan.

Flames shot up into the night sky, burning brightly despite the distance between the firehouse and where the person watched. Those flames were coming from the truck assigned to Ethan Sommerly; the bomb had been rigged to go off when the vehicle started.

There was no way Jonathan Canterbury IV could have survived that explosion like he had the plane crash. This time he was dead for certain.

And there would be no resurrection for him like the news outlets were all claiming…

He was gone forever now.

Chapter 12

Rory VanDam stared into the flames, which snapped and crackled as they consumed the wood he'd stacked within the fire ring. The last thing he wanted was to start a wildfire in the national forest surrounding Northern Lakes. The trees and brush were just now growing back from the last fire. That one had been deliberately set.

He'd hesitated over starting this one. He hadn't wanted anyone to see where he was hiding from that reporter who had come to town. After her picture of Jonathan Canterbury IV had hit the national news, she wasn't going anywhere, and now there would just be more of them. More damn reporters…

He didn't need anybody snapping *his* picture. He wasn't a missing heir. He wasn't famous. But there were some people who would recognize him.

Dangerous people…

An alarm pealed out, shattering the silence, and a horn beeped on and off.

His damn truck alarm.

What had set it off?

An animal? It must have been. This deep in the woods it couldn't have been anything else. Nobody lived around here. Maybe it was a bug. The mosquitoes dancing in and out of the flames of the campfire were probably big enough to set off his truck alarm. And so were the bats that flew overhead.

He reached for the backpack lying atop his sleeping bag and pulled out his keys. When he clicked the fob, though, nothing happened. The alarm kept ringing out.

He must have been too far away. So he jumped up from his folding chair and headed through the trees to where the lights flashed on and off in the darkness. The closer he came, the harder he pressed the fob.

But the alarm continued to peal out, drowning out the drone of the mosquitoes buzzing around his head and the sound of twigs snapping beneath his boots. When he neared the truck, he headed toward the driver's door. Since the fob wasn't working, he'd probably need to unlock it and pop up the hood to disarm the alarm.

And he needed to disarm it before he drew anyone's attention to his hiding place. But when he reached for the door, something struck him—slamming him hard against the metal. The truck shuddered with the impact, and a groan of pain slipped through his lips.

Maybe it was already too late. Maybe those dangerous people had already found him.

Fury coursed through Ethan, dulling the pain in his hands as he fisted them within the bandages and slammed one into Rory VanDam's jaw. His knuckles cracked, and pain radiated up his arm. It echoed the pain in his shoulders and back from where the explosion had slammed him against the asphalt.

Or had Annie done that? If she hadn't been holding him back, he would have been inside the truck when it had blown up. His body still vibrated with the fury and adrenaline that had coursed through him. He'd survived…but just because of Annie. She'd been like the parachute that had saved him from the crash, that had saved them both.

"You son of a bitch," he yelled as he slammed Rory into the side of his truck again.

"What the hell—" Rory began as he pulled away from him. "What are you doing?" He dodged Ethan's next blow and pointed at the flashing lights. "Shut off the damn alarm."

"I should have blown it up like you just did mine," he said. But all Ethan had done was set off the alarm to draw Rory away from his fire. He knew the guy well enough to know that, even though he was bigger than the blond guy, he had needed to take him by surprise to get the upper hand. Rory was all wiry muscle with killer survival instincts. Ethan knew he had probably honed those instincts during their time lost in the mountains.

Rory, with his short, almost white, blond hair and pale blue eyes, had been easy to see moving through the woods, while Ethan had been able to hide in the shadows. Just as he had at the firehouse, taking off in Stanley's car before anyone had seen him, he'd made damn certain he hadn't been followed. Just in case he was wrong about Rory…

Rory clicked the fob, and this time the alarm shut off. "What are you talking about?" he asked.

"Isn't it obvious?" Ethan shot back at him. "You don't have to try to kill me. Your secret is safe with me." The past five years should have made that clear to him.

Rory shook his head, though, and asked, "What secret?"

"Seriously?" Ethan chuckled at his feigned innocence. "Come on, Rory. I know I'm not the only one who changed his identity the day that plane crashed."

While Ethan had grown out his hair and beard to disguise himself, the other man had cut all his off. Maybe being clean-cut was his disguise.

"You got your facts wrong. But it happened a long time ago. It would make sense you don't remember everything accurately."

Anger coursed through him over Rory's lie. Now he understood why Tammy and Braden had gotten so ticked with him when he'd denied his true identity. Being lied to was infuriating. He cursed the man he had once considered his best friend.

They'd been through a hell of a lot together when, five years ago, they had both parachuted out of that plane. They hadn't landed anywhere near each other, and it had taken them weeks to find each other in the mountains. Weeks in which they had survived alone and then they'd helped each other stay alive until finally rescuers had found them.

"You knew I wasn't Ethan Sommerly," he said. But he'd never called him on the lie. Or so he'd thought. "So you must be the one who sent that note to Braden."

And if Rory had betrayed him once, he could have betrayed him again—when he tried to kill him.

"Why would I do that?" Rory asked. "Why would I want him looking into who isn't really who they say they are?"

There it was at last: the truth. "So who the hell are you?" Ethan wondered aloud.

"Your friend," Rory replied. "I wouldn't hurt you."

Remembering all those weeks they'd kept each other alive had Ethan's anger ebbing away. They'd been through too much together. If Rory had wanted to get rid of him, he could have done it five years ago when they'd been stuck together in the mountains.

"I wouldn't purposely hurt anyone," Rory reiterated. "Ever…"

The anger ebbed away, but now Ethan was shaking just in reaction to how close he'd come to dying when that truck had blown up. He desperately wanted to be able to figure out who wanted him dead; it was the only way he'd ever be safe.

But it wasn't Rory. Ethan believed him. But then that made Rory a better man than he was—because Ethan had hurt people.

Too many people…

Her friends had wanted to stay with her, but Tammy had insisted that she was fine. That she actually wanted to be alone.

They had probably returned to the scene of the crime. Earlier they hadn't been able to get close to the firehouse. Troopers and firefighters had quickly set up a wide perimeter around the entire area until they'd had a chance to bring in a bomb squad—to make sure there were no other explosives planted in or near the firehouse.

The explosion had not been inside this time. It had

been in the parking lot behind the building and had left behind only the burned-out skeleton of a truck.

A chill swept through her. Was there a human skeleton inside the truck? Nobody had been allowed close enough to determine if someone had been inside, but there must have been. For the truck to explode, somebody must have started it.

Stanley had said he'd heard the engine fire up just seconds before the explosion. Fortunately he'd been inside the firehouse, so he hadn't been hurt—although the force of the blast had knocked him against the fire engine he'd been polishing.

He'd been shaken up, though, and in tears when she and Courtney and Serena had seen him. And even now, tears rushed to Tammy's eyes and filled her throat as she remembered why he'd been crying.

"Ethan," he'd sobbed. "Ethan was walking to his truck…" And then he'd buried his face in the fur of his dog. Annie had been near the blast, close enough that she smelled like smoke with sections of her hair singed nearly as badly as the stove had singed Ethan's hair. Fragments of glass had matted in her hair as well. And she'd whimpered when Stanley had hugged her—either with sympathy over his pain or because she'd been hurt.

Serena had stepped in then—to comfort Stanley and to help him with his dog. Since her fiancé was Stanley's former foster brother, she had become like a big sister to him or a mother. She took care of him, but then Serena was so maternal that she took care of everyone. She'd wanted Tammy to go with her and Stanley as well.

But she'd refused. She'd insisted she was fine. She hadn't had to convince just Serena but her twin as well. Courtney had left her just a short time ago.

For some reason her friends kept thinking that Tammy cared about Ethan. That he meant something to her...

Her friends knew her well—better than she knew herself. Because Ethan did mean something to her. Or had...

Was he gone now?

Had he been inside that truck when it had exploded?

He must have been. Stanley had seen him walking toward it just before the blast.

Pain gripped her heart, squeezing it so tightly that she whimpered like the dog had. Why did it hurt so much?

It wasn't as if she'd known Ethan well. She hadn't even known that he wasn't Ethan—until she'd shaved off his beard and cut his hair. How had he come to mean so much to her—when she hadn't even known who he really was?

And why did she feel so hollow inside now? She was afraid that feeling might never go away. While she was too afraid to sleep, she'd changed into her nightgown anyway.

Then she'd remembered the wine she'd left sitting on the coffee table. Maybe a glass would calm her frayed nerves. Ever since the explosion, she had been trembling in reaction.

But when she stepped out into her living room, she heard a strange creak and saw a flash of light from the stairwell. Had she not locked the door?

Maybe she hadn't. She'd been so shell-shocked from what she'd heard, what she'd seen...

Ethan's truck burned up.

Ethan as well?

She didn't know.

Maybe she should have stayed, like Courtney had suggested, and found out for certain. But she hadn't wanted confirmation. She hadn't wanted to face the fact that he could be gone.

For good.

She shuddered at the thought.

Then she cringed at the sound of footsteps on the stairs. Heavy footsteps…

She opened her mouth to call out, to demand to know who was there. But she was afraid to find that out as well. This second explosion proved that the first had definitely been no accident. Somebody had been trying to kill Ethan.

There was a killer in Northern Lakes. Was that person coming after her now?

Fear froze her when she should have been running for her bedroom. She could lock the door and climb out the fire escape. Or she could go into the bathroom and slide the dead bolt she'd had installed on the inside of the door. But she was unable to do either. She was unable to move.

Who would want her dead anyway? Since she'd lost the weight and cleared up her complexion, people had stopped picking on her. Nobody had even inadvertently hurt her for a long while. Except for Ethan.

He'd hurt her when he'd slipped out of her bed the night before. And he'd hurt her tonight although that had been through no fault of his own.

He hadn't set that bomb in his own truck. He hadn't tried to kill himself. But why would whoever had gone after him now come after her?

She meant nothing to him. He'd proven that when he'd left her without a word after they'd made love. So she waited for her intruder, standing next to the coffee table, the wine bottle clasped in her hand. She could use it as a weapon if she needed to defend herself. But it wouldn't save her from a gun or a bomb.

Finally the person reached the top of the stairs. A big body filled the doorway. Her intruder was tall and broad and so very familiar…

Was she dreaming? Only imagining it was him?

She had to be—because there was no way he could have survived the truck exploding when he'd started it. There was no way he could be standing in her living room.

No. She was only seeing a ghost.

Chapter 13

He shouldn't have come here. Just being near her might have put her in danger. But he'd wanted to see her. No. He'd *needed* to see her.

To make certain that she was all right. That she wasn't hurt like he had hurt other people he'd cared about. But she was scared. All the color had drained from her beautiful face, leaving her eyes wide and stark with fear.

"You left your door unlocked," he said. He'd been scared when the knob had turned easily beneath his bandaged hand. He'd wondered if someone had broken into her place. But if someone had, it would have been to get to him.

Tammy had no enemies. Nobody wanted her dead. But they wanted her. At least he sure as hell did.

"You're dead," she murmured.

He shook his head. "No." A ragged sigh slipped through his lips. "Not for lack of someone trying though…"

"But I—I heard the explosion," she stammered.

He didn't doubt it. Everyone but Rory had probably heard the blast.

"I saw the truck…" And she shivered. But then she was wearing only a thin silky nightgown, so she could have been cold.

"I wasn't inside," he said.

"But Stanley heard it start up…"

He shuddered at how close he'd come to dying in the explosion. "I hit the remote starter on the key fob." If he hadn't…

He would have been inside. "Remind me I owe Annie a big bone." Hell, he owed her an entire skeleton—for making sure he hadn't become one.

"Annie?"

"The dog kept jumping on me," he said. "She wouldn't let me get to my truck. It was like she knew…"

And maybe she had. Stanley had said she'd run after something in the darkness. The person who'd planted the bomb on his truck?

If only the dog could talk…

But he wasn't the first hotshot who'd hoped that Annie could speak. If she could, she would have saved them a lot of trouble.

"Was she okay?" he asked. The dog had been knocked to the ground with him. But for a whimper of shock, she'd seemed fine though.

But he ached now. He wasn't sure if that was because the blast had knocked him to the asphalt or because Tammy stood before him wearing nothing but that sheer silk nightgown.

She was so beautiful.

"Serena was going to take her to the vet to be checked out," she said.

"Good."

"Why didn't anyone see you after the explosion?" she asked. "Where did you go?"

"I took off in Stanley's car." The teenager had left the keys in the ignition, which had been fortunate for Ethan.

"Were you chasing someone?" she prodded. "Or running away?"

He'd been chasing down a lead. But he had, inadvertently, run away. He grimaced at the twinge of guilt that struck his heart. "I shouldn't have taken off," he said, acknowledging the mistake he'd made.

Poor Stanley must have thought the worst. And so had Tammy.

She shook her head, swirling her streaked hair around her slender shoulders. "It was the right thing to do," she said. "If you hadn't…" She shivered again. "The person who set that bomb might have tried something else…"

Ethan hadn't considered that. He'd been so angry that he'd reacted without considering the consequences. If he'd been right about Rory, he would have been running into danger instead of away from it.

He just hoped he hadn't led that danger to her. But he'd been careful to make certain that he wasn't followed when he'd walked from the firehouse, where he'd dropped off Stanley's car, to her place.

"I shouldn't have come here," he said.

She nodded in agreement. "You need to talk to the police and to Braden. Or have you already spoken to all of them?"

He shook his head. "I wanted to come here first."

After confronting Rory, he'd lost steam to talk to any-one else…but her. He, especially, didn't want to speak to his family. Not now.

Or Braden…

Either encounter was going to lead to disappoint-ment for him. Because it always did with his family and because the superintendent was certain to fire him. The only one who didn't disappoint him was Tammy.

"Why?" she asked. "Why did you want to see me first?"

"To make sure you were all right." And somehow seeing her made him feel all right, or at least better than he'd been. *She* made him better…

"Nobody's trying to kill me."

Yet. But they could. They might if they realized what she meant to him. But he hadn't even realized that— until tonight—until he'd had a compelling need to see her after dropping off Stanley's car. He'd intended to go inside the firehouse to talk to Braden. But he'd been drawn here instead, drawn to her like he'd always been.

He'd had to see her before he saw anyone else. Her beauty struck him with nearly as much force as the blast had. "I should leave," he rasped.

Before he put her in danger.

But he stood motionless in the doorway, waiting for her to nod her agreement, waiting for her to tell him to leave. She placed a wine bottle that he hadn't noticed she'd been holding onto the coffee table alongside a trio of glasses.

And he felt a pang of jealousy. Was someone else with her? Was she not alone?

"You have company," he said.

She glanced down at the table. "No," she answered.

"They left when your truck exploded. Serena and Court-ney."

Relief lifted the weight from his heart, not that he had a right to feel possessive of her. Not after how he'd treated her.

How he'd snuck out the night before...

She walked toward him now, and he braced himself. He wouldn't have been surprised if she pushed him down the stairs and shouted at him to leave—especially when she extended her arms toward him. But instead of shoving him away, she wrapped her arms around his neck and pulled him toward her.

His body was warm and hard and real. "You're not a ghost," she murmured. "You're not a ghost..."

He had survived once again. *He was alive.*

Tears sprang to Tammy's eyes as relief overwhelmed her. His handsome face blurred with her vision as he lowered his head to hers.

She stroked her fingers over the stubble on his jaw, holding his face as he kissed her. And she kissed him back with all the emotion overwhelming her.

Tammy wanted him so badly, wanted to feel as con-nected to him as she had the night before. Especially when she relived how close she'd come to losing him. Forever...

Of course she knew she would lose him eventually. To his old life.

He would have to leave Northern Lakes. Even though he might not want to, there was no way his family and the media and the authorities would let him keep living under another man's identity. And because of that she should have been pulling away. She should have been protecting herself from any more pain.

But instead, she wrapped her fingers around his big wrist and tugged him across the living room and into her bedroom. When she flipped on the chandelier over the bed, she got a good look at his handsome face. He had a scrape on one cheek and when he lifted his hands toward her shoulders, the bandages were ragged and bloodied.

"Oh, my God!" she gasped. "You need to get to the hospital." The blast must have hurt him worse than he'd admitted.

He lifted one of his hands and stared down at the wrecked bandages. Then he shrugged. "That's not my blood." As if to prove it, he pulled off the already loose bandages from both hands. The skin beneath was fading from red to pink, and there were no blisters. The burns were healing.

"What did you do?" she asked. "Whose blood is that?"

He shook his head. "I made a mistake. I suspected somebody I shouldn't have…"

"Who?"

He shook his head again. "It doesn't matter. I was wrong about him." He stared down at her intently, as if wondering if he was wrong about her, too.

But he must have made up his mind because he kissed her again—passionately, hungrily—his lips nibbling at hers before he deepened the kiss. He pulled back, panting for breath, and ran his fingertips along the bare skin of her shoulders.

"I can touch you now," he murmured, his voice gruff with desire. "I can feel how silky your skin is." He dipped his head to her shoulder and slid his lips over it as well.

And she shivered as sensations raced through her body. She wanted to touch him, too, to feel the life and the power in him.

So she reached for the buttons on his shirt and pulled them free. Then she pushed the shirt from his broad shoulders. And she leaned forward and pressed a kiss over his heart, which leaped beneath her lips.

His breath audibly caught before shuddering out in a ragged sigh. "You're so damn sexy."

She smiled at the compliment, happy that he appreciated her efforts. Not that she had any makeup on now. She hadn't expected company. And she certainly hadn't expected to see him again tonight—if ever again.

But that was all she'd wanted. *He* was all she wanted.

So she reached for the button on his jeans now, undoing it before pulling down the tab of his zipper. The sound of the teeth giving way sounded like the same hiss of breath that escaped through his mouth as he clenched his jaw.

"You're driving me crazy," he said, and a muscle twitched in his cheek.

Then she slid her fingers over his erection and that twitched as well.

He groaned. "Tammy…"

And she smiled again, pleased with the power she had over such a burly giant of a man.

But then he touched her, too, and her knees began to tremble. He slid his hand beneath the hem of her nightgown, along her thigh and over the curve of her hip to her butt. "You are so damn incredible."

That was how he made her feel with sensations and

pleasure racing through her even as tension built inside her. She wanted him so badly—too badly to take it slowly. So she pushed down his jeans and boxers and freed his erection. Then she bent over to press a kiss to the head of it.

But he jerked back and groaned again. "Not so fast..."

"I want it fast," she breathed. "I want you now."

He grabbed his jeans but only to pull out a condom. This time he ripped it open and sheathed himself. But he didn't immediately plunge inside her like she wanted.

Instead he kissed her again and again and again... and as he claimed her mouth with his, he pushed down the straps of her nightgown and freed her breasts. He caressed them and stroked the nipples into taut points.

Pleasure streaked from those points to her core, making her so hot, she throbbed for him.

She sucked his tongue into her mouth, teasing it with everything she wanted to do to his body. And finally he lifted her, pushed aside her panties and gently eased inside her.

But she didn't want gentle. She wanted madness. She wanted the intensity she'd felt the other night. And she moved against him, arching and jerking until his body began to shake slightly. He moved them, still joined, to the bed, and he set the pace she needed.

Wrapping her legs and arms around him, she clung to him, matching his rhythm—taking him deeper and deeper with each of his thrusts. And finally that tension that had wound so tightly inside her shattered and she came, screaming his name. Tears stung her eyes at the intense bliss that gripped her body and her heart.

Then he tensed and joined her in release, shouting out his pleasure before he leaned forward and pressed his face into her hair. He didn't stay joined with her, though. He slipped out of her arms and out of her bed before she could even close her eyes. But he'd left his clothes on the floor. Water whooshed in the bathroom that adjoined her bedroom. And then he was back, crawling into bed with her. He sprawled out, wrapped his arm around her and rolled her up against his side.

She rested her head on his shoulder as she splayed her hand over his chest which rose and fell with his pants for breath. He'd had a minute to clean up, to splash water on his face, and droplets ran down his chin and onto her cheek. But it took him several more moments before his breathing evened out.

She smiled with satisfaction—the satisfaction he'd given her and the satisfaction she'd obviously given him. But yet she felt compelled to ask, "Are you just waiting for me to fall asleep, so you can sneak out again?"

Color flushed his face with embarrassment. "I shouldn't have done that," he said. "I'm sorry. I didn't know what to think after that, after this…"

Neither did she. So she could forgive him that. However, she wasn't sure she could forgive him for the lie he'd been living all these years—pretending to be someone else.

"What did your family say?" she asked softly.

He tensed against her. "What?"

"Did they forgive you for letting them think you died five years ago?"

"I didn't talk to them."

"But they were coming into the bar when I was leaving," she reminded him.

"I told them I'd meet them back at their hotel and then the truck exploded and…"

She stiffened. "And you forgot about them?" She hadn't been able to since she had met them. She'd thought of his mother with the tears glistening in her eyes. And she'd worried about how devastated she would be to lose him again when his truck had exploded.

"What if they heard about the explosion?" she asked. What if, like her, they thought he'd died before they'd ever gotten to talk to him again? She shoved at his shoulder now, pushing him from the bed. "You have to go to them."

"It's late," he protested.

She snorted. "So now you want to stay?" It was just because he didn't want to talk to them. "If they heard about the explosion, they won't be sleeping."

"I told you that my family isn't close, that they don't care about anything but money and appearances—"

"No," she said. "I saw your mother's face. She cares—"

He shook his head. "She's never shown it before. Not when my father passed away. Not even when my brother died…" His voice cracked, and tears glistened in his eyes. But then he blinked them back.

"He was so young," she murmured sympathetically.

"There," he said. "You show more emotion over a kid you never met than the woman who gave birth to him."

"Maybe she can't show her feelings," she suggested. "But that doesn't mean she isn't feeling them. That any of them don't care about you. You need to go to them."

"I can't—"

"You can't let them worry about you anymore. Go!" she shouted. She wanted him gone—not just so he could talk to his family. She wanted him gone before she did something stupid…like fall completely in love with him.

Because she had no doubt that if she did something that stupid, he would break her heart just as he was breaking the hearts of his family members.

"I can't go because I have no way of getting there," Ethan told her. "Someone blew up my truck., remember?"

"I—"

"And if you're going to offer me yours, you might want to rethink that." he said. "After what happened to mine. Hell, after that, you should rethink having anything to do with me."

She was rethinking it, and not just because someone was trying to kill him. It was because he was getting too close, making her feel too much. Making her *want* too much.

And she was happy with what she had, with who she was. But the Canterburys wouldn't be happy with her. She didn't have the social status someone would have to have to be involved with one of them.

Not that she wanted to be involved with one of them. She didn't even want to be involved with Ethan Sommerly. But she had a feeling that it was too late for that.

She was the first one who had broken the story. The other reporters checking into the hotel now were just chasing the story—*her* story. Brittney shouldn't have been sitting in the lobby. She should have been in the suite the Canterbury family had booked, recording their reactions when they'd heard the news. There had been an explosion at the firehouse. But by the time she'd learned about it, she'd been too late to get close to the scene.

State troopers had cordoned off the area. She'd recorded a couple of quick clips from behind the yellow crime scene tape. But she hadn't been able to get anyone to talk to her there.

And she hadn't managed that yet here either. But surely, if Jonathan Canterbury IV had died in that explosion, someone from the Huron Hotshots would have come to the hotel to inform the family. Or a state trooper would have.

That was why she'd camped out in the lobby with a cameraman. After getting that picture on her phone, Brittney Townsend had credibility now with the newsroom, enough credibility that the producer had sent her a camera crew.

"Are you going to stay up all night?" Barney asked. His eyelids kept sliding down as he struggled to stay awake.

"Get another coffee," she told him. While the other reporters had gone down to the firehouse looking for Canterbury and asking about the explosion the hotel staff must have mentioned to them, she had decided to stay put.

The story was here—with the Canterbury family.

The reporters weren't the only new arrivals to the hotel. Another couple had come into town from out East. A man and woman about Canterbury's age.

While the woman had stayed up in the room they'd booked, the man had come down to the lobby. He kept glancing over at her as if torn over whether or not to approach her. But every time he looked at her, his gaze drifted over to Barney. Was he worried about getting caught on camera?

Who was he? The woman had seemed familiar. Or maybe she had just looked like the other women

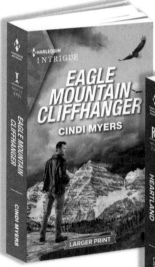

who'd arrived in town—the sister and the mother who'd dressed in designer clothes…

The fiancée.

That must have been why she'd looked familiar; she'd done the most press after her fiancé had gone down in that plane.

"Go time," Brittney whispered to Barney.

He blinked and focused on her face. "What—what's happening?"

"Get your camera ready," she said, but before he could even get up from the low seat of the lobby couch, the doors swooshed open to the outside.

And *he* walked in. If he'd been involved in this explosion, it sure hadn't killed him. Jonathan Canterbury IV was alive and well—just as she'd told the world.

But the moment he stepped inside the lobby, the man who'd been looking at her launched himself at Canterbury, fists swinging. Was this the man who'd caused the explosions? Who'd tried to kill Canterbury?

And since those attempts had failed, had he decided to kill the heir with his bare hands?

Chapter 14

Pain radiated from Ethan's jaw to the base of his skull as the blow knocked his head back. He cursed—as angry with his attacker as he was with himself for being unprepared.

He damn well knew that someone was trying to kill him. So he should have been more observant. But then he wasn't alone. Tammy stood beside him. And just her mere presence alone distracted him.

But now it made him more defensive—not of himself but of her. His attacker was not going to get close to her. He launched himself at the man, knocking him flat on the lobby floor.

The guy cursed, and Ethan recognized the voice he hadn't heard in nearly five years.

"Kip," he said as he stared down at the blond-haired guy. "What the hell are you doing here?"

"What the hell are you doing *alive*?" Kip shot the

question back at him as he surged to his feet and propelled himself at Ethan again.

He would have stepped aside if he hadn't been worried about Tammy. But he used his big body to shield hers, bracing himself so that he wouldn't move. Kip was tall, but he was skinny, and Ethan was able to easily push him away.

The guy stumbled back into one of the hotel staff. "Hey, stop! Stop throwing punches, or I'm going to call the police," the young clerk threatened them.

"Why are you fighting?" a female voice asked the question. But it wasn't Tammy.

Ethan glanced around him and noticed the camera trained on his face. And the woman standing beside the cameraman, directing him for the perfect shot. And he swore again.

"Are you not happy that Jonathan Canterbury IV survived that plane crash?" she asked Kip now.

But he ignored her as he jumped up from the floor and launched himself at Ethan again. The guy had never learned when to quit. In their boarding school and college days, he hadn't stopped drinking until he'd passed out. Maybe he wouldn't stop coming at Ethan until he knocked him out. So when Kip headed toward him again, Ethan swung out.

And a woman screamed.

It wasn't Tammy's scream either. Or the reporter's. This scream chilled his blood.

"Stop!" Helena said. "Stop fighting over me!"

Her scream froze Ethan midswing, but Kip lashed out again. His fist grazed Ethan's chin just enough to turn his head.

Yeah. He was going to have to knock him out. So he

pulled back his arm to swing again, but when he connected, it wasn't Kip's face that crumpled with pain. It was Wesley's. The guy dropped to the ground.

And Melanie screamed this time. "Jonny, what are you doing?"

"Stop," his mother commanded.

But now Wesley vaulted to his feet, bristling with rage. "You son of a bitch, I was trying to help you."

Kip shoved Wes aside and launched himself at Ethan again. Ethan pulled his fist back again to swing, but small hands caught it and held tightly to it.

"Stop," Tammy said. Her voice was soft but steely.

And he stopped.

But Kip didn't stop. He shoved at Ethan again, so hard that he stumbled back and nearly knocked down Tammy. He shouldn't have brought her here.

No. She'd brought him. He'd pointed out that his vehicle was gone, and he had returned Stanley's to the firehouse. If she wanted him to see his family, she would have to drive him. He hadn't thought that she would actually do it, and he shouldn't have let her.

He shouldn't have let her anywhere near the toxicity that was his family and his friends. He should have just had her dump him at the door of the hotel and speed off—out of the mess that was his life. After having witnessed what she had, she was certain to leave now. He doubted he would ever see her again.

She never should have come here. She should have just loaned him her vehicle to use despite his warning her against it. Even if it had gotten damaged, it wasn't as if she ever drove it that much. But she hadn't trusted that he would actually come to see his family—if she hadn't driven him here.

But the minute they'd stepped through the doors, he'd come under attack. The man who'd attacked him finally stepped back, panting for breath from all his exertion. And the woman who'd screamed just moments ago clutched at his arm. Tammy recognized her from those interviews she'd done. This was Ethan—Jonathan's former fiancée.

"What are you doing?" Helena asked him. "What were you thinking?"

Kip's face flushed, and he looked down, as if unable to meet her gaze. She had beautiful eyes, a vivid blue that was visible even from across a room. And her blond hair was perfectly pin straight without a hint of frizz. The old Tammy, the one back in high school who'd felt inferior to her beautiful friends, would have been envious or intimidated. But she'd grown up and into her own. She was happy with herself, with her life, with no reason for envy. And at the moment, all she felt was pity.

No one seemed happy, and they should have been rejoicing, thrilled that he was alive. But they were all shouting at each other—mostly at Ethan, cursing him just like the man had who'd attacked him. Ethan had called him Kip.

"It's his fault," Kip told Helena. "It's all his fault. He put everybody through hell all these years."

"You did!" the sister shouted as she turned on her brother now. And her husband nodded in agreement as he wiped a trail of blood from his swelling lip.

"You're a son of a bitch," the man told him.

And the argument escalated again with more recriminations and screaming. The older woman said nothing, though, even as her skin grew paler.

Tammy was out of place, but she'd had enough. "Stop it!" This time she raised her voice when she said it because she wanted them all to hear her. "Stop it right now!"

They looked at her as if she'd materialized out of nowhere, as if they hadn't noticed her until then. And she realized they hadn't. Maybe it was just because they'd all been caught up in the moment, but she had a feeling that wealthy and influential people like them didn't pay any attention to people they didn't know.

She felt a pang of anxiety, but then she forged ahead. "Stop fighting," she told them. "And be happy he's alive. You all thought he was dead, but he's not. You should appreciate that. You should appreciate each other."

She didn't expect them to hear her since they couldn't apparently even see her. But she added, "Take advantage of the second chance you've been given."

Then she turned on her heel and headed out the lobby doors. She wasn't going to wait around to see if they took her advice. She wasn't going to wait around for Ethan either.

But he hurried out after her. Catching her arm in his hand, he spun her around to face him. "Where are you going?" he asked her, and he almost sounded panicked over her leaving him.

"Home," she told him.

To her, Northern Lakes was home. Her salon, her apartment, her tight circle of friends…

But it had never been his home. He'd only ever stayed in it while awaiting a call to a wildfire. He hadn't lived here. And she knew that he never would. Even if Braden didn't fire him, how could he stay here? His family—his life and legacy—were miles and worlds away from Northern Lakes.

"But," he began in a sputter.

"Go," she said, and she pointed toward the lobby. "Go, talk to your family. They're your home."

"They're *hell*," he muttered darkly.

"They wouldn't be upset if they didn't care," she pointed out.

"They care more about my letting them think I died than my being alive," he said. And his brow furrowed. "Hell, one of them could be trying to take me out."

"They didn't know that you were alive until that reporter took the picture," she reminded him. "They couldn't be behind what happened with the stove. And they only just arrived in town when the truck blew up. It isn't one of them."

At least that was what she wanted to believe; that *he* would be safe with his family. *She* wouldn't be. Just the way his fiancée and his sister had looked at her had let her know that she had no place among those social-ites, which was fine with her. Her place was here with her friends and her business and the life she'd built for herself.

Ethan glanced back at the hotel. "I'm not so sure."

"You're just looking for an excuse to avoid talking to them," she said.

Was that why he'd come to her apartment? Why they'd made love again?

No. They'd made love because she'd pulled him into her bedroom because she'd wanted him. Because she couldn't resist him…

When she'd thought he was dead, she'd been thrilled

to find out he was alive. She'd wanted that second chance with him. To be with him…

But all it had really been was sex. She couldn't fall for him—for a man she didn't even really know. And what she knew of him now only confirmed that their lives and worlds were too different for them to ever be together.

"Go to your family," she urged him. "Go back to your old life."

He shook his head and murmured, his voice gruff with emotion, "I don't want that life."

He really didn't. She saw that now and she finally understood why he hadn't let anyone know that he was alive. But now that they knew, he had to deal with them and with the press. The reporter and her cameraman had stepped outside too.

"I don't think you have a choice," she told him. But she did. She could walk away. But as she did, a pang of guilt struck her.

She felt sorry for him. But how could she pity the famous heir to billions?

Because he clearly wasn't happy.

And he wasn't safe either.

Somebody wanted him dead.

He was supposed to be dead. The truck had exploded. The bomb had been rigged to the ignition, so once the motor started, the bomb would detonate. How the hell had it not killed him?

Was he invincible?

No. That wasn't possible—just like nearly every member of his family had proved. They'd all died.

And he would, too.

Soon...

He was cursed, just like the other male Canterburys. He was cursed, so that luck he'd had was only fleeting. It would run out, and so would his life.

Jonathan Michael Canterbury IV would be dead soon. And this time, he would stay dead.

Chapter 15

Watching her drive out of the lot, Ethan grimaced at the yearning ripping him apart. He wanted her to stay. But then he also wanted her to go—to get away from him and his crazy family. He wanted to keep her safe.

And she wasn't safe anywhere around him. What if she'd been with him earlier that night, if she'd gotten into the truck as he'd pressed the key fob? He shuddered to think about what would have happened to her.

No. He had to make himself stay away from her. He also had to make himself turn around and head back inside the hotel.

"Jonathan, what happened tonight at the firehouse?" the reporter asked. "Was there another attempt on your life? Do you have any idea who might be trying to carry out your family curse?"

At first he'd thought it was Rory, but his friend had

convinced him he was wrong. So if it wasn't him, it might have been one of the Canterburys, determined to cut him out of his family fortune. He considered that a possibility even though Tammy didn't believe it because she figured none of them had known he was alive. But when he walked back through the doors, they didn't look happy that he was alive. They looked at him like they wished him dead.

All but his mother. The tears were in her eyes again. Or maybe that was just a trick of the light because she blinked, and her eyes were clear, just heavily shadowed with the dark circles rimming them. She looked older than he remembered. Not that he'd seen her that often during his life, not since she'd sent him off to the boarding school. He'd spent most of his holidays with friends' families since he hadn't really felt like he'd had one of his own. Even for his brother's funeral, he'd only stayed that day before going back to college.

So had Mother even noticed that he was gone the past five years? Had any of them?

They all noticed him now, glaring at him as he walked up to them. He shouldn't have come here—to them. What he should have done was stay in bed with Tammy. He could have convinced her to not throw him out—with kisses, with caresses…

His body tensed as he thought of everything he wanted to do to her and with her. But he couldn't selfishly put her in danger again.

"Who is she?" Helena asked the question with all the jealousy of an insecure wife.

But she wasn't his wife. When he'd gone missing, she'd married Kip. Hell, she'd married Kip even before "Ethan Sommerly" had been rescued. But even if he'd had time, he wouldn't have tried to stop the wedding. He'd never met two people who deserved each other more except maybe for his sister and Wesley. No. Wesley didn't deserve his sister. For the most part the lawyer was a nice guy.

Melanie, however, was not nice. "That's the hairdresser he was leaving when that reporter snapped the picture of him," she said with a grimace of distaste.

"Hairdresser?" Helena repeated as if horrified. "Not your usual type."

He looked at her, maybe for the first time, and he didn't like what he saw. Helena wasn't the beauty he'd once thought she was. In fact, her snide tone made her quite ugly. She was the one who wasn't his type—at least not anymore.

"My type has changed," he said. For the better…

"Everything about you has changed," she remarked with a disdainful sigh.

He grinned. That was the nicest compliment she could have given him. He didn't like the guy he'd been before he'd become Ethan Sommerly. He didn't like Jonathan Canterbury at all. He'd been shallow and superficial with no true purpose in his life, just like all these people. He felt sorry for them now, and he felt sorry for the man he used to be. It was all so surreal standing here with them, reminding him whom he'd been and knowing that he could never be that man again. He had changed and fortunately, it was for the better.

"I'm sorry," Kip said as he stepped forward with his hand outstretched. "I was just so mad about you letting everybody think you died…" He released a sigh too, a ragged one of relief. "But your pretty little friend is right. We should just be grateful you're alive."

"Of course you would think she was right," Helena muttered resentfully.

Tammy *was* right—about everything.

He had needed to talk to his family; he owed them an apology. But he didn't want to continue this conversation with the cameras rolling. A couple other reporters were rushing toward the lobby now.

"Mother," he said. "Let's go up to your suite." He had no doubt she'd booked herself the best one in the hotel. Actually she would have had Wesley book it. She treated the man more like her personal secretary than her son-in-law and lawyer.

His mother froze, and the little color in her face drained away. She looked as though she'd seen a ghost, like Tammy had looked earlier after she'd heard about his truck exploding. But his mother should have realized by now that he wasn't a ghost.

"This way," Wesley said, stepping in to lead the others toward the elevator. Fortunately there was only one and only his family fit into it. No reporters could squeeze in as well. Not that Ethan would have let them.

But with the awkward silence in the elevator car, he almost wished a reporter was firing questions at him. His family didn't ask anything, though. They didn't even seem curious about why he'd stayed away or about his new life.

Maybe they knew him better than he'd realized, and they understood.

But moments later, in the suite, he realized they had only been biding their time. Maybe they'd figured the elevator had a security camera.

"This place is a dump," his sister said once they walked into the suite. It was the best one the hotel had, and by most standards, it was pretty luxurious with its thick beige carpeting and brocade wallcoverings. But apparently it wasn't fancy enough to please his sister.

Did anything please her though?

He cast a sympathetic glance at his brother-in-law. "Sorry I hit you," he said. "I didn't realize you'd come up beside Kip."

"I was trying to help you," Wesley said petulantly as he headed toward the bucket of ice sitting on the bar in the corner of the suite's living room.

"It was my fault," Kip admitted. "I shouldn't have lost it like that."

"All the drinks you had on the plane probably had something to do with that," Helena remarked, and her face flushed with anger.

Kip's face had already been flushed.

Ethan had thought it was because of the fight. But now he noticed the blood streaking through the white of his friend's eyes. Kip's drinking problem was news to no one; he'd started drinking in boarding school when they were barely teenagers. But he ignored his wife and apologized again.

Ethan shook his head. "No, I'm the one who's sorry." And not just for letting everyone think he had died. He was sorry that none of them had changed like he had. His former best friend was still a drunk. And Helena Shaw was still an unhappy snob.

She looked as critically at the suite as Melanie had. The women were startingly similar. How had he not noticed it before? Or maybe that was why he'd proposed because he'd known she would fit into the Canterbury family better than he had, just like Wesley had.

"I can't believe you've been living here, Jonny," Helena said.

And he flinched. She had always called him Jonny, too. Hell, everybody had but his mother. To her, he'd always been Jonathan.

"I don't live in Northern Lakes," he said, and his lips curved into a grin at the thought of his former fiancée seeing the tiny cabin where he spent most of his time.

"But your friend does?" Kip asked.

"The firehouse here is the base for the hotshot team I'm on."

Or he had been on...

He still wasn't sure if he'd been fired. By now Braden would know that he hadn't been inside the truck when it exploded. Ethan should have gone to see him instead of Tammy. But he didn't regret what they'd done. He only worried that he might have put her in jeopardy.

"It's too dangerous," his mother remarked, her lips pursed in a tight line of disapproval.

He was used to her looking at him like that. She had protested when he'd told her he'd signed up for the training course.

"It's not my job that's put me at risk," he said. "There were attempts on my life before the plane crash. That's why I didn't let anyone know I was alive...because I wanted to stay that way."

"Are you saying someone's trying to kill you?" his mother asked, and she lifted her hand to her throat as if she was struggling to breathe. Her fingers trembled.

And he felt a pang of regret. But he wanted to be as truthful with them as he'd been with his team. "You must have heard about the explosion earlier tonight and the other one a couple of days ago," he pointed out. "Someone is definitely trying to kill me."

Was it one of them?

Despite what Tammy believed, he wasn't certain that none of them knew he hadn't died in the plane crash. And the crash? Had that been an accident? Or had the problem with the motor cutting out been another *accident* like the ones that had that car nearly running him down and his brakes failing?

How long had someone been trying to kill him? And was that would-be killer in the room with him now?

"Somebody's trying to kill you," Braden said, his voice shaking with fury. "You can't go off on your own like that anymore." He glanced over the console at the man slumped in the passenger's seat of Braden's US Forest Service pickup truck. "You need someone to be with you at all times."

"What are you saying?" Ethan asked.

And to Braden, he would always be Ethan—no matter that the real Ethan Sommerly had probably died in that plane crash. Ethan was the man Braden knew, not Jonathan Canterbury IV. Although, after Braden had talked to his father-in-law, he did know Canterbury. Few people ever impressed Mack like Canterbury had. Mack had been training smoke jumpers for years, and Canterbury's fearlessness had wowed him.

However, that fearlessness worried Braden. It was going to get the man killed for real this time.

"I shouldn't have to say anything," he said. "Your truck blowing up said it all tonight."

"It doesn't say whether or not I still have a job," Ethan murmured.

Braden sighed, but his sigh turned into a yawn. He hadn't been to bed yet and the sky was already beginning to lighten with dawn as he drove from the hotel toward the firehouse. "I can't say one way or another," he admitted.

He had to talk to people, had to figure out the legal ramifications of what Ethan had done when he'd assumed another man's identity. Was he going to be arrested? Prosecuted?

"Is that why you called me?" Braden asked. Fury chased away his fatigue. "You didn't see fit to let me know that you were alive after the explosion, but you called me to pick you up from the hotel."

"I'm sorry," Ethan said, and a heavy sigh shook his burly body. "I'm sorry about everything."

He said the words as if he'd been uttering them for a while. And since Ethan had met with his family at the hotel, Braden could understand why he'd been apologizing. But no matter how many times he'd repeated them, there was a ring of sincerity in his words.

"I didn't mean to deceive anyone," he continued. "But I didn't trust anyone either. And I didn't know what was an accident or an attempt on my life…"

"I can understand that," Braden murmured, especially after everything that had happened to the team.

"And I wanted to leave that life behind," Ethan confessed. "I wanted to be a hotshot. Unlike my life before, I have purpose now. I can help people. And the environment, too. I appreciate it where I took it for granted before. Being a ranger, being a hotshot, that's not just what I do now… it's who I am."

Braden got that; being a hotshot wasn't just a job, it was a *calling*. One that had called Jonathan Canterbury

IV. Just as Trick and Braden's father-in-law had pointed out, no matter what name he went by, the man was damn good at his job. "You are a hotshot," he said. "You are…"

"You just don't know if I'm going to remain one," Ethan deduced.

"It's not my decision alone to make," he told him. But if it was, he would keep him on the team. "While I'm waiting on word about your status, I want you to stick close to the firehouse."

"Is that safe?" Ethan asked.

"You'll be safe if you stick close to your team."

"That's what I mean," Ethan said. "Will it be safe for everybody else if I stay close to the firehouse? Or would it be smarter for me to return to the UP?"

Braden had been to Ethan's place in the woods. He shook his head. "Too remote, too isolated," he said. "You'd be a sitting duck."

Ethan shook his head. "I know that area better than anyone else does."

Maybe that would be the safest place for him then. But Braden hesitated to send him off alone. "I still think there's more safety in numbers."

"Unless one of the number is the saboteur," he pointed out.

But Ethan obviously wasn't the saboteur. Instead he'd become the target…if the saboteur had been responsible for the two explosions. And if he wasn't, somebody else wanted this hotshot dead.

"You think it's somebody on the team?" Braden asked. After realizing the note could be referring to Ethan, he'd hoped that was all it had meant. That it hadn't been about the sabotage at all—just about him being an imposter. And if the note wasn't about the saboteur, it might mean he wasn't looking for someone on his own team. Maybe they were all innocent after all.

Ethan shrugged. "I don't know what to think."

"Neither do I," Braden admitted. About anything…

Except that he needed some sleep, or he would be of no use to anyone—least of all his team. "I'm going to drop you at the firehouse and go home for a bit."

More than he needed sleep, he needed his wife. Needed her love, her warmth, her support. And her brains. If anyone could help him figure out what was going on and what was the right thing to do, Sam was the one.

"Drop me at Tammy's," Ethan said.

Braden snorted. "No."

"I just want to check on her," he said.

Braden snorted again. "Yeah, right." He'd recognized the salon in the background of that picture the reporter had taken of Ethan.

And that was another thing that had blindsided him. He hadn't realized Ethan and Tammy were involved. But nobody else had been surprised.

No wonder he couldn't figure out who the saboteur was; he had problems seeing things that were apparently happening right in front of him.

"I just want to make sure Tammy's safe," Ethan persisted.

"Then stay away from her," Braden told him firmly. "You have someone setting off explosions to get to you. You don't want her getting hurt."

Ethan cursed but nodded in agreement. "No, I don't…"

Braden felt a pang of regret for the young woman. Tammy was a sweetheart, and while she acted like a flirt, she didn't get involved with anyone. Until now. And since she'd made an exception for Ethan, she would be hurt whether anything happened to Ethan or if he left town. But at least she would be safe.

She couldn't sleep, not in the bed that smelled like him, like musk and man and smoke.

And sex…

Tammy's body tingled and ached with wanting him again, with needing him. But Ethan was where he belonged now—with his family. With his fiancée…

That was who the gorgeous blonde was. The woman he had once loved enough to propose to, who he had intended to spend his life with before he'd assumed another man's identity. He'd told Tammy why he'd given it all up, that he'd wanted more. That he'd wanted a purpose.

She could understand that; she'd wanted the same. And she'd worked hard for everything she had, for the life she'd made herself. He had worked hard, too, as a hotshot. Nobody worked harder than those elite firefighters. But that wasn't who Ethan really was.

He was a Canterbury. A rich and powerful billionaire.

She couldn't even imagine what his life had been like before the accident, and she didn't want to fathom it. Tammy had wanted nothing permanent with him when she'd thought he was a hotshot; she wanted even less to do with him now. She liked her life as it was, within her control. If she fell for anyone, especially someone like him, she would have to change. She would have to get used to being in the public eye, and that was too much, too invasive.

But she didn't need to worry about that.

Ethan wasn't asking her for anything permanent. Not that she could expect him to be thinking about her or anything other than the fact that someone was trying to kill him…

Shivering at the thought, she reached for her robe. She couldn't sleep in the bed, so she headed out in the living room toward the couch. But as she walked, footsteps echoed hers.

Footsteps on the stairs. Not the stairs that led to the exterior door but the other stairwell—the one that led down to her office in the back of the salon. But the salon wasn't open and the only stylist she'd trusted with a key was the one who'd already had one.

Margaret wouldn't be up yet, though. Only a faint glimmer of dawn lightened the sky. And that was another reason Margaret had sold her the salon—because she hated waking up early. So who in the world was down there?

It wasn't Ethan. She'd left him at the hotel without a ride. And even if he borrowed one of his family's rental vehicles, he wouldn't come up through the salon. He would have come to the exterior door again. She'd made certain it was locked, though, when she'd come home.

She'd made sure he couldn't get inside again.

But now she wished she hadn't. She wished he was there, so he could protect her from whoever had broken into the salon. He wasn't sticking around, though, so she couldn't count on him. Not that she wanted to…

She'd learned long ago how to protect herself—from the insults, from the bullying…

She could and would protect herself from her intruder as well. But she had a feeling she might be in danger of getting more than her feelings hurt this time, especially when the shadow appeared at the top of the stairs.

It was big and burly, but it wasn't Ethan.

She felt no flicker of recognition or attraction. She felt only fear. And as it washed over her, she opened her mouth and screamed.

Chapter 16

Braden was right. He needed to stay the hell away from Tammy. It was the only way to protect her. But something told him that she wasn't safe. A niggling doubt had kept him from heading up the stairs to the bunkroom. Despite the warmth of the summer night, he shivered as a chill had raced down his spine. Something was wrong.

So once Braden's truck had pulled away from the firehouse, Ethan had slipped back outside into a mist glowing eerily in the faint light of dawn.

Hell, everything was wrong. But the only thing he was worried about, the only person, was Tammy. He knew something was wrong with her.

Maybe it was just the way she'd left; how upset she'd been with him and with his family. Hell, she'd been horrified. She hadn't realized just how dysfunctional they really were.

But now that she knew, surely she had to understand why he'd left Jonathan Canterbury IV behind him.

After so much time spent in the spotlight, he liked his solitude. Maybe that was why he hadn't wanted to go to the bunkroom. But he didn't want to be alone right now. He wanted to be with her.

But only to make sure that she was safe.

He hastened his pace until he was nearly jogging toward her place. But instead of going around the front, something compelled him to slip into the alley that wound around the back.

Or maybe *someone* compelled him to do that since that reporter always seemed to be wherever he was. Had she followed him and Braden from the hotel?

He wouldn't have put it past her. But Braden had been extra vigilant about checking the rearview mirror for a tail. After everything that had been happening lately, it made sense to be extra careful. They'd been in so much danger and none of it had had to do with the wildfires they'd fought.

A pang of guilt struck him. What if some of those accidents had been attempts to take him out—like the stove and the truck exploding?

What if someone threatened Tammy because of him?

That chill chased down his spine again as he finally reached the back entrance. A motion light came on, glittering on the glass fragments sprayed across asphalt. The glass in the back door had been shattered, and the door stood ajar.

Ethan cursed. He had been right. Tammy was in trouble. Somebody had broken into her place.

There was probably a stairwell inside the salon that led up to her apartment. He jerked open the door and rushed into the building. The back of it was pretty much just a hallway with other doors opening off it. One led to an office. Another to a break room. And another to a stairwell.

He wasn't sure if he should be quiet or loud. Sneak up on the intruder or scare him off? His size alone made it impossible for him to climb the stairs without making noise. His footsteps echoed in the stairwell. The sound of his heart, pounding madly, reverberated in his chest, too.

He was so damn scared.

And mad...

How dare someone go after Tammy? And if she'd been hurt...

Rage blinded him. He had never thought himself capable of murder until now. Now he could barely see, so he stumbled up the last couple of steps. The back stairs came up into an area that must have been her mudroom. A washer and dryer were stacked in one corner while coats hung from hooks on the wall. A couple of them had fallen to the floor as if someone had brushed against the wall.

Or struggled in the room...

He walked around the apartment, pushing open doors and peering around corners. But he didn't catch sight of the intruder—or of Tammy either. Had she been dragged off down that stairwell?

Was that how some of the coats had fallen from those hooks? Because she hadn't left of her own accord? Her purse sat on the kitchen island with her car keys lying beside it.

Where was she?

His heart continued to pound so fast and hard that his body shook. Fear gripping him, he called out, *"Tammy!"*

Oh, God, the intruder must have taken her. Must have dragged her off somewhere. He reached for his cell. But before he could punch in the emergency contact, a noise caught his attention.

Like metal sliding over metal.

A gun?

Maybe the intruder hadn't left. Maybe he was still there, hiding in the shadows getting ready to shoot. But then where was Tammy?

Was she here too?

He must not have looked hard enough. Unconcerned about his own safety, he rushed back through the apartment. That was when he noticed the door to the bathroom off her bedroom was closed. And when he tried the knob, it didn't budge. It was locked.

"Tammy?" he called out. "Are you in there?"

He heard that noise again—the scrape of metal as a dead bolt slid. He wasn't sure if she was locking or unlocking it until the door opened. She stood in the doorway, shaking. She'd put on a robe over her nightgown. But she must have been in bed when the intruder had broken into the salon.

"Are you all right?" he asked. Before she could even answer, he closed his arms around her, pulling her close.

Her body trembled against his. "Somebody was in here. Somebody got in…" She shuddered. "At first I thought it was you…"

He shook his head. "It wasn't me."

"I knew that the minute I saw him."

"You *saw* him?" Fear slammed through him at how close the intruder had come to her.

She nodded, and her soft hair swirled around her shoulders and his chin. "Just a shadow. He was big.

So big…" She trembled again. "I screamed. And then I ran."

Now fury chased away Ethan's fear. He hated that she'd been so scared. He clasped her shoulders and gently eased her away from him. "Are you okay?" he asked hoarsely. "Did he touch you?" He studied her face, which was damp with tears.

She shook her head again. "No, I ran fast and locked the door."

She was smart to have the sliding dead bolt inside the bathroom door. He'd noticed the lock earlier that evening, and now he understood why she had it. She'd made the bathroom into a safe room for instances just like tonight.

"Did he try to get in?"

She shuddered and nodded then. "He turned the knob and rattled the door. So I screamed again and kept screaming." Her voice sounded hoarse. "But nobody heard me, and I didn't have my phone to call for help."

"You're not okay," he said. And neither was he. He was more upset over her intruder than he'd been over his truck exploding. His hand shook as he pushed the emergency call button on his phone.

"What are you doing?" she asked anxiously.

"Calling the police." Hopefully they would be able to find fingerprints, something to track down the son of a bitch who'd terrorized Tammy.

And they better find him before Ethan did—because he would make damn certain that person never scared her again.

As if the break-in hadn't been bad enough…

Watching the police swarm the salon had a queasy

feeling flipping Tammy's stomach. Black powder rained all over the place as they checked for prints. Despite the mess, she was glad that Ethan had called them; she would have herself had she had her phone on her, but she'd left it in her purse on the kitchen counter.

"You're not going to find anything," she told them. She didn't even know why she was so certain, but she just had a feeling that the man had known what he was doing, that he'd broken into places before and hadn't been caught. "I'm sure he was wearing gloves."

"You said you couldn't see him clearly," Ethan reminded her.

"Not his face," Tammy said. "Just his shadow..." She shuddered as she remembered that moment when he'd come up the stairs, with how close he had been.

Trooper Wynona Wells stepped away from the tech who was scattering that black dust everywhere. "Is there anything else you can remember?"

"He was big," she said. "As big as..." And she glanced at Ethan.

The trooper looked at him now, too, intently. "As big as Mr. Sommerly? Or should I call you Mr. Canterbury?"

"Sommerly," he said.

"But is that really your name?"

Tammy felt a pang of sympathy for him. "I'm the one who called you here, Officer."

"Actually the call came in on Mr. Sommerly's cell," Trooper Wells reminded her.

Just because she hadn't had time to grab hers when she'd run from the intruder to lock herself in the bathroom.

"What were you doing here at the crack of dawn?" the trooper asked him.

"I was checking on Ms. Ingles," he said.

"You suspected someone might try to break into her place tonight?" The woman's eyes narrowed with her suspicions. Clearly she thought Ethan was the intruder.

Tammy pointed toward the banged-up cash register that had been knocked to the floor. "Somebody broke in to rob the place," she pointed out. "It had nothing to do with Ethan."

But his body was still tense, his jaw tightly clenched. He didn't believe her any more than the trooper seemed to. Any more than she did…because if the perp had wanted to rob her, he would have just taken the whole cash register or more.

"Was there anything missing from your purse?" the officer asked.

"No," Tammy admitted. She'd already told the first trooper on the scene that when she'd looked through it after the police had arrived.

"I'm not so sure this was really a theft or that some-body was just trying to make it look like one," the trooper said. And she looked at Ethan again with that suspicion.

And Tammy laughed. "You know who he is," she said. "Who he really is, so you know he wouldn't waste his time breaking into my place." He wouldn't have to. She would have let him in—against her better judge-ment, but she would have. Just as she'd welcomed him into her bed earlier that evening.

"I believe the theft was staged," Trooper Wells con-cluded, gesturing at that banged-up register. "The break-in was not about stealing money."

Tammy had already given him her body; he wouldn't have broken in for that. But her heart…

She doubted he wanted that, or he wouldn't have ignored her flirting all the years that he had. But even if he did want it, she would make sure he didn't get to lay claim to it.

"Ethan had nothing to do with the break-in," Tammy defended him. "And whoever did was probably smart enough to wear gloves, so I think your people are wasting their time trying to find fingerprints."

And wasting Tammy's time as well.

"I need to open soon," she said. "I have appointments scheduled from eight this morning until nine tonight."

"You may need to reschedule," the trooper advised.

Tammy shook her head. "That's not possible. I'm booked out for months in advance."

Trooper Wells raised a reddish-brown brow. "Really?"

Tammy took pride in the success of her salon. It hadn't been nearly as popular under Margaret's management as it was under hers. "Yes, really," she replied. "So can you and your technicians please clear out?"

"Miss Ingles, we're trying to help find your intruder," the trooper reminded her.

But Tammy had a feeling that the intruder hadn't been looking for her any more than he'd been looking for money. He'd been looking for Ethan.

No. He'd been looking for *Jonathan Canterbury IV*.

And as soon as she got rid of the trooper, Tammy intended to get rid of him, too. She wasn't worried about her business or her life, though.

She was worried about her heart. She couldn't be around him much longer and fight her feelings for him. Even now she wanted to slide her arm around his waist and lean against him, to rely on his strength.

But he had more than enough of his own problems; he didn't need to worry about her, too. And he had been worried; she'd heard it in his voice when he'd called out for her earlier. It was almost as if he'd already known she was in trouble. But of course he would have because he must have come in through the back door like the intruder had, and he would have seen the broken window and the damage.

She was in more trouble now than she'd been with the intruder. She was in danger of falling for Ethan. And that would wind up hurting her worse than the fright the intruder had given her.

Brittney had known he would wind up back here at the Northern Lakes Salon and Spa. So even though his boss had lost her earlier when he and Canterbury had left the hotel, she had known where to find him. She'd just had to wait for her damn cameraman to wake up.

His ineptness had cost her valuable coverage. The police had already been here when Barney had finally showed up, and the area had already been blocked off.

So she had to stand behind the crime scene tape and shout her questions, which made her too easy to avoid. Even when the officers began to roll up the tape and clear the scene, they continued to ignore her.

But they paid attention to the female trooper whose red hair trailed out from beneath her tan hat. So Brittney paid attention to her, too.

"Trooper!" she called out. "Trooper Wells!"

This officer had been at the firehouse the night before, too, working the explosion. The lack of sleep showed in the dark circles rimming her eyes. But she was still pretty.

She'd look good on camera. Brittney flashed her a smile. "It's great to see a woman in charge in law enforcement," she praised. "I'd love to interview you."

The trooper's lips curved into a faint smile. "Sure," she said.

And Brittney's heart lightened with hope. "You'll agree to an interview."

"I can tell you all about being a female in law enforcement," Trooper Wells replied. "I can't talk to you about any active investigations, though."

"Is that what this is?" Brittney asked with a nod toward the salon. "An active investigation?"

"That's all there seems to be lately," the trooper murmured.

"No closed cases?" Brittney asked.

The woman narrowed her eyes. "None that I care to discuss."

"Just what all has been happening in Northern Lakes lately?" Brittney wondered aloud. And why didn't she know about it?

Her source hadn't told her anything. And that was how she'd realized something was going on because it had been clear that her source was keeping information from her. That there were things he hadn't wanted to divulge.

Brittney had just happened upon the missing Canterbury heir. Her source had certainly known nothing about that, or at the very least was claiming ignorance now.

But Brittney was the one who felt stupid. She'd thought she'd discovered a story nobody else had. But now she wondered…

How many stories were there in Northern Lakes?

Chapter 17

Ignoring the tenderness of his hands, Ethan tightened his grip on the mop handle. Tammy firmed her grasp as well, tugging harder on it as she tried to take it away from him. "You're not going to win in a game of tug-of-war with me," he warned her. But she was stronger than he'd thought.

Muscles rippled in her biceps and shoulders. She'd replaced her nightgown with a summer dress that left her shoulders bare while the skirt swirled around her long, sexy legs. She obviously worked out to have the sculpted muscles she had.

He was impressed.

But then everything about her impressed the hell out of him. She was so quick-witted. So funny.

And so damn smart.

If she hadn't run like she had, if she hadn't had that lock on her bathroom door…

He shuddered to think what could have happened to her. And as he did, his grip loosened, and she pulled the mop from his hands.

"You don't have to clean up," she said.

But while she'd called around for a carpenter to fix the back door, he'd wiped off the black powder that had dusted every surface and had mopped it up from the slate floor as well. Or most of the floor.

"I'm almost done," he said as he reached for the mop again. But she held it away from him.

He could have just wound his arms around her and pulled her close to him. But he knew he wouldn't finish mopping then.

And her body was tense. She kept glancing out the front windows that overlooked the street. Was she worried about the intruder returning?

"You need to leave," she said. "I'll be opening soon."

"I'll wait until your stylists start showing up," he replied. "I don't want to leave you here alone."

"I'm not alone," she said with a nod toward the windows. "Your reporter is out there."

He grimaced. "She's not my reporter." He'd never had a good relationship with the press. From the time he was a little kid, they'd hounded him, trying to record his every misstep. Unfortunately, he'd made a lot of them in his youth although he'd been older when he'd made his biggest mistake: getting engaged to Helena Shaw. She'd been even more furious than his mother when he'd signed up for the hotshot training course, and she probably would have broken their engagement if she'd thought he would have completed it. But until that course, he'd never really completed anything. He'd kept changing his majors in college, had dropped out of law school, and hadn't found anything that had held his interest for long. Not like being a hotshot had and not like Tammy did.

"She's not the only reporter," Tammy pointed out. "Looks like more of them are starting to show up."

He groaned. "I'm sorry…about all of this."

"I'm not the one you need to apologize to," she said.

"But this break-in…" He gestured around the salon. Although he'd cleaned up most of it, streaks of black powder remained.

"Despite what the trooper seemed to think, I don't think you broke in here," she told him, and her lips curved into a slight smile.

"I didn't," he said. "But I think I'm the reason that someone did. I think I'm the one he was looking for."

She shivered. Maybe at the memory, maybe over concern for him. "You should leave," she repeated.

And though he wanted to argue further, he nodded in agreement. Braden had warned him the night before that being around her would only put her in danger. It had already been too late then. She'd already been in jeopardy. But it wasn't too late for Ethan to step away now, and to stay away from her, so that nobody would come to her to find him again.

The intruder.

Or the reporters.

Or his family…

"You should leave town," she said.

A sharp jab of pain struck his heart. But he couldn't deny that it would be in her best interests if he left. "Braden doesn't think I should go back to my ranger post."

"I don't either," she said. "I think you should go back to your old life."

This time the jab of pain was sharp enough to make him flinch. "You don't want me anywhere near Northern Lakes." Or her…

"That's not what I'm saying," she replied quietly. "Your family has spent the past five years without you. You should be with them now."

He snorted. "Because that went so well last night. You were there," he reminded her. "You saw that they're hardly rejoicing over the fact that I'm alive."

She shook her head. "They were upset that you let them believe you were dead."

He snorted again. "You don't know my family, Tammy. And you don't know for certain that one of them might not have been behind these attempts on my life…" he gestured at the back door "…or this break-in. Or even the plane crash five years ago."

She gasped. "What?"

"The wreckage was never found," he said. "So nobody knows what caused the mechanical failure."

"Sabotage?"

"It could have been…" Just like the stove and the other issues the hotshots had been having.

Maybe she was right. Maybe he did need to leave Northern Lakes. Then—if the incidents stopped—he would know that it was his fault.

That he was responsible…for all of this.

She reached out to him then, her fingers sliding along his forearm. "Ethan—"

Fists pounded against the glass of the front windows and the door. "Hello! Hello in there!" Cameras flashed.

And whatever she'd been about to say turned to curses as she turned toward the reporters who swarmed outside. Or maybe she had intended to curse him out for putting her in danger and the hotshots as well. They were her friends, too.

"They're looking for you," she said with a heavy sigh. "Go out the back."

Was she helping him escape? Or did she just not want to be seen with him anymore?

He couldn't blame her if it was the latter. He'd caused her nothing but trouble. But that was going to stop now. He would stay away from her.

For her sake.

And maybe for his as well; maybe he would be safer if he could focus again, if he could figure out who wanted him dead. He couldn't concentrate when he was near Tammy. He wanted her too badly.

Just as she'd told the trooper, the salon had been scheduled with back-to-back appointments the entire day. That, however, didn't stop people from wheedling for walk-ins. And it wasn't just the reporters who tried to get into the salon. Locals also attempted to gain entry to find out what had happened there that morning.

To find out what was going on with Tammy and Jonathan Canterbury IV…

Had she known that he was really someone else? Had she had any idea?

The questions kept coming at her until her head pounded with tension. She'd wanted to retreat to her office, but the receptionist had called her out so many times that she'd just taken over the front desk herself.

Every reporter peered around the salon like he was hiding under a dryer or in the closet. With as reluctant as he'd been to leave, maybe he was.

But Tammy had hurt his feelings when she'd suggested he should leave town. She'd seen him flinch as if she'd slapped him. She hadn't realized that going back home might put him in danger. Her suggestion had been all about keeping him safe.

And her heart...

She was so damn worried about losing it to him. And even if he didn't go now, he would go home one day. He was a Canterbury with a family legacy to uphold.

The door dinged as it opened again. Plastering on a smile, she looked up, and that smile slid away when she saw who'd entered. She wished it was reporters. Ethan's former fiancée and his sister stood in front of her instead.

"So she's just a receptionist," the fiancée told his sister, as if Tammy wasn't even there.

She didn't care enough to set them straight. "Can I help you?"

"You can stay the hell away from my brother," the sister said.

Tammy sucked in a breath—shocked at the blatant attack.

"If you think you're getting those claws into the Canterbury heir, you're sadly mistaken," Melanie continued.

Those claws had raked down his back the previous night and had probably left marks on the rippling muscles and smooth skin. The thought had Tammy's lips curving into a faint smile.

"Look how smug she is. She thinks she's already got her claws into him," his former fiancée said, as if appalled.

Tammy was the one who was appalled. She'd been bullied in school for her weight, her bad complexion, her hair...

But she'd thought the mean girls like that eventually grew up. Most of the ones who'd picked on her had apologized and befriended her. But maybe that was just here in Northern Lakes...

The two mean girls before her had yet to grow up. But Tammy had spent too much of her life being bullied to put up with such nastiness now. She stood up from behind the counter and pointed toward the door. "Get the hell out," she told them.

The sister sucked in a breath. "How dare you speak to us that way. We're potential clients. We will make sure you get fired."

Tammy had just opened her mouth to laugh when another laugh rang out from behind them. "Even you can't get the owner fired," a familiar voice remarked as the reporter stepped out from behind them.

She must have snuck into the salon with them. But for once Tammy didn't feel her usual irritation with Brittney Townsend.

"*Owner?*" Helena Shaw sputtered as she looked between the two women.

"You should have done your research," Brittney remarked. "Tammy Ingles is the sole proprietor of this place, which is the most popular salon for hundreds of miles around."

One of the only spas for hundreds of miles around, but Tammy didn't share that information. Not that she wanted to impress Ethan's family.

She didn't want anything to do with them. "And as the proprietress I have the right to refuse service to anyone I want, so get the hell out of my salon."

Melanie Canterbury gasped. "How dare you speak to us that way!"

"What way?" Tammy asked. "I've not been as bitchy as the two of you have been. Get out of here, right now, or I'll call the police and have you forcibly removed and charged with trespassing as well."

Actually she was tempted to personally throw them out. She worked out regularly. She could easily handle these two.

As if she'd read her mind, the reporter smiled and offered, "I can help you if you'd like to get rid of them now."

"So much for that interview you wanted," the sister huffed. "There is no way anyone in my family will speak to you now." Grasping her friend's arm, she turned and pulled the blonde from the salon with her. Their heels clicked against the slate floor as they hurried on their way.

Tammy smiled while the reporter sighed when the door closed behind them. "You didn't have to do that," she told Brittney. "I didn't need you to defend me. Now you've lost your interview opportunity."

"They weren't going to talk to me anyway," Brittney said.

Tammy's smile widened. "Neither am I even though you defended me."

"Why not?" Brittney asked. "They treated you like crap. You don't owe that family anything."

She shrugged. "No matter how they behave—"

"Like bitches?"

She smiled again. "No matter, they're dealing with a personal family issue. It has nothing to do with me."

"He does," Brittney said. "He was here again this morning. You're involved with Jonathan Canterbury."

"Not Jonathan Canterbury," she corrected. The man

with whom she was involved was Ethan Sommerly. But she'd pushed him away, too. She'd had to...

The reporter sighed again. "Fine. What about you? What happened at your salon that the police were here this morning?"

"Just a run-of-the-mill break-in," Tammy said. "Someone tried getting into the cash register." She pointed to the banged-up machine sitting on the counter.

Brittney narrowed her pretty pale brown eyes. "We have run-of-the-mill burglaries in Detroit. Not here..."

"You'd be surprised what all we have here in Northern Lakes," Tammy said.

"The female trooper made a similar remark to me."

"Trooper Wells."

Brittney nodded. "What was she talking about? What has been going on in this town?"

Tammy smiled at her to soften the sting when she turned her words back on her. "Sounds like you need to do your research."

Instead of being offended, the reporter laughed. "Touché."

She didn't push for any more information, just turned and walked out of the salon to join her cameraman on the sidewalk.

"You're starting to like her," Margaret remarked when she joined Tammy at the front desk.

Tammy sighed. She was. "She's just doing her job."

"She's a vulture who would do anything to get a story," Margaret warned. "She thinks you're the story."

Tammy chuckled. "I'm nothing."

"Those two snooty women wouldn't have showed up here if they thought you were nothing," her former boss pointed out. "If Ethan thought nothing of you."

"He isn't Ethan." She had to keep reminding herself of that—that he wasn't the man she'd thought he was—the one she had…

No. She hadn't fallen for either man. And knowing now who he really was, there was no way she would ever fall for him. She liked her life just the way it was with her business and her friends. But when that stove had exploded, it hadn't just turned his world upside down; it had imploded hers too.

"I told you not to go over there," Braden reminded Ethan as the exhausted firefighter joined him and Trick in Braden's already cramped office. The two big men made it feel even more cramped.

"I had to check on her," Ethan replied.

Had to… not wanted… As if he'd had no choice.

"And it was a good thing I did," he continued unrepentantly.

"You're lucky that the intruder was already gone," Braden pointed out. "Or he could have gone after you."

"You think that's why he was there?" Ethan asked. "That he was looking for me…"

"It could have been a random break-in," Trick said with the ignorance of someone new to Northern Lakes.

Braden chuckled.

"What?" Trick prodded.

Braden's amusement dried up as dread overwhelmed him. "The only bad things that have happened in this town have been because of the hotshots."

"Or because of me?" Ethan asked.

"But why break into Tammy's place looking for you?" Trick asked.

Braden shook his head. "So much for your powers

of observation," he remarked. Although he'd brought his brother-in-law onto the team to help him expose the person among them who wasn't whom he or she had appeared to be, Trick had been no better at ferreting out Ethan's real identity than Braden had been. And, apparently, he hadn't picked up on the attraction between Tammy and Ethan either.

Trick's face flushed. "Hey, it's Tammy. She flirts with everyone."

Ethan's hands fisted at his sides. "Don't you dare talk about her that way!"

Braden stood up. But if the men started swinging at each other, he wasn't sure he would be able to stop them. They were both big guys.

But he was the boss. "We're on the same team," he reminded them.

Trick nodded. "I didn't mean anything," he told Ethan. "You know I like Tammy. She's a good friend of Henrietta's, too. I'd hate to see her get hurt."

"So would I," Braden chimed in. "That's why you need to stay away from her, Ethan, until we can find who set that damn bomb in your truck."

He nodded. "I know, I know."

"The bomb in the truck…" Trick shook his head now. "It just feels different than the other *accidents* that have happened around here. Hell, from everything that's happened around here. The sabotage has always been made to look like accidents. And even the things that Louanne and Gingrich and Colleen did felt different somehow."

Braden agreed. "The truck bomb almost feels like a professional hit or something…"

The thought should have brought him relief that one of his hotshot team wasn't behind that attempt on

Ethan's life. But it brought him only fear that, with a professional after Ethan, there was no way they could protect him.

No way to keep him alive…

Chapter 18

Ethan awoke to darkness. Where the hell was he? What had happened?

The events of the last few days played through his head like a bad movie with the exception of the time he'd spent with Tammy. That was a fantasy that had his body tightening with desire. He craved her so badly.

But he needed to stay away from her.

Just that morning when he'd met with Braden and Trick, he had come to the same realization they had. The last attempt…the bomb in the truck had to have been the work of a hit man.

Was that who had broken into Tammy's place? Was that how they'd known to make it look like a burglary? The only problem was that there wasn't much crime in Northern Lakes unless it involved the hotshots.

Break-ins weren't everyday occurrences like in the big cities, like Boston where he was from, or Detroit which was a few hours south of Northern Lakes. Because of that, he'd been hard pressed to find a security firm close enough to install a system for Tammy. And to get one to come up from Detroit and install one asap, he'd had to use his name.

The one he'd never wanted to use again. His given name…and the bank accounts he hadn't accessed in nearly five years. They were still open since he hadn't officially been declared dead yet. Someone was obviously determined to make that official now.

He tensed and came fully awake. After making sure the system was going to be installed, he'd finally succumbed to sleep and had crashed in the bunkroom.

How long had he been out?

The room was dark. But he was alone. Nobody snored. Nobody barked.

Annie was okay. He'd checked on her that morning as well, and the vet had given her a clean bill of health. He needed to give her a side of beef or a dinosaur bone to show his appreciation for her saving his life.

But Stanley was probably going to keep his dog away from the firehouse until Ethan was gone. The other hotshots weren't here either, maybe staying away for the same reason. Not wanting to get caught in the crossfire…

Tammy had been right that morning. He should leave Northern Lakes. Not just for her sake or his but for everybody else's as well.

That thought propelled him up from the bunk. In a hurry to leave before anyone returned, he rushed around to collect his stuff from his locker. Then he remembered…

He had no way of leaving. No vehicle to drive. But

just as he'd used his name and his accounts to get that security system installed for Tammy, he could use it to buy a car—no matter what time it was. The owner of the car dealership down the street lived above his offices, like Tammy. He would surely open up to sell him a vehicle.

Ethan's footsteps echoed throughout the silence of the firehouse as he ran down the steps and between the engines parked in the garage bays. Nobody called out to him. Nobody else was there.

But when he pushed open the door and stepped out onto the sidewalk, he immediately knew he was no longer alone—when a fist slammed into his face.

The blow rocked him back on his heels, knocking him into the building. This wasn't Rory defending himself. Or Kip drunkenly lashing out at him.

This guy was a pro—from his size and strength and from the way he began to work Ethan over. He obviously intended to beat him to death.

But Ethan recognized Tammy's description of her intruder, and the rage he'd felt then, over how scared she'd been, coursed through him.

He wasn't going out without one hell of a fight.

She wanted to sleep. Every muscle ached with exhaustion. But the thought of going to bed…alone…filled Tammy with dread.

In addition to the dread, caffeine also hummed through her system, making her heart race while setting her nerves on edge. She'd mainlined coffee all day in order to stay awake, and now she couldn't sleep. Curled up on the couch, she finally poured herself a glass of wine from the bottle she'd opened the night before.

But before she could raise the glass to her lips, a noise drew her attention to the salon. Something pounded against the glass of either the door or the window, and then the alarm pealed out.

"Damn it!"

She hadn't wanted the alarm, hadn't appreciated that Ethan—no, Jonathan Canterbury IV—had ordered and paid for the damn thing without consulting her. But then she'd seen the relief on the faces of her stylists, and she'd accepted the system for them. So they would feel more secure.

Hearing it peal out now just scared her. She wasn't sure if she should wait for the police to arrive or if she needed to investigate. The caffeine and nerves sent her running down the steps to the salon.

And she let out a gasp at the sight of the person standing outside the glass door. Rushing over to the control panel, she punched in the pass code and shut off the alarm. Then she pulled open the door to Mrs. Edith Ludington-Canterbury.

Was she here looking for her son? Or just here to insult her like her daughter had? "The salon is closed," she said. "And it's been a very long day."

After a sleepless night.

"I want to talk about your long day," Mrs. Ludington-Canterbury said. "And I'm here alone."

Tammy arched a brow in surprise. But manners were too ingrained in her to be impolite to the woman, so she stepped back. "Please come in."

"I came to apologize," she said. "I understand that my daughter was rude to you earlier today."

"You don't have to apologize for her."

"I do because she won't," Mrs. Ludington-Canterbury insisted. "I'm sorry that I spoiled her so much that she acts like such an entitled brat."

Tammy laughed. "Apology accepted." And because she didn't want to be alone, she found herself offering, "Would you like a drink? I just poured myself a glass of wine."

The older woman smiled and accepted. "Yes, I'd like that."

"I'm not so sure about that," Tammy said. "I opened this bottle last night and didn't have a chance to drink it."

"Then it has sufficiently breathed," Mrs. Ludington-Canterbury remarked.

"This way," Tammy said as she led her through the salon to the stairwell leading up to her apartment.

The older woman looked at everything, even stopping at a stylist's station to look over the tools of the trade. "You have a lovely place here."

Tammy tensed, expecting condescension. But she heard only sincerity.

"My father was an actor," Mrs. Ludington-Canterbury said as she followed Tammy upstairs. "I spent a lot of time on movie sets with him. I had the most special relationship with one of his makeup artists." She expelled a wistful sigh. "She taught me so much about the trade. I would have loved to pursue it…"

"If you hadn't met a Canterbury?"

"I hadn't met him yet then," she said, and she accepted the glass Tammy held out to her. "But I was a Ludington. I was supposed to be in front of the camera. Not behind it."

Tammy nodded as if she understood. But she had no idea. Her family had had no expectations for her. They had no expectations for themselves either. They lived simple lives. And once again she was confronted with how profoundly different she was from this woman's son. They had nothing in common but...

Passion.

She pushed that thought from her mind—and her memories of making love with him—and focused on her surprise visitor.

"You were an actress?" Tammy asked, wondering what she might have seen her in.

"Not professionally," Mrs. Ludington-Canterbury replied. "I wasn't good enough. At least I wasn't until I got married." Color flushed her face. "I'm sorry. I don't mean to overshare."

"I love oversharing," Tammy assured her. "The minute people sit down in a stylist's chair, they seem to spill their secrets like they're on a therapist's couch."

"The stylist has more reasonable rates," Mrs. Ludington-Canterbury said. "And can make you feel better faster."

Tammy smiled at the woman's insight.

Mrs. Ludington-Canterbury sipped from the glass and nodded. "It's quite good."

Tammy took a long sip and nodded in agreement. "Yes, it is." And surprisingly so was the company.

She had expected a lot of questions—like the ones she'd fielded all day—about her relationship with Ethan. But Mrs. Ludington-Canterbury seemed more interested in the salon. Taking the bottle of wine with her, she walked back down to inspect the place.

Bemused, Tammy followed her around. It wasn't until they'd settled into the manicurist's station that the woman prodded her with a command—not a question. "Tell me about Ethan."

"*Ethan*?" Tammy repeated, surprised that his mother would refer to her son by another name.

"That's who he is now," Mrs. Ludington-Canterbury insightfully said. "He's not the boy I knew. Tell me about the man. About Ethan." She reached for a bottle of polish and held it up to inspect it. "Pretty."

Tammy smiled. "Here, I'll do your nails."

And while she did them, she told Mrs. Canterbury about her son—about the reclusive, quiet man who worked hard and supported his friends. About how, when he did speak, he could be so damn witty.

And they laughed about the stories she shared about him and the other hotshots ribbing each other. How Trent Miles loved to flirt with him like Tammy did, just to fluster him.

"They love him," Mrs. Canterbury said.

Tammy nodded.

"You love him."

Tammy tensed and sucked in a breath. "No. I… I don't even know him."

"You just told me all about him," Mrs. Canterbury said. "You know him better than I ever had."

"I didn't even know who he was," Tammy reminded her.

"No," Mrs. Canterbury corrected. "You didn't know his real name, but you knew who he was, who he *is*."

Tammy opened her mouth, but she couldn't argue. Despite his quietness, she knew Ethan better than she'd realized. "You don't mind that he's changed his name."

"It was never really his name," Mrs. Canterbury said

with a sigh. "It was his father's name and that name never really fit him. He never really fit."

Tammy nodded heartily in agreement then hastened to apologize when the woman's eyes widened in surprise. "I'm sorry. I was thinking of how different he is from your daughter." She shuddered. "And his fiancée."

Mrs. Canterbury snorted. "That little twit? All she has is her name as well. Nothing else going for her. No interests. No purpose. Ethan has found his purpose now."

"The hotshots."

She nodded.

Thinking of all the fear her friends had experienced over their significant others, Tammy felt compelled to warn her, "It's a dangerous profession."

"So is being a Canterbury."

Tammy had already determined she wasn't going to fall for Ethan or for anyone else. She didn't want to change for anyone, but she doubted that, even if she wanted, she could change enough to fit in with the Canterburys.

Though she found herself bonding with Mrs. Canterbury in a way she had never even bonded with her own mother. Her mom didn't care about hair and makeup and nails. She didn't understand how it could make someone feel so much better—even better than food.

"Let me do yours," Mrs. Canterbury offered when Tammy had finished her nails.

And she proceeded, between sips of wine, to give Tammy an expert manicure. Once she was done, she started on her own makeup, and Tammy brought down another bottle of wine. They were giggling like girls at a sleepover when the glass door rattled under a fist.

"We're closed!" Mrs. Canterbury called out in a sing-song voice.

Tammy laughed but then tensed as she noticed the dark shadow on the other side of the glass door. She'd turned off the alarm. What would happen if he smashed in this door?

Mrs. Canterbury patted her shoulder. "Don't worry. It's fine. Just wimpy Wesley…"

Tammy chortled over the nickname then realized how much she'd had to drink. Too much.

And so had Ethan's mother who lurched and nearly fell over when she stood and headed toward the door. Tammy walked with her to let in her son-in-law.

Mrs. Canterbury reached up and patted the bruise on his jaw. "You really shouldn't have gotten in the way, Wesley. Last night or now…"

"Melanie sent me to find you."

"Why?" she asked.

"To bring you to the hospital."

"I'm fine," she replied. "Just a little tipsy."

"Not for you," he said. "For Jonathan. He's been attacked."

Tammy gasped in horror.

Mrs. Canterbury reached for her hand, gripping it so tightly she'd probably smeared her manicure. "Come with me," she said.

Tammy couldn't refuse her—especially when she wanted to be there so badly herself. How badly had he been hurt?

Once again, crime scene tape roped off the area around the firehouse. "What happened now?" Brittney wondered aloud.

She'd been camped out most of the day near the salon. Obviously she should have been here instead. "What happened?" she asked a trooper.

It wasn't the female one. This one was young and male and from the interest in his eyes when he looked at her, susceptible.

So she turned on her charm, smiling and flirting with him. He glanced around, to make certain he wasn't overheard, before leaning close to whisper to her, "There was an assault involving a hotshot. The person was taken to the hospital in critical condition. He may not make it."

Brittney sucked in a breath.

What had she done when she'd reported that Jonathan Canterbury was alive? Had she put a target on his back? Or had he already had one there?

Her source hadn't been happy when she had decided to become a reporter. Had told her that it wasn't an honorable profession. Brittney had argued that there was nothing more honorable than reporting the truth.

But the excitement she'd felt over exposing that truth earlier this week dimmed. She'd felt badly today for the salon owner, too. She'd felt as though she'd exploited Tammy Ingles' relationship with the Canterbury heir. And now Brittney felt badly about Jonathan Canterbury. She didn't want anyone getting hurt because of her.

But then she reminded herself that she'd only discovered the truth because somebody had already tried to hurt him. It didn't matter what she'd reported; somebody wanted the man dead.

And it sounded as though that somebody had finally succeeded.

Chapter 19

"What happened?" Braden asked as he joined Trick in the waiting room at the hospital. They'd all spent too much time in this place, waiting on news about the condition of another hotshot.

Trick shook his head. "I don't know."

"You were supposed to be guarding him," Braden reminded his brother-in-law.

"I just stepped out for a minute while he was sleeping," Trick said. "And when I left, I made sure the doors were locked. Nobody could get in…"

But Ethan had been able to get out. He'd been found with his duffle bag. The trooper had shared that much with him but little else.

He needed to talk to Ethan…once he was able to talk. *If* Ethan was able to talk…

The doors to the parking lot opened with a whoosh of sound and hot summer air. He turned to see Tammy walking in and she held the hand of a woman Braden recognized from the news. Ethan's mother.

Not Ethan…

Jonathan Canterbury's mother. She'd already thought she'd lost her son once.

Towing the woman along with her, Tammy rushed up to Braden. "What happened? How is he?"

He glanced at Trick before shaking his head and murmuring, "I don't know."

And that killed him. He was the superintendent. The boss. He was supposed to take care of his team. He was supposed to make sure the danger was under control at all times. But for months he'd had no control.

He'd had nothing but worry and fear.

He'd already lost one team member this year, and he was damned scared that he was about to lose another.

Tammy closed her eyes, trying to shut out the fear she saw on Braden's face. But she couldn't unsee it. And she couldn't unfeel it either.

The fear coursed through her. Her nerves had already been on edge. Now they were overwrought.

And so was Mrs. Canterbury. She must have seen Braden's fear, too, because she began to shake as sobs slipped out between her lips and tears spilled down her face.

Tammy closed her arms around the woman and held onto her. "Let's not think the worst," she told her even as the worst thoughts rolled through her own mind. "We don't know anything yet. Let's wait until a doctor comes out to talk to us. To you…"

She was nothing to Ethan. Mrs. Canterbury was his next of kin.

"They'll talk to you," she assured the woman. "They'll tell you how he is."

Mrs. Canterbury held tightly to Tammy as she trembled with fear. She didn't let go until the outside doors to the waiting room whooshed open again and someone ran in screaming, "Let her go!"

Tammy stepped back and met the venomous gaze of the woman's daughter.

"Get your hands off my mother," Melanie yelled at her. "You money-grubbing—"

"Shut up!" Mrs. Canterbury yelled as she swung around to confront her daughter. "I don't want to hear one more nasty word out of your filthy mouth."

Melanie gasped. But she ignored her mother and turned on Tammy again. "What have you done? Have you poisoned my mother against me?"

"*You're* poison," Mrs. Canterbury said, and she turned toward her son-in-law who'd just scrambled into the waiting room to catch up with his wife. "Shut your wife up, Wes, or you'll be redoing my will to disinherit her."

Melanie gasped again. But when she opened her mouth, Wesley grabbed her arm. Before she could say anything, he pulled her toward the doors, which whooshed open again.

"Wow," Tammy murmured with respect.

Mrs. Canterbury was one tough lady. But then she'd had to be to have survived all the losses she'd suffered courtesy of the Canterbury curse.

Had it struck again?

As if the same thought had just occurred to her, Mrs. Canterbury grasped Tammy's hand again and squeezed it. She wasn't offering comfort, though. She was looking for it when she whispered, "I can't lose him again."

"You won't," Tammy said. And she hoped she was right.

"I lost him even before the plane crash," Mrs. Canterbury admitted brokenly. "Long before. I was so afraid of losing him like I lost his father and his brother that I pushed him away from me. I sent him to boarding school and barely made time to see him because I didn't want it to hurt when I lost him to that damn curse. I was so certain that there was no hope for him to survive it." She squeezed Tammy's hand so tightly that she winced. "But it hurt even more when the plane crashed because I knew I'd missed out on so much. I missed so much of his life. I didn't even know who he was."

"He's going to be fine," Tammy assured her again. "He's strong. Like you."

He had survived a plane crash and two explosions. Certainly he could survive this, too. He had to.

For his mother.

And for her…

With the scene his sister had made, nobody had noticed Ethan slip out of the ER into the waiting room. But he noticed them—noticed how his mother clung to Tammy for comfort.

He knew Tammy was used to it; she always stepped in to comfort and assure her friends like this whenever they were worried and scared. But he had never seen his mother so distraught. Even when she'd buried his dad and his younger brother, she'd been perfectly composed.

She'd never acted like she cared. But he couldn't deny the fear in her voice or the stricken look on her face that was damp with tears. While he was grateful Tammy had offered her comfort, he wished she hadn't made a promise she wouldn't be able to keep.

But he acknowledged that his heart had lifted when he'd stepped out and found Tammy waiting for him. She hadn't come when the stove had exploded. And he'd been disappointed even as he'd tried to convince himself that he didn't want anyone worrying about him.

Especially now...

Then she looked away from his mother and met his gaze, and he lost his train of thought. He lost everything but that overwhelming attraction and connection with her. While no one else had noticed him, she had.

"Ethan!" she exclaimed.

His mother whirled around, and all the color drained from her face as if she'd seen a ghost. But he was alive.

He wasn't supposed to be.

Somebody had probably paid that man a lot of money to beat him to death. Too much...

Because he hadn't succeeded.

Tammy rushed over to him and raised her hand to his face, gently skimming her fingers over his swollen jaw. "Are you all right?"

He nodded.

"You look like hell," Trick remarked.

He glared at him with the eye that wasn't starting to swell shut. "You should see the other guy." Then he turned back to Tammy and repeated, "Actually, *you* should take a look at him." Not that he necessarily wanted her to know what he'd done to the guy. But then he'd been fighting for his life. "See if you can identify him as the person who broke into your salon."

His mother paled. "Someone broke into your place?"

Tammy nodded. "Yes. Probably just looking for money…"

But his mother wasn't fooled. She looked at Ethan for confirmation. And he shook his head. "Probably looking for me."

"What happened?" Trick asked. "How did he get into the firehouse? I had locked the place up when I stepped out." His broad shoulders slumped with guilt. He must have been assigned to protect Ethan like he'd been assigned to protect the other hotshots when they'd been in danger.

But had anyone been in *this* kind of danger? He was glad that Trick had left before the guy had attacked him. Ethan didn't want him to get hurt, not when the nomadic hotshot had just finally settled into Northern Lakes and found love with Hank.

"He ambushed me when I stepped out of the firehouse," Ethan said.

"You should have stayed inside," Braden admonished him. "You know you're in danger."

Far more danger than he'd even realized—if the guys were right and a hired killer had been sent to take him out.

"I was going to leave," Ethan admitted.

Tammy tensed, and her green eyes widened with surprise. She'd suggested that he do it. But apparently she hadn't expected him to act on her suggestion.

"Why?" Braden asked.

"I thought it might be safer for everyone," he said, and he found himself glancing at Tammy again. He hadn't wanted anyone going after her to get to him again.

"You're not going anywhere," Trooper Wells informed

him as she joined them in the waiting room. "You are not to leave town until the prosecutor determines if he's going to file charges against you."

"Against *my son*?" his mother asked, and her voice had gone all cold and snooty just the way he'd always heard it. He'd never heard her talk the way she had with Tammy. "He's done nothing wrong."

"He's spent the past five years impersonating another man," the trooper reminded them all. "That is illegal."

His mother shook her head dismissively. "He did that for his own protection. Surely you can understand now that it was necessary for his survival."

Did she believe that? Or was she only spinning the story to get him out of trouble? Of course his mother was usually too blunt to tell a lie, which had always aggravated his politician father.

"The prosecutor may also file assault charges against you," the trooper said.

"For defending myself?" Ethan asked in astonishment.

Trooper Wells studied his bruised face. "You are conscious with no broken bones. The other man can't say the same."

"Let me see him," Tammy interjected. "Let me see if he's the man who broke into my salon."

The trooper turned toward her now. "You said you didn't get a good look at him," she reminded Tammy.

"I saw how big he was," she said.

The officer still looked doubtful.

"Who is he?" Braden asked. "Did he have identification on him?"

Trooper Wells shook her head. "Not that we found."

But she looked at Ethan again, as if she suspected him of picking the guy's pocket.

His mother made a tsking sound with her tongue against her teeth. "If you think my son robbed some thug, you are seriously mistaken," she said, and there was a warning in her chilly tone. She turned toward the doors and gestured toward her son-in-law who stood outside with her daughter. "Our lawyer will let you know the consequences of slandering a Canterbury."

Ethan groaned. "Mother, let her do her job," he said.

"Did you fingerprint the guy?" Trick asked the question.

The trooper nodded.

"Then you'll find out soon enough who he is," Trick said. "And it'll prove that he came after Ethan."

Only if he had a record. If he didn't, there was no way to prove that he was a hired assassin—unless he confessed. And Ethan didn't expect him to do that.

His mother stepped closer to him and tentatively touched his face like Tammy had. She stared at him with eyes wide with wonder. "We will sort out the legal issues," she promised him. "And I can hire you bodyguards. I will make sure that you stay safe this time."

He wasn't worried about just himself, though. He was concerned about his team. He was even worried about his family. But most of all he was afraid for Tammy.

And the only way that any of them would be safe was if he left town—or if he figured out who was trying to kill him and stopped that person.

But who the hell had hired the thug to take him out? And was that the only one who'd been hired or were there more assassins out there, waiting to try for him again?

Chapter 20

Tammy watched as Ethan searched the salon and now her apartment as if he expected somebody else to jump out and attack him. "You had that alarm installed," she reminded him. And she hadn't thanked him. Instead she'd been irritated with him.

"And you didn't have it on," he reminded her, and now the irritation was in his gruff voice.

She smiled. "Your mother was in a hurry to get to the hospital, so we rushed out of here when your brother-in-law came to get her."

"What was my mother doing here?" he asked. "Besides drinking?" He'd already picked up one of the wine-glasses from the manicurist table when he'd searched the salon. Now he grabbed the cork she'd left on the kitchen island.

She smiled and held up her hands. "My nails."

"What?" He furrowed his brow furrowed, which moved the swollen skin around his bruised eye. And a groan slipped out of his lips.

"Your mother did my nails," Tammy said. "And I did hers."

He grimaced. "What—were you two going to have a slumber party?"

"We probably would have if your brother-in-law hadn't showed up," she said then sighed to feign disappointment. "Too bad you got hurt."

"I wonder how Wesley found out about that…" he murmured.

"The reporter," Tammy said. "She knows everything that's happening in Northern Lakes."

He nodded then his brow puckered again. "Maybe there's a reason for that. Maybe she has something to do with it."

Tammy shook her head. "She's young and ambitious but she's actually pretty nice."

He touched his head now as if checking to see if it was still there. "Maybe I do have a concussion. You like the reporter and you and my mother were doing each other's nails. Did you have tea with the mad hatter too?"

She chuckled. Even badly hurt, the man still had his sense of humor. "No. I like the reporter because she offered to help me throw out your ex and your sister when they were giving me a hard time earlier today."

He cursed.

"That's why your mother was here," she said. "She came to apologize."

"For Helena?" he asked.

"For your sister," she said. "She only took responsibility for her."

He shook his head. "I don't understand her at all…"

"Who? Your sister…or Helena?"

"My mother," he said.

"She loves you," she told him.

But he shook his head again. "No. She couldn't wait to ship me off to boarding school the minute my father died." And his voice was gruff as if the loss of his father still affected him.

"Were you close to him?"

He nodded. "Closer than I ever was to my mother. My father actually paid attention to me. Looked at me. My mother never did."

"That's because she was worried about losing you, too," she said. "Like she lost her husband and your brother. He was so young."

"And so stupid," Ethan bitterly remarked. "Overdosing at just fourteen years old. Bored rich kids will try anything and have the money to get whatever they want."

"Were you like that?"

"I've done some stupid stuff in my youth. But I never did drugs," he said. "I didn't trust anybody enough to get messed up around them. David shouldn't have trusted anyone either. His little boarding school friends didn't help him when he overdosed. If they had called for help, he would have lived. But they hadn't wanted to put their families through a scandal."

"I'm sorry," she whispered. Closing the distance between them, she linked her arms around his waist. "I can't even imagine how hard that must have been…"

He stared down at her, his dark eyes even darker with sorrow and something else. "*I'm* sorry," he said. "So sorry that you're getting caught up in the mess that is my life."

She rose up on tiptoe and brushed a soft kiss along his swollen jaw. "Yeah, it sucks."

He chuckled. "I can always count on you for your bluntness. That's probably why you and my mother hit it off so well."

"I like your mother," she said.

He laughed harder then winced as the skin tightened over his jaw. She pressed another kiss to it, and he stopped laughing as his body tensed. Then he lowered his head and kissed her back—on her mouth.

He kissed her deeply. So deeply that her toes curled in her shoes and she curled her fingers into his shirt. Tammy wanted to tug it off and over his head. She wanted to make love with him again—just in case something happened to him, just in case she never saw him again.

But every time she got close to him, she risked falling for him. She risked her heart. But that wasn't all she risked.

She tensed, and so did he. Lifting his head, he glanced around the apartment. "Did you hear something? Is someone trying to get in?" he asked.

She shook her head and reminded him, "You put the alarm on. I'm safe."

"No thanks to me," he grumbled.

"You paid for the alarm," she said. And she didn't offer to reimburse him. She'd never needed one before—had never had any issues until she got involved with the Canterbury heir and his curse.

"It was the least I could do," he said, "after what happened to your salon."

"It's fine. You helped me clean it up."

"And you," he said. "You were scared."

"I'm tougher than I look," she insisted, and her lips curved into a small smile of satisfaction. "Your sister and ex found that out today. I learned a long time ago how to deal with bullies like them."

He touched her jaw, tilting her face up to his. But he didn't kiss her again. Instead, he stared at her, his dark eyes full of concern. "Who bullied you?"

She shrugged. "You know school…it was hard on me. I was the typical ugly duckling, which made me a target for everyone who wanted to feel better about themselves by taking me down even farther than I already was."

He shook his head. "I can't imagine that—"

"Me being ugly?"

He gasped. "You were never ugly!"

"You didn't know me then," she interjected, her heart contracting as she realized he might have bullied her, too, like the other popular kids had.

"Your beauty comes from within," he said. "You were *never* ugly. You are too kind, too supportive, too strong…"

"I didn't feel strong back then," she admitted. "I felt weak and helpless…" And out of control of her own life, of her own body. She never wanted to feel that way again.

"You're strong now," he said. "Strong enough to handle the bullies like your school friends and my sister and Helena. But not the guy who broke in here." He grimaced. "He could have hurt you."

She touched his jaw again. "He hurt you."

"I'll be fine."

But even he didn't sound convinced. After everything that had happened, he couldn't deny that there were people after him. "I need to leave," he said.

And she nodded in agreement.

"I need to leave Northern Lakes."

"I know," she said. Ever since she'd found out who he really was, she'd known that he would leave. But still she felt a pang of regret—of loss. She hid it with a smile, though, the way she'd always hid her pain. "Don't worry about me. I knew this was just a fling."

He tensed. "You did?"

"That's all I was looking for," she said. "It's all I'm ever looking for."

He flinched now. "That's good to know that you don't care about me then. That you don't care if you'll ever see me again."

"Ethan…" she murmured. But he'd already turned away and headed toward the stairs.

The door opened, and the alarm pealed out along with his curses. She ran down to punch in the pass code. But when he started out the door, she grabbed his arm and pulled him back.

"You know that we're too different," she told him. "You belong to a different world than I do. One that I don't want to be part of…"

He didn't argue with her—didn't offer to stay in Northern Lakes, with her. He didn't say another word. He just pulled his arm from her grasp and walked away.

And she wondered if she would ever see him again.

Was he leaving tonight? Was he leaving for good? If whoever was trying to kill him caught up with him again, he might be leaving forever.

Ethan shouldn't have gone back to the salon with her. But he'd wanted to make sure that the alarm had been installed; he'd wanted to make sure that she would be safe. Because he was leaving…

His heart ached with disappointment that Tammy hadn't been disappointed. She'd probably been relieved since she'd only wanted a fling. He was the one who'd wanted more. But he couldn't have it. Not now…

It didn't matter that the trooper had warned him against leaving town. He knew that if he stuck around, he would be a dead man. Or worse, someone else would get hurt as collateral damage.

He couldn't risk anyone else's life. But after how upset his mother had been at the hospital, he had to see her. He had to see his sister, too, but not because she'd been upset. They were all in the suite when Wesley opened the door.

Not just his family but his ex-fiancée and former best friend as well. He'd already started to wonder if his killer—at least the person who'd hired the person to kill him—was in this room. A hotshot wouldn't hire someone else to do his dirty work. If one of the team wanted him dead, he would have killed him with his own bare hands—not hired someone else to try to beat him to death.

So which one of his loyal family and friends had already known he wasn't dead? Which one of them hadn't been that surprised when he or she had seen the picture of him on the news?

"I'm so glad you came back to the suite tonight," his mother said with a smile. "I don't think you should stay at that firehouse."

"I shouldn't," he agreed. Annie had already been hurt because of him. Of course she was such a big, strong dog that she was fine. But he didn't want to risk anyone else getting harmed.

"So you'll stay here," she said.

He shook his head as he chuckled. "Hell, no. I escaped this pit of vipers once. I'm not crawling back in."

His mother gasped then giggled. And he wondered just how much wine she'd had with Tammy. But he smiled at her. He'd once thought she was the most venomous of all the vipers, but he'd misjudged her.

"What the hell's wrong with you?" Melanie asked him.

"What the hell's wrong with *you*?" he asked. "Why would you and you—" he turned on his ex-fiancée "—go to Tammy's salon and hassle her? You don't even know her."

"Do you?" Helena asked. "She's obviously just after your money."

He sucked in a breath. But before he could say anything, before he could even think of a response, his mother jumped in to defend Tammy. "She didn't know who he was. She had no idea all these years."

But they hadn't been together for all these years. They'd only just gotten intimate after she'd shaved off his disguise. When they'd made love, she'd known exactly who he was. She had been the only one who'd known then. Was that why she'd finally gone beyond flirting with him? Was she after his money?

But then why tell him to leave town? If she wanted his money, wouldn't she have wanted him to stay? Or to go with him? But she'd insisted she'd wanted no part of his life, so that would include his money.

"She doesn't want my inheritance," he said, and he looked at his sister. "But somebody else must or otherwise there wouldn't have been all these attempts on my life."

His sister pressed a hand to her throat, looking outraged. "Who the hell do you think you're talking to?" she demanded to know.

And he grimaced. "A very selfish, spoiled person."

"Mother!" she exclaimed, as if looking for maternal defense. But he'd heard what their mother had told her at the hospital.

And even if Edith Ludington-Canterbury had sobered up, she hadn't changed her mind. "He's right." She glanced at her son-in-law. "Poor Wesley."

"*Poor Wesley!*" his sister exclaimed.

"What about us?" Kip asked. "We can't get any of your money. So what's our motive?"

"I don't know," Ethan honestly admitted. "What is your motive?" He glanced at Helena. "Why did you come here?"

Her face flushed with embarrassment. And he knew. She'd expected him to want her back, to break up their marriage. No wonder Kip had attacked him. It even gave him a motive for wanting to kill him.

He looked at his old friend, but Kip looked away, unable to meet his gaze.

"Go home," he told them all. "There's nothing for you here in Northern Lakes."

"What about you?" his mother asked. "Are you leaving too?"

He nodded. "It's for the best for everyone." Especially for Tammy. So she wouldn't be put in danger again.

Wesley cleared his throat. "But the trooper told you not to leave town."

His mother sniffed disdainfully. "She can't charge him with anything."

Wesley opened his mouth, but he knew better than to argue with his mother-in-law. So he closed it again.

"She'll find out soon enough who the guy that attacked me is," Ethan said. "Hopefully she'll find out who hired him as well, and then this will all be over."

"Then what will you do?" his mother asked.

He shrugged. He had no idea if he would have a job anymore. Or what the future held for him. He just knew that he had to leave town.

"Once it's safe," he said, "I'll be in touch."

His mother stepped toward him, like she had at the hospital, and touched his face. "Be careful," she urged him, and tears glistened in her eyes along with something he'd never noticed before.

Love.

He hadn't thought she was capable of it until that moment. His mother did love him. Guilt struck him hard for all the years he'd let her think he was dead. "I'm sorry," he rasped.

She nodded. "I know."

It had been easy to stay away from them the past five years, but he found it hard now to walk away from his mother. But just like with Tammy, it was safer for her to not be around him.

He had confirmation of that just a short time later as he drove his new truck toward the firehouse. While he'd waited at the hospital for the trooper to take his statement, he'd called and had the truck delivered to the hospital. He hadn't cared what kind it was, just that it was fast. He needed to get the hell out of Northern Lakes.

After he stopped at the firehouse. He was just going to say goodbye—that was all. After all the years of lying to Braden, he owed the man the truth.

Just as he turned the corner onto the Main Street, shots rang out and the rear window of the truck shattered. "Damn it!" He ducked low and pressed hard on the accelerator.

He had his answer now. More than one assassin *had* been hired to kill him.

How many more?

Was there only one shooter? Because the gunfire continued, bullets pinging off the metal of the truck, and he wasn't sure how he was going to avoid getting hit.

He pressed harder on the accelerator, but he realized he was driving straight toward the shooter, not away from him. Another ambush had been set up at the firehouse. And he wasn't sure how in the world he was going to survive this one.

Braden shut his office door behind Trick and motioned for him to stay silent as the trooper's voice emanated from the cell phone lying on his palm. "So you got back a hit on the guy's fingerprints already?" he asked eagerly. "That was fast."

"He was in the system," she said. "A lot. He's wanted in connection to several beating deaths."

"So now you have no doubt that Ethan was acting in self-defense?" he asked her.

"I still don't want him to leave town," Trooper Wells said. "I want to question him further, find out why someone would be trying to kill him."

"I don't think he knows," Braden said. "Has the hired hit man regained consciousness? Have you questioned him yet?"

"He is conscious," she said. "But the only word he uttered was *lawyer.*"

Braden cursed.

"So I have to wait until his attorney arrives to question him further. But he's under arrest."

"You took him to jail."

"The hospital won't release him yet," she said.

"Please keep me posted," Braden implored her. He didn't want to lose Ethan.

Before the trooper replied, somebody pounded hard on his door. Trick pulled it open with his finger pressed to his lips.

But Stanley didn't even notice. "Somebody's shooting," he said. "I can hear the shots. They're close. And Annie is howling."

Then Braden heard them, too, and he jumped up from his chair so abruptly that it toppled over against the concrete block wall.

"Shooting?" a voice called out from the cell in his hand.

"Yes," he said. "Send police."

But it wouldn't matter how close the troopers were; they weren't going to get there in time.

Chapter 21

Maybe he was wrong. Maybe it was a hotshot who wanted him dead—because the shooter was at the firehouse. As Ethan headed toward it, the windshield shattered too. But unlike the rear window, the glass stayed intact. It was just impossible to see through it, though. So he steered toward the curb, threw the truck into Park and jumped out, leaving the motor running.

He had to find the shooter, had to sneak up and overpower the son of a bitch. The last light of dusk disappeared, leaving only the glow of the headlamps illuminating the area. Ethan slipped into the shadows. Keeping low to the ground, he moved toward the firehouse.

Light flashed near the side of the building as more shots rang out. Bullets struck the concrete, sending up puffs of cement into the night. All his focus on the shooter, Ethan barely registered the sound of footsteps coming up behind him until a heavy weight struck him, knocking him flat on the ground.

"What the hell…"

"Get down," a deep voice ordered. "You're going to get your head shot off."

"I was down," Ethan told Trent Miles.

The sound of their voices drew the shooter's attention and generated more gunfire. He heard the sound of bullets striking the ground near them. Dragging Trent with him, Ethan scrambled across the sidewalk.

The firehouse suddenly came alive as all the garage bays opened. Annie, barking ferociously, lunged out, but someone caught her, holding her tightly. The sudden commotion stopped the gunfire as the shooter ran off in the other direction, away from the street.

Ethan bounded to his feet. "He is not getting away." He raced off in pursuit of the shooter.

He was not alone; Trent ran beside him. "How are we going to stop him?" he asked Ethan. "He has a gun."

"Go back!" he said as he shoved his friend. He didn't want Trent getting shot.

"You're not going after him alone," Trent insisted.

More shots were fired, bullets whizzing close to Ethan and Trent's heads. The flash of the barrel pinpointed the shooter's location. They were gaining on him. But he hadn't run out of bullets yet.

Ethan was so furious that he didn't care. He rushed forward, toward where the shooter had darted into the small patch of woods behind the firehouse. A subdivision was on the other side of those trees—homes where families slept. He couldn't let the assassin get into one of those houses. So he leapt toward the shadow running in the darkness and knocked him flat onto the ground.

Curses were uttered. His. Trent's. The shooter's…

Then, as all three of them grappled for the gun, more shots rang out. With as close as they were, the bullets could not miss this time.

The gunshots were worse than the explosion. That had been one blast disrupting the night. The gunfire just kept ringing out over and over, and with the sound of each shot, Tammy flinched—imagining those bullets striking Ethan.

She had no doubt the shooter was aiming for him. He was the one somebody wanted dead.

Had that person succeeded?

While other people stayed holed up in their houses during the gunfire, Tammy ran out into the night. She ran down the street toward the firehouse. It was all lit up as if there was a fire. Annie barked ferociously while Stanley held tightly to her, his arms wrapped around her neck to hold her back.

"Are you okay?" she asked.

Tears streaked his face, but he nodded.

And tears sprang to Tammy's eyes too as fear overwhelmed her. "Is everybody else?"

He shook his head. "I don't know. I heard the gunshots. Then Braden and Trick came out, and the shooter ran off. But they were chasing him."

"Braden and Trick?" Maybe Ethan hadn't been involved. But who else would the shooter have been trying to hit? Were all the hotshots under attack?

"They went, too," Stanley confirmed. "But Ethan and Trent were ahead of them. They ran right after the guy."

Relief washed through her. Since Ethan had been able to run, he must not have been hit.

"Then there was more gunfire," Stanley continued. "Until it stopped."

It had stopped. What did that mean?

Had they stopped the shooter? Or had he succeeded in killing Ethan, so he'd stopped firing?

Stanley must have been as scared as she was because more tears rolled down his face. Tammy reached out and covered his hand on the dog's fur. Hers was shaking.

Sirens replaced the sound of gunshots as police vehicles rolled up to the firehouse. A paramedic rig followed.

"Where's the shooter?" Trooper Wells asked as she ran up to them.

Before they could answer, Trick McRooney rushed up from the darkness, panting for breath. "This way!" he yelled. But he wasn't talking to the trooper; he was pointing to the paramedic—to Owen James who had also arrived. "We need medical attention. This way!"

They all started off across the parking lot behind the firehouse. And Tammy instinctively started forward too. But Stanley grabbed for her hand again. "No, Miss Ingles," he said. "You shouldn't go."

"But…" If it was Ethan…

What if Ethan had been shot? Or worse?

She shuddered.

And Stanley repeated, "You shouldn't go."

"I have to know," she murmured.

"What?" a familiar voice asked.

She wished it was Ethan's. But it was that reporter. With a sigh she turned toward Brittney Townsend. "How are you *always* around?"

Brittney's smile flashed in the glow of the light pouring from the firehouse. "Because I'm good at my job…" Her smile slipped, though. "But it looks like I'm a little late this time. What happened?"

"I don't know…"

Except that someone had been hit or Trick wouldn't have urged Owen to hurry.

Who?

More people rushed up. More reporters descended on the area. And more troopers and hotshots and some of her friends.

The troopers tried to keep order in the chaos, attempting to push back the crowd of onlookers and the reporters. But there was pandemonium.

And there was panic in Tammy, pressing on her lungs—making it hard for her to breathe…until she saw him in the crowd.

He was with the paramedics, not on the stretcher they carried but walking beside it. Trooper Wells was with him and his boss and Trick McRooney.

He was alive.

So the panic should have eased. But Tammy didn't feel better. Even if they'd caught whoever had been shooting at him, she doubted the attempts on his life would end. He'd put one person in the hospital but somebody else had been sent after him.

Whoever was trying to kill Ethan wasn't going to stop until he was dead.

Brittney rushed toward the group that emerged from the woods. And not just because she was chasing a story. Fear pounded in her heart because she recognized one of the men. Blood was sprayed across his face. But when she rushed toward him, he shook his head.

He didn't want to talk to her.

He never wanted to talk to her lately.

Which was the reason she'd showed up in Northern Lakes in the first place. She hadn't wanted to lose her source. But he was so much more than a source to her. He was her brother.

"Step back, Ms. Townsend," the female trooper told her. "If you continue to interfere in this investigation, I will arrest you for obstruction."

Brittney lifted her hands as if the trooper was holding her up. "I'm not interfering," she protested. "I'm reporting." But she had no idea what the story was.

Then she looked at the stretcher. A blood-soaked sheet covered the body. Somebody had died. As the paramedics carried the stretcher, an arm slipped from beneath the sheet and dangled.

And Brittney gasped as she recognized the ink. "He's a gang member," she said. "From Detroit."

Trooper Wells stopped. "You recognize him?"

Brittney gestured at the sheet covering his face. "I recognize his tattoo."

The trooper grabbed the arm of the closest paramedic. "Stop." Then she pulled back the sheet herself and showed Brittney the face of the dead man. "Do you recognize *him*?"

She studied his face for a long moment before she shook her head. "No."

The officer turned toward Trent. "What about you? You're from Detroit. Do you recognize him?"

Trent snorted. "Detroit is a huge city. I don't know everybody there."

"I'm not asking about everybody," Trooper Wells said. "I'm asking about this person who tried to shoot your friend."

Trent shook his head.

But Brittney wondered…

And from the glance the others shot him, it was clear they wondered, too.

Was he telling the truth?

Or did her brother know more than he was admitting?

Chapter 22

The trooper had to wait for the hit man's lawyer to arrive at the hospital to talk to him, but Ethan didn't. Hell, he wasn't just going to talk to him. He was going to negotiate. The man had been paid to kill him. He cared more about money than human life. So if money meant that much to him, maybe he would give up who'd hired him for a price.

And Ethan could afford to pay more than whoever was trying to kill him. He had a hell of a lot of money from all the trust funds he'd already inherited.

He couldn't pay the shooter who'd tried to gun him down at the firehouse, though. Dead men didn't need money. It was too damn bad the killer had gotten shot himself—for so many reasons. One. He was young. And it was just such a waste. And two, he couldn't talk.

He couldn't tell Ethan who had hired him. And it

was clear that he *had* been hired. The only thing they'd found on him was a wad of cash and a copy of that picture the reporter had taken of Ethan the night he'd left Tammy's place.

Where was the other hit man's wad of cash? Where was his picture of Ethan?

He intended to ask him all of that. But Trooper Wells stood between him and the door to the hit man's hospital room.

"You can't go in there," she said.

"Why not?"

"You already put him in that bed," she said. "I don't want you to put him in the morgue like the last guy who came after you."

"I didn't pull that trigger," he reminded her. She'd already tested his hands for gunshot residue. He hadn't had any on him. While he'd taken the guy down, Trent Miles was the one who'd piled on top of him.

He could have been shot. Ethan shuddered to think how close he'd come to losing one of his best friends. Trent had had residue on his hands as he was the one who'd fought for the gun. When it had gone off, it had been pointing at the kid instead of Trent.

But it had been too close.

And Tammy had been too close as well.

He'd seen her at the firehouse. She must have run over when she'd heard the gunshots. She should have stayed inside her place with the alarm engaged.

But what the hell good was her alarm? If the shooter had come after her, he could have shot and killed her before the police responded.

"We're lucky he's the only one who died," Ethan

pointed out to her. "We have to find out who's behind this."

It was the only way to stop the attempts for good. That was what Ethan needed to do. Sure, he could have followed through on his plan to go into hiding, but that wouldn't track down his would-be killer. And while he didn't want to put his friends or family or Tammy in jeopardy, he didn't want to leave them either. He had to end this—for everyone's sake.

"You can't beat the truth out of him," Trooper Wells warned him.

He'd tried a bit of that already when he'd tussled with the guy. "I'm going to buy it out of him," he said. "You forget who I am, Trooper."

She grimaced. "You're the one who forgot. Or who wanted everyone to forget…until it serves your purpose."

That had been his problem with being Jonathan Michael Canterbury IV; he'd had no purpose. Not in that life…

He'd been famous for his family—not for anything he'd done. But Ethan had a purpose now, one that would stay with him no matter what people called him.

"Let it serve a purpose now," he said. "I can get the guy to talk. I can give him more money than whoever paid him to kill me."

"He's not going to need money in jail."

"He can use it for a lawyer to try to keep him out," Ethan said.

She sighed, but finally, she stepped out of his way.

And Ethan reached for the doorknob, turned it and pushed open the door. A curtain had been pulled, blocking off the bed from the doorway. Ethan jerked it aside and cursed.

"What?" Trooper Wells asked as she appeared beside him. Then she cursed too. "Where is he? Where the hell is he?"

Gone.

The bed was empty but for the pair of handcuffs clipped to the side rail. Somehow he'd gotten out of them and apparently out of the open window as well.

Ethan swore again.

He was too late.

He had never killed anyone before. At least not with his own hands.

Or gun.

Well, it wasn't his gun. But he'd used it. The forest was eerily silent after the noise of the gunshot that had reverberated throughout it, sending birds flying up from the trees. Even the ground had seemed to shudder beneath his feet. But it was quiet and still now that it was over.

He stared down at the body lying under the trees. What should he do now?

Bury it?

Leave it?

It wasn't as if he was going to be sticking around this damn town. Once he had what he wanted, he'd be leaving. He would probably be long gone before anyone even found the body. It wasn't as if anyone would link him to the murder anyway.

To any of the murders.

Nobody suspected him. Nobody knew what he was really capable of.

* * *

Was he gone?

Tammy hadn't seen him all day. She hadn't seen anyone who'd seen him either. He must have left. Maybe even last night, after the shooting, or had that been this morning?

All the sleepless nights were catching up with her. Tammy had barely been able to keep her eyes open that day. And she had never been as happy to turn over the Closed sign as she was now. But before she could engage the alarm, a face appeared on the other side of the glass.

She gasped and stepped back. And the door she had yet to lock pushed open.

Ethan's friend—the one with the thinning blond hair—stepped inside, grinning at her. "Hey, there, gorgeous!" he greeted her.

And the acrid odor of alcohol struck her like a blow. She stepped back.

"You've got a busy place here," he said. "Took a while to empty out."

Apparently he'd been watching and waiting for everyone to leave. Knowing he'd been out there, stalking her, had her shivering.

"What do you want?" she asked.

"Just to talk to you," he said.

She doubted that with the way his gaze kept running up and down her body. She worked too hard to stay in shape to cover up, but she wished now she wasn't wearing such a short, form-fitting dress.

But just because she had didn't mean she welcomed this kind of ogling. "I don't want to talk to you," she told him. She didn't want to talk to any of Ethan's family but his mother. And maybe his brother-in-law. She actually felt a little sorry for that guy.

But this man…

She shuddered again as she remembered how Kip had attacked Ethan in the lobby. Goose bumps rose on her skin as her discomfort turned to fear. "You need to leave," she told him. And she would have opened up the door to show him out, but he stood between her and it.

He stood between her and the security control panel as well. But maybe she could get to the reception desk which had a panic button installed along the edge of it.

She stepped back, but he followed her. And before she could turn and run, he wrapped his hands around her waist and jerked her up against his body.

The smell of booze overwhelmed her, making her want to gag. "Let me go!" she shouted at him.

"C'mon," he said. "You're friends with Jonny. That makes you friends with me, too."

She squirmed and tried to get away. But his body hardened, and he started breathing heavy.

"Oh, yeah," he groaned.

Tears sprang to her eyes. She was scared but she was also furious. "Let me go!" she yelled again.

"C'mon, honey," he murmured drunkenly. "Jonny and I share everything."

She pounded on his chest. "Not me!"

"What—don't I have enough money for you?" he asked. "You're just like Helena. I was good enough for her when Jonny was dead. But now that he's back, she wants him—just like you do."

"I don't care about you and your wife," Tammy said. "I just want you to let me go!" She raised her knee and drove it into his groin. "Now!"

He cursed and doubled over, and she ran for the door. But when she reached for it, he caught her again and pulled her back.

She was not going down without a fight. So she jabbed her elbows back into his body as she screamed for help. Where was Ethan when she needed him?

Where had he gone?

Chapter 23

He had a shadow. A big, burly, red-haired giant of a shadow that kept snapping twigs beneath his enormous feet. Ethan turned back and cursed him. "What the hell are you doing?"

"What our boss told me to do," Trick replied. "I'm not letting you out of my sight again."

"I'm just meeting up with Rory." The guy had called him a little bit ago and had reported hearing a shot fired in the woods. These woods…which seemed eerily quiet now but for Trick crashing around behind him.

"And haven't you learned yet that you can't trust anyone?" Trick asked.

"Says the man following me around," Ethan grumbled.

"I have no reason to want you dead," Trick said. Then he sighed. "But neither does Rory…"

Rory actually did—if he wanted to keep his secret,

whatever that was. Ethan didn't know it; he just knew that he had one, like Ethan had had one.

"Why didn't he come down to the firehouse?" Trick asked. "What's he doing hiding out in the woods?"

Hiding. Just as Trick had said.

"He heard a shot earlier," Ethan said.

"So?" Trick asked. "It was in the woods. It was probably a hunter."

Rory was a ranger, like him, so he knew the difference between gunshots. "It didn't sound like a hunting rifle to him."

"Then he should have called the police," Trick said. "Not you."

A chill rushed over Ethan's skin. That was true. But then Rory probably didn't want to talk to the police either. Why not?

Just what the hell was his secret?

And where was he?

"Rory!" he called out. His voice echoed back before dissolving into that eerie silence again.

"This is weird," Trick murmured.

"Too quiet," Ethan agreed.

They both turned around, peering into the woods around them. A flash of color among the briars caught Ethan's attention. He rushed over to pluck the piece of green material from the briars.

"Somebody lost a piece of a shirt or something," he murmured.

"He lost more than that," Trick said, and he pointed toward the body lying a short distance from them.

The green was a piece of the hospital scrubs the guy wore. A doctor? An orderly?

Ethan walked closer and stared down into the battered face of his assailant. And a ragged sigh escaped his lips.

"He's dead, right?" Trick asked.

Ethan pointed toward the gaping hole in his chest. "I'd say so…"

"Who did this?" Trick asked.

"Somebody who didn't want him talking," Ethan said. Which meant he probably would have talked—had the killer not gotten to him first. "Damn it."

Trick pulled out his cell. "We need to call the trooper. Let her know we found her escapee."

"Too late…" He couldn't talk now. Just like the gang member couldn't talk.

Both had died without being able to reveal who'd hired them. Was that a coincidence?

It had to be. It wasn't as if Trent had purposely killed the guy…

Or Rory…

Or…

Ethan's head pounded. After the assailant escaped from the hospital, he'd told the trooper that he couldn't trust anyone. He hadn't realized how right he'd been until now.

Had Rory calling him been a trap?

Maybe he was working with Trent and… Trick?

He looked at his red-haired shadow again.

Trick cursed. "No reception." He glanced up and noticed Ethan's stare. "What?"

Ethan shook his head and shook off the paranoia. "I'm losing it," he admitted. "I'm beginning to suspect everyone."

Trick sighed. "Now you know how I've felt since

Braden asked me to help him out—to find whoever on the team wasn't who he thought they were."

"Was that note really about me?" he wondered. Or had it been about Rory?

Trick shrugged. "I don't know. I don't even know if it has anything to do with the equipment getting sabotaged."

Ethan tensed. "The stove thing…"

"Yes?"

"It wasn't that serious—not like the truck bomb and the shooting and…" He glanced down at the killer who'd tried beating him to death.

"No. It barely even damaged the kitchen," Trick said.

"So maybe that was like the other things…the equipment failures." Ethan's brow furrowed as thoughts continued to run through his head. "But then the reporter took my picture, and everybody found out I'm alive."

"And the person who wants you dead wasn't happy," Trick finished for him.

So it had to be someone who'd come to town after the report, which meant that it probably had to be someone from his family or his friend or ex-fiancée, someone who knew him from his former life. The life someone was determined to end for him…

Tammy couldn't stop shaking. The guy was gone. Finally her protests had penetrated his alcohol-soaked brain and he'd figured out she wasn't interested. But maybe she should have called the police like she'd threatened.

It wasn't okay what he'd done. The guy was dangerous and delusional. He'd actually believed that she would have gone from Ethan to him. But then he'd probably gotten the idea that she would because Ethan's former fiancée had. And Helena Shaw was supposed to have loved Jonathan.

Tammy shuddered with revulsion for both of them. Hopefully they would leave town soon since Ethan must have already. Where had he gone?

Back to the estate where he'd grown up?

She hoped not. She hated to think of him with those people. And she couldn't help but wonder if it was one of them who wanted him dead.

Sure. She'd been the one telling him that it couldn't be, that they hadn't known he'd existed until the reporter had published that picture of him without his beard.

But what if the stove explosion and everything else that happened afterward had been unrelated? Needing to talk to someone, she picked up her cell from the island in her apartment. But before she could punch in the contact for any of her friends, someone pounded on the door downstairs.

Hoping the drunk hadn't returned, she slowly descended the stairs and called out, "Who is it?"

"Wesley Bergman, Miss Ingles."

Wesley...

The brother-in-law. He hadn't struck her as creepy like Ethan's old friend, but she didn't unlock the door. "What do you want?"

"I'm here for my mother-in-law," he replied.

"She's not here," Tammy replied. "I haven't corrupted her again tonight." But she smiled as she remembered the fun they'd had—until Wesley had come to bring them to the hospital.

"I'm here at her request," he said. "She'd like to see you before she leaves town. Can you open the door?"

Tammy's brow furrowed. If Mrs. Ludington-Canterbury was with him, she would have done her own talking. "She's not here," Tammy said. So she had no reason to open the door.

"No," he said. "She's back at the hotel. She asked that I bring you to see her."

Tammy wasn't entirely convinced but maybe Mrs. Canterbury had wanted to avoid the reporters, so she was staying in her suite until they left. She turned the dead bolt and opened the door. "You don't have to drive me," she told him. "I can drive myself."

Wesley smiled. "The Canterburys are used to having cars and drivers," he informed her.

"You're not a driver."

"I'm whatever they want me to be," he said.

That pang of sympathy for him struck her again. "I'm sorry." He deserved to be treated better, but then what did he expect when he'd married someone like Melanie?

Why had he married someone like her?

And now a frisson of unease passed through her. She stepped back a bit. "I can drive myself to the hotel," she repeated.

But Wesley pulled something from the pocket of his suit jacket and pointed it at her. "I'm sorry, too, Miss Ingles, but you are coming with me. Right now."

Was he carrying out someone else's wishes or his own? Tammy didn't know, and she didn't think it mattered at the moment. Because from the look on his face, she had no doubt he would pull the trigger of the gun he grasped, if she didn't leave with him.

She'd lost him. Again.

Where the hell did Ethan Sommerly or Jonathan

Canterbury or whatever he called himself keep disappearing to?

No matter where else he went, eventually he would come back here. To her. So Brittney had camped out near the salon again. Not close enough for Tammy to notice her and get annoyed again, though.

But near enough that Brittney could monitor, through the long-range lens on her camera, who came and went. Despite being closed, the place had stayed busy.

First the greasy-haired frat boy had paid her a visit. Brittney had almost had to step in to help her with that one, but before she'd had a chance to approach the building, Tammy had dealt with him on her own—just like she'd dealt with the bitches that had harassed her the other day.

She was a strong woman. And as a fierce woman herself, Brittney respected her. They probably would have been friends—if Brittney hadn't exposed Tammy's boyfriend for who he really was.

But the fact that Jonathan Michael Canterbury IV had been living under an assumed name and working as a hotshot in Northern Lakes, Michigan was the most insignificant part of the story. Someone wanted him dead.

And how long had that person been trying to kill him? And had Ethan or Jonathan or whatever he called himself been the only one hurt?

Brittney was only assigned the fluff at her station: the restaurant openings, the concert coverage, the community interest outreach stuff. But she'd known from her source that there was something going on with the hotshots. She'd known because her brother had stopped confiding in her. In fact he'd been awfully evasive about his work and especially about the hotshots.

But she hadn't realized how much danger they were in until last night. But was it only the hotshots who were at risk? Or was it the people close to them as well?

She lifted her camera and peered through her lens as Tammy stepped out of the stairwell that led up to her apartment. The man with her wasn't Canterbury, but he was married to one.

It wasn't him that gave Brittney pause, though. It was the expression on the woman's face. Even when she'd been rejecting the unwelcome advances of Canterbury's friend, Tammy Ingles hadn't looked as scared as she did now. She'd dealt with him, though.

She looked as if she didn't know what to do now.

Brittney froze for a moment, too, before she rushed from the shadows of the alley across the street. Her heart pounded like crazy with the fear coursing through her, the fear she'd seen on Tammy's beautiful face. But before Brittney could cross the road and approach them, they climbed into a car the guy had left running at the curb. No. *He* climbed in on the passenger's side and dragged Tammy in behind him.

Then he closed the door and sped off in the car.

Brittney lifted her camera again and snapped a photo of the license plate. She had a feeling they might need it to find Tammy Ingles—because Brittney had a horrible feeling that the salon owner had just been abducted.

Cursing herself for not stepping in sooner, she pulled out her cell phone and punched in a number she called often. Her older half brother had always been there when she needed him—even when he was irritated with her, like he'd looked earlier when she'd showed up at the shooting at the firehouse.

"Don't hang up on me," she told Trent. "I need your help."

"No—"

"Not for me," she interjected before he could refuse. "I need your help for Tammy Ingles. I think she's in danger."

Chapter 24

Ethan glanced down at his cell phone, but the number calling him was unknown. He had no damn time for some telemarketer or, worse yet, a reporter who'd tracked down his number. In fact, he had no time for anything but the truth, which was long overdue.

"What are you two doing here?" he asked as he stepped inside his mother's suite.

Kip glanced up from where he sat on the couch, a towel in his lap. Startled, he jerked and sent ice cubes tumbling across the couch and the carpet around it. "What—"

"Shouldn't that ice be in your glass?" Helena asked her husband. "Or are you too drunk to realize that?" Her blue eyes narrowed. "What's wrong with you?"

Ethan wondered, too, so he stepped closer to the guy. "What happened?" he asked.

"Your damn girlfriend attacked me."

Ethan's hand shot out then and he jerked Kip up from the couch, sending more ice cubes flying around the room. "Did you hurt her?!"

"Hurt her," Kip sputtered. "She just about neutered me."

"Somebody should have done that a long time ago," Helena muttered as she served herself a drink at the bar. Lifting the glass as if toasting, she said, "Maybe your little friend isn't the money-grubbing whore I thought she was, Jonny."

Ethan let Kip drop back onto the couch. His former best friend had money; he could have hired those assassins. But why? Out of jealousy? Had he always wanted everything Ethan had?

So he asked again, "What are the two of you doing here? You're not my family. You're not my friends anymore." If they had ever really been...

"You and I were supposed to get married," Helena reminded him.

And he grimaced at the thought. "But you married someone else."

"Only because I thought you were dead!" she exclaimed.

"She came here hoping that you'd want her back," Kip explained.

"And why did you come here? To fight for her?" he asked. Was that why Kip had attacked him in the lobby? Out of jealousy? Was he jealous enough to try to have him killed?

Kip laughed. "Hell, no. To give you my blessing."

Helena flipped him off. Those two definitely deserved each other; they were both miserable people.

Like his sister...

Melanie stood to gain the most from his death. He hadn't married Helena, so she had nothing to gain. But if Jonathan Canterbury IV was really dead, his sister would become the sole heir to the Canterbury fortune.

"Where's Melanie?" he asked as he glanced around the room again. But these two were the only people in his mother's suite.

Helena shrugged.

"And my mother?" he asked as fear gripped him. Melanie would inherit even more if his mother died, too.

Helena shrugged again.

His cell vibrated, flashing the same unknown number at him. Then someone pounded on the door.

"Ethan!" Trick called out. "Are you in there?"

Sighing, he opened the door.

"What the hell are you doing?" the auburn-haired hotshot asked him. "You took off from that crime scene in the woods before I even noticed you slipped away. You know I'm supposed to stick with you. And why aren't you answering your phone?"

"It's not your number that keeps popping up," he said. Trick McRooney was in his contacts just like every other hotshot on the twenty-member team.

"No, it's my number," a female voice remarked as the reporter walked into the room.

Ethan groaned. "I don't have time for you now." He never had time for the press.

"You're going to want to listen to her," Trent Miles said as he walked in behind the woman. The two of them looked oddly similar to each other with those same pale brown eyes.

"What's going on?" Ethan demanded to know.

"I'm worried about Tammy," she told him. "I was

staking out her place to see if you'd show up and first I saw him…" She pointed toward where Kip sat on the couch, scooping ice cubes back into the towel on his lap. "Then, after she fended him off and tossed him out on his slimy ass, your brother-in-law showed up."

Ethan cursed over Tammy having to deal with first Kip and then Wesley.

"You don't know that he has anything to do with this," Trent told the reporter. "You're just jumping to conclusions again."

"I saw the look on her face," Brittney Townsend told him. "She looked scared, even more scared than when this schmuck tried attacking her."

"You just watched?" Trent asked Brittney in horror. "You didn't try to help?"

"Tammy is tough as nails. She got rid of him before I could even get across the street. She can handle herself," the reporter said.

That was true. Tammy was smart and strong. But she was in more danger now than she'd ever been because it suddenly occurred to Ethan who stood to gain the most if Jonathan Canterbury IV was dead: Wesley. He had to the one who'd been trying to kill him. He had either been acting on his own or on the orders of Ethan's sister. They wanted him dead and out of the way, and probably his mother as well, so they inherited the entire fortune. And they had no compulsion against using Tammy to get what they wanted.

"Where are they?" Ethan asked as he tried to squeeze out the door. But more hotshots than Trent and Trick had showed up; the others had lined up in the hallway outside the room. "Are they at her place?"

Brittney shook her head. "No. He got her in the car."

She held up her camera. "I have a plate number. But I wasn't able to follow them. He was driving too fast."

Wesley wouldn't have brought her back here. Where the hell would he have brought her?

His cell rang again, but the reporter was here so she wasn't calling him. It was Tammy. He quickly accepted the call. "Hello?"

"Hey, Jonny," Wes greeted him as casually as if he was checking in to see how everything was going.

But there was nothing casual about this call. Ethan knew that. "What have you done with her?" Ethan asked.

"Nothing yet," Wesley said.

"What do you want?"

"You know," Wesley told him.

Money. It was all about the damn money.

"How?" Ethan asked. "Everybody knows I'm alive now."

"Which is unfortunate since I'd already started the paperwork to declare you legally dead," Wes said. "I had to wait five years. And we were so close…then that damn picture showed up all over the news."

"I'll sign off the inheritance," Ethan offered. "I'll give you everything."

"Yes, you will."

"But you can't hurt her," he demanded. "I'll meet you. I'll sign whatever you want—"

"No!" The scream echoed in the background. "Don't do it!" Tammy cried. "Don't—"

A sharp noise cut off her voice as skin slapped skin. Ethan felt the sting of it through the phone and grimaced with the pain. He had such a connection with her that it was as if he could feel what she felt. The pain and the fear.

"Don't you dare lay another hand on her!" he warned Wes. "Or you won't get a damn dime out of me."

"Don't tell me what to do," Wesley said coldly. "I'm so damn sick of you Canterburys telling me what to do. You're going to do what I say from now on." And he listed his demands before disconnecting the phone call.

Ethan would do what his brother-in-law had told him to do—despite Tammy yelling that he shouldn't. He would do *anything* to get Tammy back. But he wasn't sure that would be possible.

Or if Wesley would kill her first.

He was going to kill her. That was why she'd screamed, and now her face burned from the slap he'd given her. Tied to a chair, she hadn't been able to move to avoid the blow. She wasn't even able to untangle her hair from around her face.

Wesley clicked off her cell phone and smashed it against the boards of the hardwood floor. "Why would you tell him not to help you?" he snapped. "Or is it that you don't want him to give up the money? Was my mother-in-law wrong? Is that really all you've been interested in from him?"

She shook her head. No. She loved Ethan. And now she wished like hell she'd told him so. His mother had been right that day in the hospital; pushing him away hadn't changed her feelings for him. It didn't matter if they were together or not, if he was a hotshot or an heir to billions. She was still terrified that he was in danger.

And she was more afraid of what was going to happen to him than she was for herself.

"I know you're going to kill me anyway," she said. "And that you're going to kill him too."

He stared at her for a moment as if the thought hadn't occurred to him. Then he smirked. "I guess you're smarter than I thought. Certainly smarter than my wife thinks you are."

"Is she involved?" Tammy asked, as she tried tugging at the ends of the rope he had tied around her wrists.

With juggling the gun from hand to hand when he'd bound her to the chair, the rope wasn't that tight. She had to be able to work it loose. She just needed time.

And she didn't have much before Ethan would get here. She had to get loose and she had to get the gun away from Wesley before he could use it on either of them.

It was their only chance…

Wesley tensed as he thought of his wife. Not that long ago he'd driven her and his mother-in-law to the airport. He'd promised he would take care of Ethan and be home with Melanie soon.

She had no idea how he intended to take care of her brother, though. Her dear Jonny…

Despite how mercilessly she teased him, Melanie loved Jonny. She would hate to lose him. But eventually she would see that it was for the best.

She just couldn't ever learn that he was responsible. It would have to stay his little secret. So the hairdresser was right. She and Jonny would both have to die—no matter what promises he'd made to them.

He couldn't let either of them reveal what he'd done. That was why he'd killed the incompetent hit man after he'd gotten the call to act as his lawyer. The guy had threatened that if Wesley didn't help him escape, that he would negotiate himself a deal with the police.

So Wesley had worked a deal of his own.

He'd ended the guy's life and the threat he posed. Just like he would end this woman's life.

She knew it. He saw the fear in her pretty green eyes. She trembled too against the chair. Then he realized she wasn't shaking because she was scared.

She was shaking because she was untying herself. He whirled toward her with the gun. But she scrambled up and swung the chair at him.

He squeezed the trigger and fired.

Chapter 25

The woods around the cabin where Wesley had told him to come were as eerily quiet as the woods where he and Trick had found the dead hit man. Somehow, even his team was being totally silent.

But they were out there. His fellow hotshots wouldn't let him go off alone. Ethan wouldn't have let them get involved—if it wasn't for Tammy. He didn't want anything to happen to her, so he'd been willing to let them risk their lives for hers.

That was why he hadn't called the police either. Wesley had sworn that if he heard a siren, he would shoot Tammy. And Ethan hadn't trusted the sometimes overzealous troopers to not arrive with sirens blaring.

"This is crazy," Trick murmured from somewhere behind him.

His shadow moved quietly this time. And the setting sun hid his presence.

"We're firefighters, not FBI agents," Trick continued.

There hadn't been enough time to call in the FBI. Wesley had wanted to meet quickly to settle things.

To kill him…

That was what the man intended to do. Ethan knew it. He just hoped that he hadn't killed Tammy first. But she'd been alive during the call.

She'd screamed to warn him. Like the reporter had said, she was smart and strong.

And resourceful…

She would survive. She *had* to.

He couldn't imagine a world without her in it—even if they weren't together. But he wanted to be with her so damn badly that his body ached. And not from the beating he'd endured.

Thanks to Wesley…

He still couldn't believe that his brother-in-law was behind all of this. Wesley had always seemed so mild-mannered, so patient and kind. But apparently he'd just been biding his time until he could inherit the Canterbury fortune.

How had Ethan been so wrong about him?

"There it is," Trick murmured in the darkness as he and Ethan drew near the cabin.

Ethan raised his hand to his mouth, so Wesley wouldn't see his lips moving if he was watching through one of the windows. "Make sure you and the others stay out of sight." He'd never forgive himself if anything happened to Tammy because of him, because he'd screwed up. He lowered his hand and approached the cabin.

It wasn't much bigger than a deer hunting blind. Since it was in the middle of a heavily wooded area, that must have been what it was used for. It wasn't on one of the many lakes in the area. And it was certainly secluded.

That was why Wesley must have chosen it. Because it would be the perfect place to commit murder.

Murders.

No wires were connected to the wood paneled building. There was no power, so no lights. The door stood open, though, and the fading sun washed across the floor, which was spattered with blood.

His heart flipped and swelled with fear that choked him. He rushed inside but it was easy to see the tiny place was empty but for a small table, a bed and a broken chair.

Had it been the chair that had caused the bleeding? Or a bullet? As he walked around the small space, his foot slipped on the hard wood floor, his sole skidding against something small and round and hard. Then a spent shell rolled across the blood-spattered boards.

A gun had been fired in the small space. And a gun fired this close wouldn't have missed.

But if she was dead, what had Wesley done to her body? Why hadn't he left her here like he'd left the dead hit man in the woods nearby?

He hurried out of the cabin just as gunfire rang out. And in that moment Ethan knew—she wasn't dead yet. But if they didn't find them—and stop Wesley—she would be dead soon.

Tammy ducked low as the bullets rained all around her. Bark chipped off the tree trunks near her. Leaves dropped and branches snapped.

And she kept running, just as fast and furiously as she'd raced out of the cabin after swinging that chair at

Wesley's head. She'd knocked him down. If she hadn't, he would have shot her for certain then.

He would likely shoot her soon, though—if she couldn't escape him.

The branches and briars scraped and scratched her bare feet. Even before they'd arrived at the cabin, she'd lost her shoes somewhere along the path to it. First one heel had broken off, then the other. Wesley hadn't cared and had just kept urging her to hurry, the gun barrel against her back.

Of course he hadn't cared about her shoes. He'd intended to kill her all along. How long had he been trying to take out his brother-in-law?

Was he responsible for that plane crash all those years ago? How evil was this man?

Evil enough that he kept firing his gun. He must have been gaining on her—because she could hear branches snapping all around her and brush rustling. It was as if he was suddenly everywhere.

Or maybe it only seemed that way because darkness was falling. The last of the sun began to slip away into the shadows of all the trees. She wore a light-colored dress though—so light that she stood out like a flame in the dark. No matter where she ran, he would be able to see her.

To find her…

To kill her.

"*Damn you!*" Wesley yelled.

That pesky little hairdresser was ruining everything. Jonny would be at the cabin soon—if he wasn't already. He would know that Wesley had set a trap for him.

That he didn't intend to let him live any more than he intended to let his little girlfriend live.

"Come back here!" he shouted at her.

He could hear her crashing through the trees and the underbrush. She was close.

She had to be.

Barefoot, she couldn't have gotten much ahead of him—no matter how fast she'd been running. And she had been surprisingly fast. But then she knew she was running for her life.

So she wasn't likely to stop and come back. She knew he intended to kill her. And Jonny probably knew the same. Because Wes's plan was falling apart, and he could see it all slipping away from him.

Melanie.

The estate.

All the money.

And then he saw her, the flicker of lightness in the shadows. And he raised his gun and squeezed the trigger.

Chapter 26

The gun glinted in the shadows, drawing Ethan's attention. He saw the barrel rise, spotted it pointing toward the light in the darkness. Toward Tammy...

He shouted. "Get down!" And launched himself at his brother-in-law. The gun went off, the metal hot against Ethan's hand as he wrested it from Wesley's grip. He tossed it into the trees as he slammed his fist into the guy's already damp face. Blood flowed from Wesley's nose, running over Ethan's knuckles. But he hadn't broken it; Tammy must have—with the chair.

"Is she all right?" he called out to the others.

"She's fine," Trent Miles called back from the darkness. It was complete now that the sun had set.

"Nobody was hit?" he asked with concern. This was his problem—not theirs, but they were all there—just like when they were called out to a fire. Every member of the team had had his back.

"Do you have him?" Trick asked, and he nearly tripped over where they lay sprawled on the ground.

Ethan held Wesley down with his weight and with his arm against the guy's throat. "Yeah. The gun fell into the brush somewhere."

Trick hesitated a moment. "You didn't kill him?"

Ethan eased his grip slightly and Wesley gasped for air.

"You should have stayed dead," his brother-in-law hissed weakly. "Just a few more weeks and you would have been legally dead…"

Because no body had been found, Wesley would have had to wait five years for the courts to declare Jonathan Michael Canterbury IV officially deceased.

"That was you, wasn't it?" Ethan asked. "The plane malfunction. You were behind that just like you were behind the stove. Somehow you knew I was alive. You knew where I was. And you tried to kill me."

"What—what are you talking about?" Wesley sputtered. "I didn't touch any stove."

But Ethan noticed that he didn't deny messing with the plane. He had to have been behind the other things, too, that had happened before the plane crash. The car nearly running him down, the brake failure and then the things that had happened recently. Like the stove and…

"One of your hit men rigged it for you then, just like he rigged the truck to blow up," Ethan said.

"I didn't hire any hit men until I saw that picture of you," Wesley said, "until I knew you had survived the crash, just like you survived me trying to run you over and your brakes going out. For someone who's supposed to be cursed, you were so damned lucky…"

Then maybe the stove had been the work of the saboteur. But not the other.

"The plane crash," Ethan repeated, and the guilt he'd carried for the past five years nearly crushed him. "You were responsible for that." Innocent people had undoubtedly perished because of him. The real Ethan Sommerly and the pilot…

Wesley shook his head against the ground. "No, not that. I tried running you over and had my mechanic mess with your brakes. But the plane…that must have been the curse…"

Ethan snorted. "There *is* no curse." He felt like a fool that he'd ever considered there might be. Everything that had happened to Ethan had been because of Wesley, not the curse.

Certainly his family had had some bad luck. But mostly bad health and accidents had claimed his ancestors' lives. His dad had had a heart condition from birth, worsened by the stress of his high-profile political career. And his brother had gotten into things he shouldn't have and hadn't had the friends Ethan had. The Canterburys only real curse was not being able to trust the people close to them, people like Wesley and whoever had rigged that stove to explode.

While Ethan didn't believe in the curse, he knew he wasn't out of danger yet. None of the hotshots were. If Wesley really hadn't rigged the stove, someone else had.

And if someone was going after hotshots, whoever was close to them was in danger, too.

Tammy had already been through enough because of him. While he ached to go to her, to hold her, to be with her, he knew the best thing he could do for her was to stay away.

That was the only way she would truly stay safe.

Days had passed since Ethan's brother-in-law had been arrested. Days of visits from her friends checking on her, but no visit from Ethan.

Not even a card. Or a text...

No. *I'm sorry my brother-in-law tried to kill you...*

No. *I'm sorry for breaking your heart...*

And her heart *was* broken. She wasn't even sure when she'd given it to him, but she had. And just like Wesley Bergman had smashed her cell phone, Ethan had tossed her heart aside and shattered it into pieces, too.

"Are you okay?" Henrietta asked as she paused at the top of the stairwell to the exterior door.

The salon was closed. Margaret must have done it because Tammy hadn't even gone down today. She hadn't wanted to see anyone. But her friends kept turning up.

Serena and Courtney had just left before Henrietta had stopped in for a visit.

"I'm fine," Tammy assured the female hotshot.

Henrietta narrowed her dark eyes. "Why don't I believe you?"

Because she wasn't a very good liar. She never had been. As Ethan had pointed out, she was too blunt.

Maybe it was the wine she'd had earlier, but a confession bubbled up along with her anger. "I'm mad," she admitted. "All of you have come by to check on me but him. What does he think? That I'm after his money? Or that I'm not good enough for the heir to the Canterbury fortune?"

Henrietta shook her head. "Of course not. He was

willing to give up everything for you. He was going to sign off on his inheritance."

"That wouldn't have been legal," Tammy said. "Wesley was going to kill him."

"He knew that," Henrietta told her. "And he insisted on going to meet him anyway, so he could save you. He was willing to give up his life for yours. So I think you mean a great deal to him."

"Then why hasn't he checked on me?" she asked, and her voice cracked with the hurt of what she'd felt was his rejection. She had been afraid that, like all those boys in high school, he didn't think she was pretty enough or sexy enough or smart enough to be with. That was why she'd vowed to stay single, so that she would never feel *not enough* again. "Why is he staying away?"

"You're close to us," Henrietta said. "You know that things have been happening that look like accidents that aren't accidents."

"Like the stove?" She'd overheard Wesley Bergman's denial of any involvement in that incident. So someone else had rigged the stove to explode.

Henrietta nodded. "Yes, among other things."

"Is it someone on the team?" Tammy asked.

Henrietta shrugged. "I hope not. But we don't know for sure. We just know that someone keeps sabotaging our equipment."

"And people are getting hurt," Tammy finished for her, remembering how the fire had singed Ethan's beard and hair and his hands.

"I think that's the real reason he's staying away," Henrietta said. "So that you don't get hurt again."

"I'm not a hotshot," Tammy said. "I'll be fine." But if something happened to Ethan…

It wouldn't matter if they were together or not, she would still be devastated.

She walked over and hugged her friend. "Please be careful," she said as worry for all of them overwhelmed her.

Henrietta hugged her back. "I'm tough," she said. "Like you." She pulled back and smiled at Tammy. "Sure you don't want to be a hotshot? You kicked ass getting away from that psycho. You broke his nose."

Tammy shook her head. "No. I love my salon."

But that wasn't all she loved. She waved Henrietta off. Then she picked up her new cell phone. Fortunately, she'd been able to save the SIM card from her broken one, so all her information had transferred to the new one. She punched in his contact.

She wasn't certain that he would answer. But after a couple of rings, his deep voice rumbled in her ear. "Hello?"

She froze for a moment until she remembered what he'd appreciated most about her. Her bluntness. So she spoke from her heart. "I need you."

Then she stiffened again as she waited for his rejection. But she heard a whoosh of air, as if the wind rattled the phone. "I'm close. I'll be there right away," he said.

By the time she walked down the stairs, he was at her door, pounding on it. "Are you all right?" he asked the moment it opened.

And she smiled. "I am now."

Henrietta had been right. He'd only stayed away to protect her, and he must not have stayed far away to get there as fast as he had.

"What is it?" he asked as he peered around the place. "Did the alarm go off?"

She shook her head. "I didn't set it."

He cursed. "I got you that to keep you safe."

"I don't want you to keep me safe," she said.

His brow furrowed. "But you said you needed me."

"I do," she replied. She looped her arms around his neck and pulled his head down for her kiss. And she kissed him with all the passion and love she felt for him.

He pulled back, panting for breath. "Tammy, I don't want you to get hurt. And that saboteur is still messing with the team."

"People get hurt," she said. "My whole adolescence people picked on me and hurt my feelings. But I survived."

"I wish I'd been here then," he bit out, his jaw clenching with anger. He must have shaved again for there was just a faint growth of stubble on his chin. "I wouldn't have let anyone pick on you. I wish you hadn't had to go through that."

"It made me strong," she said. "It made me a survivor. You don't have to worry about me. All you have to do is love me—like I love you."

He sucked in a breath, and his dark eyes widened with shock.

And just in case he harbored any doubts that she was after his money, she said, "I love you as Ethan Sommerly, as the man who speaks little but when he does, it matters. The man who's funny and loyal and smart. That's the man I fell for, probably years ago. But I was scared then. I was scared of falling for anyone because I worked hard for my life, for my self-esteem, for control…and I didn't trust anyone enough to give that up…" Until now. Until *him*.

"You were hurt growing up," he said. "And you felt

helpless. And I understand that you didn't want to feel like that again. I didn't know who to trust either. I didn't have real friends growing up. I had friends like Kip and Helena…"

She sighed. "I was a hell of a lot luckier than you were. I had Courtney and Serena."

"Well, I was *cursed*," he reminded her with a smile that let her know he didn't really believe that anymore. "Until that plane crashed, and after that… I found real friends. But more importantly than that, I found myself."

She smiled. "You do understand."

He nodded. "That's why I never acted on my feelings for you. I didn't want to fall for you and tell you the truth and risk you rejecting who I am now, who I want to be always."

"That's the man I love," she assured him. "*You're* the man I love."

"And you're the woman I love," he said gruffly. "And respect so damn much. You're so strong and so smart, and there isn't one thing I would ever want to change about you."

Her breath shuddered out with her relief. She believed him. She believed in *them*.

He wrapped his arms around her. "And I'll make sure that nobody ever hurts you again."

"With your family, I'm not sure that's possible," she reminded him but she was just teasing. Mostly.

"My mother loves you," he assured her.

"Your sister certainly doesn't."

"Melanie has actually been wanting to talk to you," he shared. "To apologize for what Wesley put you through."

"That wasn't her fault," Tammy said, and she believed that she hadn't been involved. "She really loves her Jonny. She wouldn't have done anything to put you in danger. But I know she doesn't love me."

"Yet," he said. "But she will." He swung her up in his arms and started up the steps, carrying her as if she weighed nothing.

"What about you?" she asked. "Do you really love me?" She could hardly believe that she had truly found that person who would accept her as she was. No. Not just accept her but appreciate her.

"With all my heart," he rasped. And she felt his heart pounding hard in his chest, pounding as fast and furiously as hers was.

"I love you," she said. "So much..."

He released a sigh of relief. "I thought you'd never forgive me for not being truthful about who I am."

"You were truthful," she said. "You are much more Ethan Sommerly than you ever were Jonathan Canterbury IV."

And he expelled another rough breath.

She would have thought it was because they reached the top of the stairs, but he continued to carry her through the kitchen and living room and down the hall. He carried her easily—with no exertion.

"You do understand me," he said and the relief in his voice echoed the sigh, "better than anyone ever has, better than I even understood myself."

"The first moment we met I felt like I knew you," she admitted. "When I found out who you were, I figured that was why—that I had recognized you as Jonathan Canterbury. But I didn't until I shaved off your singed beard."

He swept her through her bedroom doorway and onto

her bed. And once she settled onto the mattress, he ran a hand over his jaw. "I shaved..." He knocked a piece of bloody tissue from a nick on his chin.

"I see that," she said.

"I prefer when you shave me."

"I will from now on," she promised. "Well, whenever you're in Northern Lakes."

He tensed. "Why wouldn't I be in Northern Lakes?"

"You're a ranger in the UP," she said. Her eyes widened as she considered what might have happened. "Or did you get fired?"

He shook his head. "I quit."

She gasped with shock. "Why? You love being a hotshot!"

"I love being a hotshot," he said. "And I didn't quit the Huron Hotshots, and fortunately Braden didn't fire me either. I just quit being a ranger because I don't want to hide out in the woods anymore. I want to be with you."

"But you've been staying away from me."

"Only because I didn't want to put you in danger," he said. "Because of the saboteur. Once we catch that person I would have been pounding down your door begging for another chance with you."

"I have an alarm system now," she warned him with a smile. "You wouldn't get in."

"Aw. You wouldn't have let me in?" he asked. But he was grinning, too, as they slipped into their old, flirtatious manner.

She smiled. "I will *always* let you in," she said. "I just might not let you out." She reached for him, pulling him down onto the bed with her.

He kissed her as passionately as she had him. "I

might not want to get out," he growled. "In fact, I never want to leave…"

He would—for a fire. But she was fine with that because she knew he would always come back to her. The Canterbury curse was broken. She wasn't worried about losing him and she wasn't worried about losing herself. They both knew who they were and loved each other as they were. That was all Tammy had ever wanted—*he* was all she had ever wanted whether he was clean-shaven or had his long beard. She would take him however he was because she knew just as she was his, he was her soul mate.

"She's still here," Braden remarked as he slid into the corner booth next to his brother-in-law.

"Who?" Trick asked.

He pointed at the reporter who sat at the bar. "I thought she'd leave after she filed her big story about the Canterburys."

"That wasn't the story that brought her here," Trick reminded him.

Needlessly.

He sighed. "I know. She got wind of the things happening around here—of the sabotage."

"That Bergman guy had nothing to do with the stove thing," Trick said.

"I know." He'd suspected as much for a while now. Ethan hadn't been specifically targeted until after the reporter had taken that picture of him and all the national news stations had picked it up.

Anyone could have started the stove and had it blow up on them. It had just been Ethan's bad luck that he had been the one. Or had that been his curse?

Hell, maybe all the hotshots were cursed.

"We have to figure out who's doing this," Braden said.

"We will," Trick assured him.

They would. Eventually. But how many more people would get hurt before the saboteur was stopped?

* * * * *

HARLEQUIN
PLUS

Try the best multimedia subscription service for romance readers like you!

Read, Watch and Play.

Experience the easiest way to get the romance content you crave.

Start your **FREE TRIAL** at
www.harlequinplus.com/freetrial.